*Also by Ann Hood*

Somewhere Off the Coast of Maine
Waiting to Vanish
Three-Legged Horse
Something Blue

# Places
## to Stay the
# Night

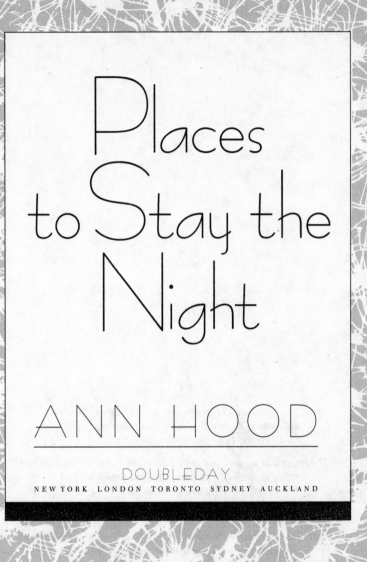

# Places to Stay the Night

# ANN HOOD

DOUBLEDAY

NEW YORK  LONDON  TORONTO  SYDNEY  AUCKLAND

PUBLISHED BY DOUBLEDAY
a division of Bantam Doubleday Dell Publishing Group, Inc.
666 Fifth Avenue, New York, NY 10103

DOUBLEDAY and the portrayal of an anchor with a dolphin are trademarks
of Doubleday, a division of Bantam Doubleday Dell
Publishing Group, Inc.

Book design by Chris Welch

*For Gail
and
For Gina and June*

# ACKNOWLEDGMENTS

I would like to give a very special thanks to my parents, Melissa Hood, Gail Hochman, Bob Reiss, Pete May, Rob Weisbach, Marianne Merola, and especially Deb Futter.

# Places to Stay the Night

# Summer

When *Libby Holliday* finally left her family, she went to Los Angeles, to Hollywood. She did not go to become a movie star. She was thirty-six years old and her days of becoming a starlet, an ingenue, someone like Sandra Dee in those Tammy movies, were long gone. She went because she thought it was her last chance. Because she thought that if she spent one more day in Holly, Massachusetts, one more day looking at a husband she did not love and two teenage children who frightened her the way strangers in dark shopping mall parking lots frightened her, one more day in that house, that room, that bed, she would certainly shrivel up and die.

Libby woke up that morning and knew it was time to leave. It was a beautiful summer day, early June, the kind of morning when it seems things are about to happen. Warm air that still holds the faintest touch of spring. A pale blue sky with puffs of clouds way up high. It was a day that children draw when they're very young, using brightly colored Crayolas, the sun a yellow triangle in one corner, its rays shooting out at a small house with oversize flowers growing beside it and fat lines of thick green grass.

Every Saturday, her husband, Tom Harper, got out of bed early to get to his garage in town. On the Saturday Libby left, the clock radio went off as usual. But instead of leaping out of bed, Tom rolled into her, pressed himself against her, his erection poking at her. He smelled like sleep, sour and musty as a cellar.

"Why did you change the station?" Libby said. Her voice sounded too loud in the still morning air. "You know I like it on Lite-105."

Tom didn't answer. He pretended he didn't hear and nuzzled her neck, his face like a piece of sandpaper against her skin.

"You know I hate talk radio," Libby said. "I hate the way those people who call in are so needy. And how they tell their problems to just anybody who will listen."

Tom reached down and yanked on her nightgown. It would wrinkle, Libby thought. He was always too rough, too eager. The voice on the radio was shouting now, about those missiles that were costing a fortune and didn't work. She had seen a piece on *60 Minutes* about that and she'd written a letter to George Bush, complaining. Libby always wrote letters when something displeased her—a bad meal in a restaurant, pantyhose that ran too easily, weathermen who never predicted the weather accurately.

And she always heard back too. Sometimes a company sent coupons or gift certificates, though that was not why she did it. George Bush wrote her a very nice reply that she kept with her important papers, birth certificates and marriage license and bank books.

Tom was spreading her legs now, breathing hard.

Libby turned her head, away from him, so that her gaze settled out the window and onto that beautiful summer morning—the sky, the distant clouds. By habit she lifted her legs and wrapped them around her husband's back, placed her hands lightly on his shoulder blades, and thought about the things she couldn't see out her window. She thought about sprawling cities glittering in sunlight, deserts burning hot, snow-capped mountains and long endless stretches of highways.

Libby knew that other women, like her best friend Sue, imagined famous men during sex. They pretended it was Richard Gere or Kevin Costner pushing into them and maybe that fantasy would actually excite them. But not Libby. It was true that as a teenager, she had cut Tom's face from all the wallet-size prom pictures that came in the special photo package and replaced them with Robert Redford's face, cut from magazines. It wasn't his face exactly. It was Robert Redford as the Sundance Kid, in that movie. Back then, Libby had been thrilled by the idea of danger, of a handsome outlaw carrying her out of Massachusetts into the Wild West. Or even farther away, to Bolivia where they would rob banks and make love.

Somewhere she still had a dozen pictures of herself in a white prom gown sprinkled with daisies and Robert Redford's face glued to Tom's tuxedoed body. But that fantasy had faded over the years. Instead, it was something even more distant that excited Libby now. It was whatever lay outside this bedroom window. As Tom's movements grew stronger, faster, Libby stared out at that perfect blue sky, imagined herself tossed into it, gaining momentum, hurtling forward, westward, not knowing where she would land. And as it sometimes happened, the thought thrilled her and despite herself she came, clutching at Tom, looking away.

He crumpled into a heavy heap on top of her.

"Good morning," he whispered sweetly in her ear, his breath warm and yeasty.

She still looked away, waiting for her heartbeat to return to normal.

Tom pulled away from her and kissed her lightly on the lips before he bounded from the bed. Libby heard his footsteps, heavy on the floor as he walked out of the room to the bathroom. She used to think he moved with great grace. She imagined him in school, running across football fields and baseball diamonds, light and surefooted, always securing a victory.

The sound of the shower blasting on filled her ears, but still Libby's heart raced. A cloud floated by, wispy as angel hair. The shower stopped and Tom came back in, bringing steam and the smell of Old Spice. She listened to him as he opened drawers and slammed them shut, all the too familiar sounds of Saturday mornings. He sat on the bed to pull on his socks, and the bed dipped and creaked.

"I know you're awake," he told her. He slapped her thigh playfully. He got up and came to stand over her. "Libby?" he said.

She kept her eyes half closed so as not to block out her view of the sky completely. Tom sighed and kissed her cheek, his breath fresh now, full of mint toothpaste.

"Love you," he whispered. He stared down at her a moment before he left, closing the door softly behind him.

When she knew for sure he was gone, when she heard his footsteps fading on the stairway and distant kitchen noises—tea kettle, toaster, the hum of the downstairs radio—Libby opened her eyes wide. She did not try to calm her heart. Instead she pressed her hand to her chest and felt it beating quickly beneath her fingers.

The front door slammed shut and Libby got up from the bed and went to the window. It was funny how lying down it was impossible to see what was out there. But standing in front of it everything became clear. She could see the yellow of a forklift through the bright green leaves. Libby watched as Tom got into his red pickup truck. From where she stood, he seemed very small.

There was a time when Tom Harper had seemed bigger than life, not only to Libby but to the whole town. He had been a hero of sorts, six foot four and built solid as stone. All the girls in Holly had wanted him, and sometimes Libby thought that was the only reason she went out with him. She was the one who got everything. She was pretty, with blond hair and blue eyes. She was smart. It was only natural that she win Tom Harper too, that they got voted Class Cuties and Class Couple, that they got crowned Prom King and Queen, that they got married and lived happily ever after.

Libby gripped the windowsill, felt the paint flake in her hands as she watched Tom go. She stood like that until even the smoke from his exhaust pipe had disappeared and there was no sign of him at all. Then she turned from the window, and with her heart still pounding hard, she started to pack her things.

*Dana felt as if* she had been expecting her mother to leave forever. She knew that someday she would come home from school and find the house empty, or wake up one morning and discover that while she'd slept, Libby had packed up and gone. So she wasn't surprised when the day finally came. She just followed her mother outside and watched the baby-blue VW Rabbit disappear down the road, past the cornfields, until it was completely out of sight. It reminded Dana of that movie *Field of Dreams*, the way the ghosts walked into the cornfields and vanished. Except that was a movie and this was real life. *Her* life.

Standing there in the early summer heat, watching her mother go, Dana made herself think about other things, things that didn't matter. How in geometry you can make things that don't make sense seem true. Like: God loves boys. Boys love sex. Therefore God loves sex. She just kept thinking about stupid things until she felt numb, as if there was a big dead spot where her heart was supposed to be.

She woke up that morning to the sounds of her mother packing her bags and the radio tuned to Lite-105, playing old songs real loud.

"What's going on?" Dana had asked, standing in the bedroom doorway peering in. She'd asked that even though she knew exactly what was happening.

Libby was dressed in white pants and a blue and white polka dot sheer blouse. Everything matched—earrings, sandals, belt. Like all of her outfits, she'd planned this one out, every detail, right down to the seashell pink lipstick and coordinated blush. She was dressed as if she was going somewhere. She was singing along with Kenny Rogers on the radio, and she didn't turn toward Dana when Dana spoke to her. Instead, she just kept singing and neatly placing folded clothes into her matching set of lavender American Tourister luggage.

Dana swallowed hard. "You're leaving us," she said, trying to keep her voice from cracking. Instead, it came out flat, a monotone.

"You could look at it that way," Libby said. "Or, you could look at it like I'm going to find myself."

Dana nodded.

Once, her mother had told her that determination was everything. That if you set your mind to something, you should just do it. No looking back. She watched as her mother zipped up the smallest bag. She seemed very determined. No looking back.

"Well," Dana said, her voice still flat and steady, even though something else was rising up in her stomach, something wild and hysterical. "Where is it you're going?"

"Los Angeles," Libby said. "Hollywood." Then she looked up at Dana, for the first time.

Dana saw the carefully applied blue eyeliner around her mother's eyes, and the blue Ultra-Thick mascara on her lashes. Libby's eyes were so blue —clear and shiny. To Dana, the effect was as if someone had dipped her mother in Easter egg dye.

"Please don't look so sad," Libby said. She flashed Dana her perfect white teeth. "Come on," she said, reaching out to her. "Give me a hand here."

Every morning, Libby flossed her teeth, then brushed them, then polished them with Pearl Drops Tooth Polish and rinsed her mouth with Lister-Mint. Dana was sure her mother had the cleanest teeth in all of Massachusetts. In all of the United States even.

Libby patted the big suitcase on the bed. The suitcase had made the quilt underneath bunch up and Dana had the urge to straighten it out.

"You sit," Libby said. "I'll zip."

Dana walked into the bedroom. Her mother's perfume always choked her and the smell caught in her throat now. It was Beautiful, by Estée Lauder. They should call it Gross, Troy always whispered to Dana when their mother walked by them, leaving a heavy trail of perfume behind her.

Libby patted the suitcase again, and Dana climbed on top of it. Behind her mother, she saw all the bureau drawers, opened and emptied except for the heart-shaped sachets she ordered from the Victoria's Secret catalogue. The closet was open too. Hangers covered in peach satin and stitched with bows and fake pearls hung empty from the rods.

For an instant, Libby seemed to hesitate. She looked first around the room, then at Dana. Dana thought her mother was going to reach out to her. But then the moment passed.

Libby sighed. "Well," she said, "I've got a long drive. I don't want to lose any daylight, do I?"

Dana tried to catch her breath but she got a mouthful of Beautiful instead. It caught in her throat, and brought tears to her eyes.

5

*No one was home* that morning except Dana. Her father had gone to work early, as he did every Saturday. He said more cars broke down and more things went wrong on Saturday than any other day of the week. Things were sure going wrong this Saturday, Dana thought as she stared down the empty road. She felt sweat trickling down her neck, making her T-shirt stick to her back, but she still didn't go inside right away. It was as if she was afraid of the house now that her mother had left.

A car started to move up the road, toward Dana. She tried not to even think that it could be Libby, changing her mind, coming home before she even got as far as the next county.

"If this is her, I'll be real nice to her from now on," Dana whispered. She supposed she was bargaining with God, even though she had decided long ago that she was an atheist. "I'll do my hair the way she wants. I won't wear my jeans anymore. I'll take the SATs." Dana thought of the advice her mother always gave her, then added, aping her, "I'll make something of myself."

She watched the car turn the corner, realized it wasn't her mother's Rabbit at all. It was Caitlin's Pontiac Sunbird. Dana could see the crumpled front fender and dented driver's door from here. She took a big breath, and remembered why she had become an atheist in the first place. It seemed to her God never came through on his end of the deal.

"Hey," Caitlin said as she got out of the car.

The dented door didn't open, so Caitlin climbed over the bucket seats and out the passenger's side. Dana and Caitlin had been best friends since they were born, one month apart. Their mothers were best friends. Before Caitlin's father died, their fathers had been best friends. They were linked. When they were six, they had poked their fingers with a safety pin and rubbed their blood together.

"I'm on my way to your father's garage," Caitlin said. "See if he can fix the door."

That feeling started rising up again in Dana's stomach. She touched her friend's arm.

"What?" Caitlin said.

"She did it," Dana said. Her voice wasn't flat now. It was thick, ready to explode. Beautiful burned in her throat, and she gagged a little.

Caitlin's small green eyes darted toward the house, then back to Dana. "Who?" she said. "Your mom?"

Dana knew if she opened her mouth, she would start to cry, so she nodded instead.

"What did she do?"

Dana gulped. "Left," she said finally. "She left us."

*Harper's Garage was* always full on Saturday mornings. This morning Tom had just finished unlocking everything, yanking open the big garage door and checking his notebook of repairs for the day, when Jake Fontainbleu pulled up in his new four-door Mitsubishi Montero.

"Hey," Tom said, "how was the trip?"

Jake was Tom's age but seemed older. He had thinning hair and a big soft belly that drooped over the top of his jeans.

"The car ran like a dream," Jake said.

The two men stepped back to admire the Mitsubishi. They both appreciated anything that ran smoothly, the hum of a finely tuned engine, gears that shifted without incident.

"Of course," Jake said, "the kids drove me fucking nuts. Fought about everything. Who was going to sit where and for how long. I mean, how many times can you sing 'Ninety-Nine Bottles of Beer,' right?"

Tom laughed.

"Brought you something," Jake said. He reached into his back pocket and pulled out a map, the creases still crisp.

Tom had been collecting maps for as long as he could remember. Something about them, the way the lines connected places to each other, the way you could put your finger on one place and trace a route to somewhere else, fascinated him. When he was a kid, every gas station used to sell road maps, and he'd buy them and study them, seeing how Washington, D.C., nestled into Maryland and Virginia, or following the New Jersey Turnpike, or the old Route 66, cross-country.

Tom Harper knew how to get places. People stopped in the garage to ask him for directions before they left on trips. And when those same people came home, they brought him new maps. He had maps of Indian ruins in New Mexico, subway maps from New York City and Barcelona and Tokyo, topographic maps of the Rockies. But his favorites were still road maps.

"This here," Jake told him as he unfolded the map, "is Yellowstone." He pointed to various spots. "Grizzlies here. Old Faithful. A campground."

But Tom was not listening. His eyes were taking it in, the thin red lines

7

and alternate blue ones, the map's own symbols speaking to him like a new language.

*Tom Harper had opened* the garage when he was only nineteen years old, and it had never let him down. In high school, he had been a hero. He had won basketball and baseball games and championships for the Holly Huskies every year. He had raised money so the town could have Christmas lights and a monument for Vietnam vets. Everyone knew Tom Harper, and everyone stopped by his garage on Saturday morning. They called him Harp. They always had, and as a high school star the papers had loved to use the alliteration with great admiration. HOLLY HUSKIES' HARP HIGHLIGHTS HERE!!!! HARP HAS HUSKIES HOPPIN'!!!!

His sister, Mandy, sold coffee and doughnuts at the garage on Saturdays, and Tom talked to everybody who came in. There wasn't anybody who disliked him. Even the ones who talked about Libby behind his back, who laughed at her crazy schemes or whispered that she was locking herself in her room, acting crazy, still held no grudges against him. They felt sorry for him.

He didn't even care. He had fallen in love with Libby back in ninth grade when she sat next to him in Mrs. Heinz's English class. Tom was a terrible student, and he was bored by everything except sports, cars, and sneaking glimpses of Libby Holliday. He still remembered everything they read that year: *The Red Badge of Courage* and *Julius Caesar* and poems by Emily Dickinson and Edgar Allan Poe. He tried to say something in class every day, to get Libby's attention. He told the teacher that *The Red Badge of Courage* had changed his life. That Edgar Allan Poe was his hero. He memorized the "Et tu, Brute?" speech for extra credit.

But nothing ever worked. Libby did not seem to notice him no matter what he did. She seemed special even then, apart from everyone else. Some guys called her the ice princess. Her hair was white-blond, her eyes pale blue, her skin fair, like someone from Sweden or Norway instead of Holly, Massachusetts. She got her clothes at Filene's and Lord and Taylor's in Boston, and everything matched just right. She had shoes and sweaters and pocketbooks, all the same color. She wore a silver charm bracelet with charms from a jewelry store in New York. They arrived, he later learned, tucked into a small velvet bag in a bright blue box. Tom used to get dizzy just sitting next to her.

And she still made him dizzy, even though they'd been married for eighteen years, and had two kids. Even though as time went on, she paid less and less attention to him and spent most of her time alone in her room. For the past year, she'd looked at him as if he were a stranger. When he spoke, she'd say politely, "My, isn't that interesting?" or "Is that so?" Then she'd smile and go back to whatever it was she'd been doing—giving herself a manicure or facial, combing her hair, or just simply staring. His buddies used to say Libby Holliday had cast a spell on him, and Tom wasn't sure they were wrong. Nothing she did could drive him away.

The summer after he'd graduated from high school, Tom left Massachusetts and hitchhiked around the country. He went as far south as Key West, as far east as Block Island, as far north as Canada, and all the way west to Los Angeles. He saw palm trees, redwoods, aspens, and birches. He saw both oceans and the Gulf of Mexico, skyscrapers, Dodger and Three River Stadium, the Liberty Bell, the Grand Canyon, and the Golden Gate Bridge. And the happiest part of his trip was the day he got back home to Holly.

Libby wanted him to tell her every detail of his trip. "What did you see?" she kept asking. "What was it like?" He tried to explain how he felt about everything, how now that he'd seen the rest of the country he was somehow satisfied with himself, sure that there was no place he'd rather stay than right here, tucked in this small corner of the world. But Libby didn't understand any of it. Even then she imagined that she did not belong in Holly, that her real life lay beyond it somewhere.

"We could go out there," she told him. "To California or Arizona. We could start a life somewhere new." Tom had laughed at the idea. "Why would we want to leave everyone we know? Our families, our friends. Everything." He hadn't wanted to sound afraid of the notion, but he was. He knew that part of what he'd missed out there was the familiarity of life in Holly. The smells, the feel, the sameness of each day here. He couldn't tell her that he'd been frightened to eat alone, and usually bought fast food that he ate right in his car, with the radio on for company.

"We could have a front yard with cactus growing in it," she was saying. "Orange and avocado trees. A pink stucco house."

Those blue eyes of hers glistened while she talked. They looked off in the distance, at some future that Tom couldn't even begin to see.

"Hey," he'd told her, pulling her closer to him, "look at that moon." He'd looked up at it himself, searching for the man in the moon's face on its surface.

"Or we could live in a little house right on the beach in Florida," she'd said, sounding almost desperate. "I'd collect seashells, and driftwood, and hang wind chimes to catch the ocean breeze."

"You nut," he'd laughed. "You read too much." He'd tried to believe she was only dreaming about impossible things, the way he sometimes did. His crazy dreams had him driving a Porsche, or playing shortstop for the Red Sox. Things that he knew were never going to happen.

Even back before they were married, when she got pregnant and took off for New York City to have an abortion, he still loved her. He went after her and stopped her before she even reached the state line and let her cry and rant about how he had ruined her life by getting her knocked up. They had sat like that all night, in his car, and in the end they had driven into Boston and gotten married instead. Then he'd taken her to a Red Sox game, box seats. He caught a foul ball hit by Carlton Fisk that they kept on the mantel above their fireplace the way other people kept a wedding photo in a fancy frame. Only Libby would do something crazy like that. It was the sort of thing no one else knew about her.

That Saturday morning his daughter Dana walked in with her face all blotchy and red, Tom Harper considered himself the luckiest guy in the world. His house was a mess. His son was smoking dope. His wife was usually locked away in their bedroom. And he couldn't be happier.

*When Dana walked in,* Jake Fontainbleu was working his way through a Boston cream doughnut and telling Mandy about his trip. Tom looked up from the map of Yellowstone when the bell over the door tinkled and saw Dana holding on to Sue's kid Caitlin as if she'd fall over if she let go. He had one thought when he saw her: something bad had happened to Troy. A car accident. A drug overdose. Something real bad.

Jake was saying how his one kid wouldn't get out of the car the whole time because she was so afraid of bears and Tom looked right at his daughter's swollen eyes and said, "What? Tell me."

It seemed like everybody stopped talking and stared at the two of them. Bad news hung in the air with the smell of motor oil and coffee.

"Mr. Harper," Caitlin said, "I think you'd better come outside."

He'd never liked Sue's kid much. She was too skinny, and too bossy, a real wiseass. All of her clothes hung on her as if they were made out of old potato sacks or something. The kid made him squirm. But this morning, he listened to her and followed Caitlin and Dana outside.

Dana made him uncomfortable too. She looked just like him, a face that worked better on men, on him and Troy. He'd wanted a daughter just like Libby, blond and delicate. Beautiful. You'd never even know Dana had thick strawberry blond hair. She chopped it all weird, using his electric razor on the sides. Right now she'd shaved a peace sign on one side, some other blurry design on the other. A skull or something he couldn't make out. It was hard to tell if she was a boy or a girl if you didn't know. She always wore jeans. She never put on perfume or makeup. She was a real oddball.

"Dad," she said, looking away from him.

Caitlin nudged Dana with her bony elbow but all Dana did was gulp as if she was drowning and needed air.

"Is he in the hospital?" Tom said. "Or is it worse than that?" He couldn't bring himself to say the word "dead," but it was right there on his tongue.

Dana looked at him, surprised. "It's Mom," she said. "She left us. She went away."

"To Los Angeles," Caitlin added.

Tom grabbed the edges of the hood of Gale Strand's Impala. "Libby?" he said, to be sure he'd heard right. "Los Angeles?"

Dana started to cry, heavy sobs that shook her and made that peace sign on her head jump. "I always knew she'd do this," she was saying.

Tom closed his eyes, trying to figure out exactly what had happened. But he could only think of one thing—how quickly luck could leave a person, how fast life could change from great to awful. And then he thought of something else: How could he live without Libby?

*There were thunderstorms* all that summer before Renata Handy took her daughter Millie and moved back to Holly, Massachusetts.

"The angels are bowling," Millie would tell her.

"Angels don't bowl," Renata always answered.

But Millie's faith in magic and angels could not be shaken. She was eight years old and still thought anything was possible.

"Some do," she'd say. "Some play harps and some sing with beautiful voices—"

"Angelic voices, you could say. Right, Millie?" Renata tested her daughter constantly. She took her to science exhibits at the IBM building. She read to her from *Discover* and *Psychology Today*. She gave her facts, evidence, hard proof that there was no Loch Ness monster. No fairies. No angels bowling in the sky.

"Yes," Millie said, sighing. "A choir of angels—"

"Oh, no," Renata groaned. "Now she's quoting Christmas carols." God was another thing altogether. She hadn't even started on God yet.

Millie climbed onto her mother's lap. She was a small child with a cloud of dark curls and deep-set blue-black eyes. Those eyes were the color of bruises. Bruises that were still tender, bruises that hurt. When Renata put her arms around Millie, she felt as if she was hugging a pile of pick-up sticks.

"Mama," Millie said, pressing her head against Renata's chest. "Angels are lovely."

"Are they?" Millie's hair tickled Renata's chin, and she placed her large hand on top of her daughter's head to flatten the curls.

Outside their window, thunder rumbled.

"They have long blond hair—" Millie said.

"What about the brunette ones? What about Chinese angels? Eskimo angels? They can't all be blond."

"And white silk robes and big gold wings." Millie stretched her arms up high to show just how big their wings were. Then she faced her mother and made a circle with her hands. She held the circle over Renata's head, straining to reach. "And they have a shiny gold plate right here. Over their heads."

Renata laughed. "It's not a plate, Mill. It's a halo."

Millie did not let her hands drop. She narrowed her eyes. "If there are no angels, how come you know that?"

The thunder roared again, rumbling and cracking and shaking the windows.

Millie dropped her hands and smiled. "Sounds like a spare to me," she said.


*Renata Handy was thirty-five* years old and she felt as if she were twice that. She had left Holly for New York City the day after she graduated from high school. She packed all of her belongings in a laundry bag shaped like a smiling hippopotamus. The bus ride took four hours, but to Renata, it had seemed more like a ride on a spaceship, as if she had landed on the moon, or Mars. Or any place, worlds, light-years, from Holly.

Back then, she had thought she would be an artist. But somehow, all these years later she was still a waitress. A waitress who had long ago stopped talking about her art. There had been a few shows at the art school, a few teachers who claimed she showed promise. But now, when people asked, Renata no longer said she was an artist. She told them the truth. "I'm a waitress," she said.

Sometimes, when she worked the early shift at Goldilox, if she happened to glance at a newspaper someone left behind, she would see a review of someone's work whom she had known. Someone who had made it to Leo Castelli or Mary Boone. Someone who had long ago left the fifth-floor walk-up in the bad neighborhood for somewhere with newly painted walls and lots of space. Somewhere with a courtyard in the back, and flower boxes in the windows, and large leafy plants that did not die.

There were times, when her feet ached and she felt cranky, or when she watched Millie tremble in fright at a group of passing teenagers, or when she read those reviews in the *New York Times,* that Renata thought about leaving New York. She tried to think of a place that would return the sense of promise and hope she'd felt the day she stepped off the bus here. She imagined Santa Fe, her and Millie living in a Georgia O'Keeffe landscape. She imagined them driving down Hollywood Boulevard in a convertible, living in a cabin in Oregon, or a houseboat down South.

But as soon as she got the image of them in a new place fixed in her mind —Millie tilting her head toward an ocean breeze, the two of them roller-skating on a boardwalk—reality would set in. Moving, she told herself, was expensive. And difficult. It involved packing everything she had accumulated all of these years, labeling boxes, loading things into a truck. It involved renting the truck in the first place. It involved uprooting Millie. Uprooting herself.

So they just stayed put.


"Mama," Millie asked Renata as they stood in front of Monet's *Water Lilies* at the Museum of Modern Art, "don't you want to fall in love?"

Renata looked at the paintings in front of her. Lately she had been feeling blue, a slow sadness creeping into her. She'd read an article in the *Times* about light deprivation causing depression. It had been a gray rainy summer so far. Her apartment looked out onto an air shaft. Renata decided that if anyone suffered from light deprivation it was her. So she had come here to see these paintings. Supposedly, she'd read, Monet's paintings had helped chronic sufferers of this condition. So far, though, the blurry pastels had made Renata feel worse.

"I never did get turned on by Impressionism," she said.

Millie tugged at her jacket sleeve. "You're avoiding the question."

Renata glanced down at the top of Millie's head. The rain made her dark curls even springier. Once Millie had asked Renata to iron her hair so that it would be straight. Like Demi Moore's, Millie had said. Renata had done it too. Millie had kneeled on a chair and rested her head on the ironing board. Renata placed a towel beneath her hair and another on top of it, then ironed her daughter's curls away. "Beautiful women have long straight hair," Millie told her. For a few hours, Millie had her wish. But by late afternoon, her curls had returned, stubborn and bouncy.

"Don't you want to meet your prince and ride into the sunset on a white horse?" Millie said. "Don't you want to go to fancy balls and wear a white wedding gown?"

"No," Renata said, "I don't. And it's cowboys who ride off into the sunset, not princes."

Millie looked up at her mother and shook her head. "You're too practical," she said. "In a fairy tale, you can have your prince do anything you want. Cook your dinner. Turn straw into gold. Ride into the sunset."

"You know," Renata said, turning away from Millie's stare, pretending to focus on the Monets in front of her, "I understand the importance historically and artistically of the contribution of Monet, but I find him too soft somehow. Too easy."

Millie sighed. "Fine, Mama. Let's go in the other room then and look at the dribbles."

Renata followed Millie through the maze of rooms to the Jackson Pollocks.

"I did these in kindergarten," Millie said.

It wasn't light deprivation at all, Renata thought, trying to make sense of her uneasiness. It was something bigger. There used to be a time when she would chart her stars, get her palm read, burn a white candle while she slept. Anything for answers. But she was past that kind of thinking. She closed her eyes. The feeling was definitely there, and growing larger. Renata wasn't sure even if it was sadness. It seemed bigger than that somehow.

"Let's go," she said to Millie.

On the subway back downtown, Millie read the advertisements out loud. Roach killer, abortion counseling, AIDS hotline. She even read the ones in

Spanish. Then she turned to Renata. "I wish you'd fall in love. Even if he wasn't a prince. Even if he was a regular guy. I wish you'd fall in love and we would live with this man and all eat dinner together like on television. Those children always seem so happy."

"They're pretending," Renata told her. "Making believe. In real life, they're not leading these perfect lives, you know."

"Maybe they are," Millie insisted. Then, softly she read, " 'Acme Beauty School. You too can train to be a beautician, licensed electrologist, manicurist, and more.' "

She was angry at Renata, like the time they went to see *Peter Pan* and Renata told her how Sandy Duncan was able to fly. She had carefully pointed out the wires that stretched across the theater, showed her where the machine was that hoisted the actress upward. Millie hadn't talked to her for days that time.

"Hey," Renata said, nudging Millie, "don't be mad at me."

Millie narrowed her eyes. "Why can't the Huxtables be happy? For real?"

Renata shook her head. "Because," she said, trying to keep her voice even, "there are no Huxtables."

Millie stared straight ahead. " 'You mean,' " she read quietly, under her breath, " 'Jose is HIV positive? Now I'm really scared. Maybe I will get tested after all.' "

At first, it *was* as if someone had died. Everyone came and brought casseroles and cakes and sat around the living room looking sad. Dana kept thanking everyone for coming. She laid all the food out on the kitchen counters, the way they did after funerals, and made the big urn of coffee. She even put on a black dress that used to be her mother's a long time ago. The dress had long sleeves and a high neck, and it made Dana sweat. But she didn't know what else would be appropriate, so she kept it on.

When Troy finally came home on Sunday afternoon, he pushed through the crowd in the living room and went right over to Dana.

He had on a white T-shirt and she could see one of his tattoos peeking out from under the sleeve. It was the yin and yang. Dana was sure her brother had no idea what it even meant. He had four tattoos in all, and his girlfriend, Nadine, had three. They'd gotten them in Albany.

"Did somebody die or something?" he said.

"Mom left."

Troy had thick eyebrows, like Matt Dillon's. When he frowned, they joined together and made a long line like a caterpillar crawling across his forehead.

"What's that supposed to mean?" he said.

He smelled all stale and smoky, and Dana stepped away from him. "You stink," she said.

"Yeah? Well, so do you."

She didn't argue. Sue and Caitlin had just come in with more food. They were dressed in black too.

"Yesterday," Dana told Troy, "she packed her stuff and drove off to Los Angeles."

"No shit," he said.

"What does she think?" Dana laughed. "She's going to be a star or something?"

Troy lit a cigarette. "She's fucking nuts," he said. His eyes moved across the room. "What's everyone doing here anyway?"

"Bringing casseroles," she said. "Somebody brought that string bean kind you like. The one with the fried onions on top and the cream of mushroom soup."

"No shit," he said again.

"And somebody brought that good coconut cake. With the cherries and pineapple."

Troy nodded. "She'll be back," he said, bunching up his eyebrows again. "Don't you think?"

Dana looked over at their father. He was sitting in the Naugahyde La-Z-Boy, all slumped and old-looking, holding on tight to a bottle of beer, while some ladies from the church talked to him in real quiet voices.

"I don't know," she said. "She took everything with her."

"Well, she can bring it all back," Troy said angrily. "A person can bring stuff back just as easy as they take it away."

"Sure," Dana said. Her father was nodding now. He hadn't shaved since yesterday, a sure sign that Libby was gone. She hated facial hair, so Tom always shaved real close, and splashed on Old Spice afterward.

Caitlin came over to them. She had a casserole of hamburger meat with crushed Fritos on top.

"I told my mother this is the most disgusting stuff in the world," Caitlin said. She held the dish away from her as if it were a dead rat or something.

Troy picked some Fritos off the top and tasted them. "Good," he said.

Caitlin's black dress was shiny in spots, and stray threads hung from the hem. She'd bought it at Goodwill and thought it looked sophisticated.

"There's lots of good food in the kitchen," Dana told her.

"Your father looks just awful," Caitlin said.

The three of them turned toward Tom. He was working on another beer and still nodding at the church ladies.

"They're trying to convert him," Troy said.

Dana laughed. "Good luck."

"Why is Nadine sitting in the car?" Caitlin said.

Troy shrugged. "She doesn't like coming in."

"But it's like ninety degrees out there. She's baking," Caitlin said. She poked Troy's arm. "Did you get another tattoo?"

He pulled up his sleeve and showed her the latest one, Yosemite Sam.

"Ugh," Caitlin said. "That is so Neanderthal."

"Nadine got a rosebud right on her ass," he said. He said it proudly.

Dana and Caitlin rolled their eyes at each other.

"You know," Caitlin said, her voice soft. "Your mom had the right idea. Getting out of here. Moving on."

"Yeah," Dana said. But she wasn't sure she really agreed. She just said yeah and nodded her head, the way her father was doing with the ladies from church.

*"You are not going to* believe this," Troy told Nadine.

She had her head hung out the window, face up toward the sun. The thing about Nadine was she never tanned. Instead, she got all hot pink and blotchy, as if she had hives or something.

Troy sighed. "Put your head in the car. You'll burn."

"I used sun screen," she said, but brought her head back inside anyway. "Number forty-five."

The car smelled like her sweat. Troy frowned. Usually he found something sexy about that, but right now it was turning his stomach.

"You're not going to believe this," he said again.

"Like that museum in Florida I told you about?" she said. "Believe It or Not? Believe it or not, a guy slapped another guy's face for like three months. Without stopping."

"Nadine—"

"In Russia," she added, as if it mattered.

"My old lady left," Troy said. "She went to Hollywood to become a fucking movie star."

Nadine laughed. "Give me a break," she said. "I mean, she's ancient."

The old couple who lived down the road knocked on the side of Troy's car.

"Why are you sitting here like this?" the old lady, Mrs. Yarrow, said. She peered inside, her nose twitching like a rabbit's. "Who's the girl?"

Mr. Yarrow tugged on her arm. "Come on," he said. "Tom needs to see that we came. This one's a lost cause. You know that."

Troy watched the extra flesh on Mrs. Yarrow's upper arm sway and sag.

"Nice to meet you too," Nadine said as they walked away.

Troy backed out of the driveway, making sure the tires spit gravel as he went. He was a lost cause to everybody. He and Dana, who was only eleven months older, were in the same grade at school. But for the past few years, she'd walked by him in the hallways as if she'd never seen him before, as if he were a stranger. Just a week or two ago his mother had come into his room and sat on his bed and told him so herself. "I have done everything I can to make you respectable. To make you somebody." That was a joke. She was a terrible mother. He hardly ever even saw her. Sometimes he did things just so she'd notice him. When he was a kid, he used to do things like beat up other kids and cut school. There were always truant officers dragging him home, and teachers calling his mother, and parents banging on the door at night with their bruised sons as evidence. The principal had looked at him and said, "You are going to be nothing except a juvenile delinquent, Troy Harper." She had shaken her head, all her tight white curls bouncing around. "To think your father was something great."

Lately, Troy had done worse things. He'd stolen cars with his buddies. Taken them for joy rides until they ran out of gas, then abandoned them. He got a girl pregnant last year, someone who had dropped out of school way before Troy ever met her and already had a kid even though she was only seventeen. Troy's father had paid for an abortion. He took drugs, came home so high he couldn't even answer his mother's questions. "What are you on now?" she would ask him. "Where have you been?" But he'd be too stoned to respond.

Then, in the winter, he met Nadine at a party. And he really went wild. He brought her home all the time, both of them drunk or stoned, until his mother told him Nadine wasn't allowed in the house anymore. He started staying overnight at Nadine's. He hardly ever went to school. When his mother asked him why he was ruining his life, he laughed.

Sometimes, Nadine asked him if he loved her. Sure, he always told her. Of course. But he knew he was lying. It was her wildness he loved. The way she would do anything, try anything, say anything. She was always shoplifting, bringing him new sweaters and after-shave. Expensive stuff. She had a racket where she stole things from stores and then returned them for cash. He and his buddies had started fooling around with girls when they were in junior high. But it was always the same, hurried and in the dark, still half dressed. Even the girl he'd gotten pregnant, he'd hardly seen her face. But Nadine would do anything. She'd let him do anything. His father seemed to know that. He'd taken Troy aside and said, "Stop thinking with your dick." All Troy had done was laugh at that.

He wasn't sure where any of this was leading. He didn't even really care. The truth was, he liked Nadine. He liked the things she'd let him do with her, the things she thought up herself. He liked being high all the time. Or at least, until today when he walked in and saw all those people, he did. But something clicked in his gut when his sister told him their mother had left. It was as if he'd gone one step too far, as if he'd made her go away. He had shaken his head, trying to clear the fog there. But he couldn't shake the feeling.

He tried again now, shaking his head. He even pulled over to the side of the road, and squeezed his eyes shut hard so he could see squiggles and stars on the back of his eyelids.

"What's wrong?" Nadine said.

Troy opened his eyes and looked right at her, like it was the first time.

"You miss your mama?" she said.

"Shut up."

Nadine lit a joint and passed it to him. For a moment he thought about refusing it. He thought about dumping Nadine and driving to California himself, finding his mother and bringing her back. Maybe it wasn't too late.

"You love me?" Nadine whispered.

"Yeah," he said. He looked in the opposite direction, away from her.

"Say it."

He took the joint and sucked on it hard.

"Say it," Nadine said.

"No," he told her. "I don't say it." He pulled back onto the road.

"Actions speak louder than words," Nadine said. "Right?"

He thought about his mother getting in her car and driving away. That sure as hell said a lot.

Nadine reached over and unzipped his jeans. This was one of her favorite things to do—give him a blow job while he drove. He looked down at the back of her head, moving slowly up and down. For the first time, he wondered if he even liked Nadine.

"As for me," she said, when he was done, "I'm perfectly happy that you're a lost cause. I wouldn't want it any other way."

*Goldilox was a diner in* the East Village that was built to look dated. Everything was stainless steel and Formica. The booths were cracked red vinyl. The counter had stools with mustard yellow seats. There was a jukebox filled with Glenn Miller, Louis Armstrong, Frank Sinatra. Outside was a blinking neon sign of a martini glass. Above the olive the letters G-O-L-D-I-L-O-X slowly lit up, one by one, then flashed GOLDILOX in bright blue before beginning to slowly spell it out again.

Millie liked to pretend she was in *Happy Days* whenever she went into the diner. She liked to be the Fonz. Renata was not a mother who monitored how much television Millie watched. She felt television was a good thing. She taught Millie all the words to the theme songs from *The Beverly Hillbillies* and *F Troop*. She taught her the names of all the characters on the old *Dick Van Dyke Show*. The people who came into Goldilox had kids who hugged large Babar and Madeline books, who watched *National Geographic Specials* and listened to Mozart. But Renata knew better.

On Mondays Renata worked the early shift and got out at three, and Millie liked to come and get her and walk her home. Today, the sky hung low and gray again. More storms on the way. Earlier that week, a family picnicking in Prospect Park had been struck by lightning and killed. Some people thought this was the beginning of Armageddon. The beginning of the end.

"It's environmental," Renata explained to Millie. "Global warming." There were answers to everything, she thought. If people only looked for them.

When Millie came in that afternoon, the restaurant was almost empty. She sat on one of the stools at the counter, spinning as fast as she could.

"Give Millie a milkshake," Liz told Renata. Liz was the owner. She was tall, though not as tall as Renata, and resembled the Wicked Witch in *The Wizard of Oz*. Millie was afraid of her.

Renata mixed the milk and ice cream and syrup in the silver container, then started to whip it.

"Back home," she told Liz, "we call these frappes."

"I thought frappes were after-dinner drinks," Liz said. She never looked at people when she talked to them. Her eyes always darted around the restaurant. "Hey! Who has section two?" she shouted. "There's a fourtop there that needs cleaning pronto!" When a busboy ran past, she said, looking at the front door, "You know, like crème de menthe frappe."

Millie liked her milkshakes thick and Renata made this one so thick it was almost impossible to pour it into a glass.

"That's fra-*pay*," she told Liz. She spooned the drink into the glass, smiling. Millie would love this one.

"Whatever," Liz said, then walked away.

Renata turned toward where Millie had been spinning on her stool. But her daughter had stopped and was resting her head on the shiny counter.

"Did you make yourself sick?" Renata asked her.

Millie nodded. She did not lift her head.

"I made you the thickest milkshake ever," Renata said.

Millie smiled but did not lift her head.

"Hey," Renata said. She touched her daughter's forehead. It did not feel warm, but this was not a technique that Renata had mastered.

Millie opened her eyes. "Is the world ending?"

"Yes," Renata said. "But not in our lifetime."

"Maria Ramone's mother said it's not. She said on the last day the skies will open and all people will be judged."

Renata sat on the stool next to Millie and spilled her tips onto the counter. "That's stupid," she said.

"Mama?"

Renata didn't answer. As soon as they got home she would go across the hall and tell Maria's mother to stop telling Millie stupid lies.

"I feel dizzy," Millie whispered.

Renata glanced over. Her head was still resting on the counter. The milkshake was sitting untouched. She tried to remember if there was a flu going around. From someplace far away she could hear thunder.

"Does anything hurt?" Renata asked.

Millie shook her head. "I just feel funny. Like I'm drunk."

Renata frowned. "Are you afraid about what Mrs. Ramone told you? About Judgment Day?"

Millie lifted her head slowly. She blinked as if she was struggling to focus, then pretended she was just acting funny. "Nothing scares the Fonz," she said. "Nothing."

*The rain started as* soon as they stepped outside.

"Shit," Renata said. She grabbed Millie's hand again and started to run.

"I can't, Mama," Millie said.

"Of course you can," Renata told her.

"No, Mama," Millie said, the hint of a whine creeping into her voice. "I'm all off balance."

Renata slowed down a little. She glanced back at Millie. She had her mouth open slightly, and her eyes were as round as saucers. She even seemed to be dragging her leg a little, the way she did when she pretended she was the Ghost of Christmas Past after they watched Mister Magoo play Scrooge on television. Millie was terrified. Renata decided she was really going to give it to Mrs. Ramone.

By the time they reached their building, they were drenched, and Renata had to carry Millie up all four flights of stairs.

"Listen," Renata said, "there's no such thing as Judgment Day. Remember I told you about global warming? About cutting down the trees in the Amazon? About using aerosol cans?" As she talked she stripped her daughter, whose body had grown as limp as a rag doll. "About freon and car exhaust?"

Their one plant, a coleus that sat in a tiny plastic green pot on the windowsill, crashed to the floor. It had been a gift from Jack, the man Renata sometimes slept with. When he gave it to them, he'd assured Millie that it was impossible to kill a coleus. "But we've even killed cactus," Millie had told him. "These things," he'd said, "are invincible."

Now there it was, in a heap of dirt, on the floor.

But Millie hardly seemed to notice. Not long ago, she had named everything in the apartment. The plant was Penelope. The sofa, Sylvester. Even an old lamp had a name, Joseph. Maybe, Renata thought, glancing over at Penelope scattered across the floor, Penelope's life could still be saved. She could replant it. Jack had told her the plant needed a bigger pot, more soil.

Millie's eyes were half closed, but when the next round of thunder came, she smiled and said, "Tater wagons."

Renata wrapped a blanket around her. "Tater wagons?"

"That's what Old Man Dardowitz said. He said that's the tater wagons coming." Her voice did sound like she was a little drunk, Renata thought.

Renata smoothed back her daughter's hair, as if to erase all the myths inside Millie's head. "Mrs. Ramone is bad enough," she said, "but Old Man Dardowitz. Really, Millie."

He was a man who lived on the street, huddled in a corner, dressed in rags. Cats followed him everywhere. The kinds of cats that made people nervous—one-eyed or ribs showing or ears chewed up. There was a tiger-striped one with a harelip, long teeth protruding, drool dripping. But they all loved the old man.

"He knows wonderful stories," Millie said.

"Thunder is a scientific phenomenon, Millie," Renata said.

She put on the old lamp, and the television, ignoring the spilled plant for now.

"I'll be back in a few minutes," she told her daughter.

Millie nodded, and waved.

"It's just the flu," Renata said. "Vitamin C. Plenty of fluids. Sleep."

*"Mrs. Ramone,"* Renata said. "May I come in?"

Mrs. Ramone was short and squat, like a jeep. She smelled of fried foods and garlic, and always wore black. A crucifix hung on a tarnished chain around her neck, and she had a habit of rubbing it whenever Renata spoke to her. She was younger than Renata, but still somehow Renata called her Mrs. Ramone. As far as she knew, there was no Mr. Ramone. The five children who clung to the woman's knees and arms could have sprung from anywhere.

Mrs. Ramone did not step back to let Renata inside.

"We're eating," she said. "Go away."

"Listen," Renata said, leaning against the door frame, "I don't want you telling Millie any more stories. You frighten her with all this talk about the sky opening up and people being judged."

Mrs. Ramone's face remained impassive. Her eyes were as dark as a well. She had a hairy upper lip, sideburns.

"I like to tell her the truth about things," Renata added.

One of the Ramone children was staring straight up at Renata, until the oldest, a boy who stuttered badly, elbowed him. Then the little boy looked away. Renata thought the older boy actually spat, as if to ward off evil.

"You see," Renata continued, "we don't believe in things like that. I guess you could say we are atheists even."

Mrs. Ramone pressed harder on her crucifix. She muttered something in Spanish that Renata could not understand.

"You see," Renata said again, but Mrs. Ramone was shooing her children inside, turning her back on Renata, closing the door.

*Jack was tall, with* long hands and feet that reminded Renata of skis. He was from Trinidad, and she'd known him since they'd both moved to New York and taken art classes together. Sometimes Renata liked to think he was Millie's father. Jack thought that was a ridiculous notion. His children, he said, would surely be dark-skinned. At least as dark as coffee, or chocolate.

Anybody could be Millie's father. She was conceived at a time when Renata had been indiscriminate, when she lost herself to strangers every night. She worked at a jazz club then, in the West Village. It was the time when she realized she would never be an artist, not really. She drank a lot, and never went home alone from work. She did not bother to ask the men their names. She didn't care. Their faces were a blur too. So that when she looked at Millie, it was as if the little girl had come from thin air. She was completely unlike Renata in every way—temperament, appearance, point of view. Like all those Ramone children, Millie seemed to have nothing to do with a man at all. Nothing to do with Renata. And when Millie asked who her father was, Renata told her the truth—"I don't know."

But Jack was as close to a father as Millie could have. He copied famous paintings onto sidewalks with colored chalk all around the city. She sometimes went with him, watching as he worked. When she was little, Millie thought he was Leonardo da Vinci.

This summer, he was copying *Starry Night* on lower Broadway. All the rain was making his job difficult. So he spent a lot of time telling Millie stories about artists. She worried about van Gogh cutting off his ear. And Michelangelo painting on his back like that. True stories bothered Millie too.

Tonight, Jack came by as Renata watched Millie sleeping on the couch.

"She's worried," Renata told him.

"What does a little girl like her have to worry about?"

"The sky opening and swallowing her up."

Jack laughed. He had a voice as deep and rumbling as the thunder outside. "Shit," he said.

The room was completely dark except for the light from the television. Jack stroked Renata's face. She saw streaks of colored chalk, blue and pink and green, in the creases of his palms. She closed her eyes and let him stroke her face, her neck, her breasts over her T-shirt. When Millie was born, Renata stopped sleeping around. The only man she had sex with now was Jack, and that was only occasionally, when one of them was lonely.

He lit up a joint, and she heard his sharp intake of smoke, then a pause before he released it from his lungs. She took it from him almost greedily. Something about today, about Millie's lethargy, Mrs. Ramone's curses, had upset her. If Jack had not come to her tonight, she would have gone out in the rain, walked down Broadway to his puddle of colored stars, and brought him home with her.

*Renata stumbled into the* living room where Millie slept. The funny clock on the table, the one that Millie loved with the two fifties teenagers dancing and the words IT'S MASHED POTATO TIME, read almost eleven.

"Millie?" she said.

The little girl was still on the couch, naked, wrapped in the blanket, just as Renata had left her the night before. Renata felt a moment of panic, until she saw Millie's chest rise and then fall.

"You scared me for a minute," Renata said, laughing nervously.

"I don't feel so good," Millie told her.

Renata frowned. "You don't look so good either," she said. Then she added, "That flu."

"I've been lying here," Millie said, "waiting for you to get up. I called and called but I guess you didn't hear."

Renata leaned closer to Millie. It looked like her face was drooping slightly on one side, the way Renata's grandfather's had after his stroke. "Why didn't you come and get me?" Renata said.

"My legs are too shaky."

Diseases were coming into Renata's mind at a rapid rate. Pneumonia. Mono. Lyme disease. And wasn't there a rare encephalitis outbreak on Long Island this summer?

"Millie? Does your neck hurt?"

The little girl nodded.

"And your head?"

She nodded again.

Renata shivered. She tried to remember if Millie had any mosquito bites, tried to remember her scratching. But her mind was racing with too many other things.

And then, as Renata tried to figure out what was wrong and what she should do, Millie's right arm started to twitch.

"Millie?" Renata said. And then stupidly she added, "Stop doing that." She remembered how just a few days ago—or was it last week?—Millie had seemed to drop everything she touched. Plates of food and a glass of juice and pens and crayons. Renata had made a mental note to enroll Millie in dance class in the fall to help her coordination. She had meant to start calling around but hadn't gotten to it yet. She'd only gotten as far as imagining Millie in a glittering tutu, a rhinestone tiara on her head like a little princess.

"Millie," Renata said, "you're scaring me."

"I'm scaring *me*," Millie said.

Renata wrapped Millie in one of her own T-shirts, the very one that Jack had lifted from her so gently last night. She pulled the blanket around Millie tighter and hurried out the door. In the hall they passed Mrs. Ramone, out of breath, bags of groceries tied to a little cart. When Renata pushed past, the woman made the sign of the cross.


*The doctor in the emergency room* looked like a high school student. His voice cracked when he spoke, stray hairs sprouted here and there on his face from a sloppy shave. Renata wanted to shout for someone older, someone wise who could treat encephalitis. An encephalitis specialist. But her voice came out calm and even as she answered the doctor's questions.

"Her head hurts," she reminded him. Did she have to make this diagnosis herself?

"Everything's all blurry," Millie said.

This surprised Renata. It filled her with relief. "Why, she probably just needs glasses," she said, almost giddy. Why hadn't Millie said that earlier? It explained everything, the headache and the clumsiness and the dizzy spells.

"When did it start?" the doctor asked.

He had beady eyes. Renata didn't like that about him. His name, pinned above the stethoscope in his pocket, seemed to have no vowels.

Again, her voice was calm. "Yesterday," she said.

"April," Millie told him.

The doctor's head shot up. "April?" he asked, his voice cracking again.

"Millie," Renata said, her heart starting to pound again, "you got sick yesterday."

"Remember that day Jack took us on the boat?"

"The Circle Line," Renata said, looking at the doctor. She suddenly felt like she had to prove she was a good mother. "One of our little excursions," she said.

"That's the day I got sick. I could hardly see the Statue of Liberty's face."

"But why didn't you mention it to me?" Renata said. She remembered how that day Millie had dropped her soda and she had scolded her. Looking back at the doctor, she added, "She never said a word until yesterday."

"I thought it would go away," Millie said, sighing.


*Renata thought encephalitis* would be bad. It would be touch and go for a while, she thought. There would be intravenous, the intensive care unit, hushed voices. Then Millie would open her eyes and ask for some Baskin-Robbins bubble gum ice cream. She would look around surprised at where she was. She would giggle and say, "Can we go home now?"

Encephalitis would be bad. But this was worse. This doctor who still had acne, who didn't shave carefully, whose voice still hadn't finished changing, was telling her that Millie had something called a neuroblastoma. He said it as if everyone knew what that was.

"Speak English," Renata said.

"A brain tumor," he squeaked.

"No," Renata told him, surprised that her voice still sounded so calm.

She had been in the hospital for twelve hours, sitting on this hard plastic turquoise chair drinking bad coffee from a vending machine. Whenever they wheeled Millie past, Renata leapt up and made jokes. She grabbed her daughter's hand and squeezed it. She made her promises. They would get goldfish, a cat. They would grow plants that wouldn't die.

"I want another doctor," she said. "I want to take Millie home."

He sat down beside her and took both of her hands in his. She was surprised at how cool and dry his hands were, and slender like a teenage girl's.

"Just take it out," Renata said.

The doctor sighed and told her to make an appointment with a pediatric neurologist. A Doctor Jinx.

"Jinx?" Renata said. "What kind of name is that for a doctor?" Certainly not one that could save someone's life.

"It's up to Jinx, of course," the doctor told her. "But my guess is radiation."

"There's been a mistake," Renata told him as he shook her hand.

He nodded. He had dandruff too, big flakes that clung to his sideburns. "I know how you feel," he told her.


*It did not seem right that* Millie was in a room with children who were not really sick. A girl whose leg was in a cast and suspended from a sling. Another who had her tonsils out. There was an empty bed, and then Millie, dressed in a hospital johnny decorated with *Sesame Street* characters. Renata noticed that the other children wore their own pajamas and she felt embarrassed.

"There's been a mistake," she told Millie.

Already a bruise had formed on the back of Millie's hand where an IV was hooked up.

"Tomorrow I'm talking to a new doctor who will straighten all of this out."

Millie said, "I thought you got to eat Popsicles when you were in the hospital. And ice cream."

Renata smiled. Children with brain tumors had no appetite. She was sure of that.

"I'll go tell a nurse to get you some. Okay?"

Millie nodded.

Renata noticed that these other children had teddy bears with them, dolls, familiar things. But Millie was only here for the night, she reminded herself. She didn't need anything like that.

The door was blocked by the arrival of a new patient, someone for the empty bed. It was a girl Millie's age, with long blond braids and a fading tan. Everyone around her was cheerful, making jokes and laughing. The girl clutched a stuffed zebra. When she smiled two dimples appeared in her cheeks.

"It's been a scary few days," the woman told Renata. Her voice sounded nervous, high strung. "We were at our place in Sag Harbor and she got bitten by a mosquito."

Renata turned and watched as they lifted the little girl from the gurney to the bed.

"Encephalitis," the girl's mother said. "You hear these things on the news and you think it can't happen to you."

Renata nodded.

"They didn't think she'd make it," the girl's mother said. "They said it was fifty-fifty."

Renata nodded again. They had given this woman odds, at least. She would take fifty-fifty right now. She thought of the doctor's smooth hands holding hers.

Behind her, the little girl's family huddled around her bed while a nurse snapped their picture.

In unison, they all said, "Cheese."

"This is the first time I've seen you smile in days, Gretchen," the mother said.

Renata left the room to find someone who could get Millie's ice cream. But the nurse's station was empty, the hallway deserted.

*The room was dark, filled* with the steady sounds of children's breathing. Renata sat beside Millie's bed, studying her face. Not memorizing it, she told herself, but looking for clues. Someone who was going to die would not have eaten all of her dinner, or giggled with the little girl who'd survived encephalitis, or look so calm and unconcerned.

There's been a mistake, Renata told herself again.

The sky lit up with late summer heat lightning. Then the thunder started again, Loud, close.

Millie opened her eyes.

"Mama," she said.

Renata pressed her fingers to her little girl's lips. "Shhhhh," she whispered. "Listen."

"What?" Millie said.

"The angels," Renata told her. "The angels are bowling."

aitlin *was always saying* that part of the problem with life was its predictability. She sighed like an actress and moaned, "No surprises." And as usual, Dana agreed. They listed all the boring things in their lives—

school, working at Pizza Pizzazz, and their boyfriends. Mike and Kevin were exactly like every other boy in school. "No surprises," Caitlin said.

They had been with them since seventh grade when Gayla Lobrowski had a Halloween party in her basement and after bobbing for apples and eating junk food everyone played spin the bottle and paired off. It seemed strange to Dana that most of those original pairings were still intact. Mike was the first boy she had kissed. He was there when she had her first drink and her first cigarette. He had taught her how to drive and waited while she took her driving test to make sure she passed.

But more and more lately she found that she hardly listened when he spoke. He never had anything to *say*, really. He didn't seem to have ideas or opinions about anything. His favorite phrase was "status quo." "How's everything?" Dana would ask him and Mike would say, "Status quo, babe." He was the school's star wrestler until he broke his arm last season. Now he mostly watched TV, got drunk, and talked about *The Simpsons*. Sometimes, sitting next to him on the couch in front of the television set, Dana went to sleep, even if it was only eight o'clock. She just slept until he took her home.

The night after her mother left, she tried to explain how she felt to Mike. But his eyes kept drifting to the old *M\*A\*S\*H* rerun on the television.

"You have to listen to me," Dana finally screamed at him. "My mother is gone!"

Mike's eyes settled on her briefly. "With your mother," he said, "that's sort of status quo, don't you think? I mean, even when she was there, she wasn't there. You know what I mean?"

"I hate you!" Dana yelled.

The next night he showed up with flowers. He stole them from graves but she still thought it was sweet.

"I'm a jerk," he told her, and nuzzled her neck and told her he was really sorry about her mother.

Sometimes, like right then, kissing Mike felt as sweet as it had that first night in Gayla Lobrowski's basement when he'd nudged the beer bottle so it pointed at her. Besides Caitlin, no one knew as much about her as Mike did.

"You are a jerk," she told him, but she hugged him real close when she said it.

They went to Joe's Diner for burgers and then to the quarry. Sitting in the car with a Madonna tape playing, Mike said, "Remember that first time I kissed you? You were wearing a witch costume."

"Uh-huh," Dana said.

"Even with a green face you looked cute."

Dana stared out the window, past the quarry. She wondered where her mother was right now.

"Hey," Mike was saying. He tugged on her hand.

"What?" She turned toward him and he had a weird look on his face. "What?" she said again.

"I got you this," he said. And he held up a ring, a thin gold band with a heart in the middle and the tiniest speck of a diamond chip in the middle of that.

"What is it?" Dana said, even though she knew.

"It's like a pre-engagement ring. You know."

It looked so tiny in his big hand. All the girls were getting pre-engaged this year. That was how it worked. Pre-engaged before senior year, engaged that Christmas or Valentine's Day, married after graduation. It was like one of her father's maps—you knew exactly where all the lines led. Dana could almost hear Caitlin's theatrical sigh. No surprises.

"Come on," Mike said, tugging at her finger. "Put it on."

She wanted to say no. She wanted to tell him that she and Caitlin were leaving, that they were going to lead unpredictable lives. But he looked so happy right then. He remembered she was a witch that Halloween night. He had cheated just to kiss her, nudging the bottle in her direction. So she held out her hand to him and tried to smile.


*"I'm getting out of here,"* Libby had told Tom on their very first date.

They were sixteen years old and Tom had sat through two years of English classes next to her before he got the courage to ask her out. He had taken her to Pittsfield for an Italian dinner at a real restaurant. They'd sat in a booth with a candle burning in a red globe wrapped with white net. The place mats had games on them. "Find the Thing That Doesn't Belong," one of them said. And Tom had found it—a fish was sitting in a tree, next to a robin's nest. "Dumb," Libby had said.

After dinner they'd gone to see the movie *Butterflies Are Free*, and she'd let him hold her hand the whole time. He couldn't concentrate on any of it, not on the dinner or Goldie Hawn helping the blind guy in the movie or anything. All he could think of was that Libby Holliday was sitting beside him. He had to admit he was a little afraid of her. She used one word to sum up exactly how she felt. The games on the place mat were dumb. The spaghetti was okay. The movie was heart-wrenching. And his car was cool.

And now they had driven the long way back to Holly so he could pull off a back road next to a cornfield and try to kiss her. "Kiss the ice princess?" Mitch had said earlier. "Good luck. You'll probably turn into the Abominable Snowman." Tom had spent the whole week planning every step of this date. He didn't want anything to go wrong. By the end of the night he wanted Libby Holliday to be his.

They sat in his car with the radio turned on low. The car was a 1972 copper Firebird with a thick white racing stripe and a V-8 engine.

That's when she said it the first time. "I'm getting out of here."

For an instant, Tom thought she meant out of the car. He hadn't even tried to kiss her yet.

"Out of Holly," she said, as if she could read his mind.

"Yeah?" he said. It was a silly notion. They were sixteen years old and there was noplace else to go. But he played along.

"I am so sick of all this corn," she moaned, laying her head back on the seat.

He studied her profile, the way her hair clung to the seat, the shape of her neck, her long eyelashes cast downward. Tom leaned over and kissed her as softly as he could right on the neck. She didn't open her eyes.

"How fast does this go?" she whispered.

Again he was confused. How fast does what go? he thought. Already he could feel himself hard inside his pants.

"This," she said, again as if she had read his mind. She patted the top of the stick shift.

"Fast," he whispered back. Steppenwolf was on the radio. "Magic Carpet Ride." "Real fast," he said.

"Let's do it," she said. She opened her eyes and looked right into his.

He was still leaning across her, his face only inches from hers.

"You got it," he said.

He tried to adjust his still hard penis so he could drive. Out of the corner of his eye, Tom was sure she had seen him do it, and that she'd smiled. He was so sure he'd been right all along. She wasn't an ice princess at all. She was wild. He shifted into first, and made her climb. At eighty he glanced away for a second, and saw Libby leaning out the window, screaming "Faster!"

He pressed down harder on the accelerator. They were over a hundred now, and still she wanted more. He could hardly see out the windshield, the tires were kicking up so much dust. And later, when they'd gone as fast as they could, and he'd pulled back off the road, and Libby was flushed and panting from the ride, he'd started at that long white neck, and slid his

32

tongue up it, across her chin, to her mouth, taking her sweat and a layer of dust with him. That was how he thought of her still, tasting like dust on his tongue.

*Holly, Massachusetts, was famous* once a year, at Christmas time. Along with other towns across the country, like Santa Claus, Maine, and Mistletoe, Iowa, and Christmas Tree, Washington, people sent their Christmas cards there to be postmarked. Holly even used a special postmark in December. It had a sprig of holly in the stamp, right between the HOLLY and the MA.

To Tom, that made Holly even more special. It made the town seem almost magical. So did the way the moon fell across the high stalks of corn that bordered the outskirts of town, and the way each spring everyone chipped in to clean and repair the buildings in the town square. Once, a film crew had shown up to investigate the possibility of using Holly in a movie. It was that perfect a place. And even though they decided to film their movie somewhere in Canada instead, their consideration only reaffirmed Tom's certainty that it was the best place to grow up, and to grow old.

That was one of the reasons he couldn't believe that Libby had left. Why would she want to be in a city like Los Angeles, with traffic and smog and dangerous gangs? He should have listened to her more, taken her on vacations to other places so she could appreciate Holly the way he did. When they were first married, she used to drive to a travel agency in Albany and bring back brochures of Greece and Italy, Hawaii and Bermuda. "Look at this," she'd say, pointing to one of the brochures. "Pink sand." Tom would study the pictures of happy couples pedaling mopeds past bright purple flowers, or sunbathing on pink sand beaches, or eating grilled fish in a fancy restaurant. It would all seem distant and frivolous somehow. And as she read to him about optional excursions on glass-bottom boats and snorkeling lessons at coral reefs, he would get a knot in his stomach. Why couldn't she be satisfied with what they had, with what was right here? For Tom, their small square house, with the babies crawling around and the two of them sitting on the couch with their feet in each other's laps, was all he wanted.

Sometimes, after she'd laid out all the travel brochures in front of him on the coffee table and read each one's highlights, he'd say, "I've got a better idea. Let's stay right here and make more babies." He used to say he wanted nine, his own baseball team. Then Libby's mouth would form into a straight, tight line as she carefully folded each brochure, smoothing the creases, running her fingers almost lovingly across the photographs of volcanoes and high-rise hotels. There was a drawer full of those brochures still, and after she left him, Tom sometimes pulled them out late at night and studied them, wondering what pleasure these places could have brought Libby and if their power could have somehow kept her here, where she belonged.

*For as long as she* could remember, Libby Holliday had been trying to leave her family. She liked to think that the first time, when she was just eighteen years old, fresh out of high school and thinking she could become a movie star, she took Dana with her. Sort of. Libby was seven weeks pregnant and Dana was the size of a tadpole, floating inside her, forcing her to throw up every morning, ruining her plans.

It was true that when she left Holly and Tom that first time, Libby was headed for New York City and, maybe, an abortion. But as time passed she could almost convince herself that she would have backed out, that she would not have gone through with it. Instead, Libby liked to think she would have had Dana and together they would have conquered the world. All the time she read about movie stars with children they'd had before they'd made it. She saw them on *Entertainment Tonight,* Suzanne Somers and Raquel Welch, too many to name, really. And there they were, famous, their children grown, everything having worked out neatly.

Of course, Libby didn't make it to New York at all, so in a way it was easy to rewrite the scene. It was much harder to accept the fact that what she did was let Tom find her and marry her and to settle down into the most ordinary, the dullest possible life. For so long Libby had thought she was special, but in the end she was no different from Sue or Dee-Dee or any other girl from school.

In those early years, she thought about leaving all the time. She would get in her car and drive to the Vermont border, then just sit there, unable to cross it. Once she got as far as Winsted, Connecticut, only to turn back at the sound of a baby crying in a McDonald's when she stopped for lunch. That little baby cried hard, her face turning purple, her eyes squeezed shut. Libby didn't even finish her Big Mac, she just got in the car and drove home.

Having Dana and Troy eleven months apart made leaving twice as hard. She kept her figure, even after two babies. At night, while everyone was asleep, she studied Tom's maps, tracing the routes west. Libby started to make lists of what she'd take and what she'd leave behind. She read about movie stars, how old they were when they got started. She kept thinking she still had time.

On her twenty-fifth birthday, she decided it was now or never. Libby went over to Sue's and told her she was leaving. "I'll come with you," Sue said. "Maybe I could get a job out there too. Doing hair and makeup. Something like that." They decided to leave bright and early the next morning. Libby crept out before anyone woke up. She didn't pause to study her children's faces, the way a woman in a movie might. She just left. Sue was waiting on the porch with Caitlin. She'd dressed Caitlin as if she was going to a party, in a bright yellow dress with ruffles and bows, little white ankle socks and shiny patent leather shoes.

"Where are we dropping her?" Libby asked as they pulled out. "Your mother's?"

She would never forget that day, the air crackling with possibility, the sky just starting to turn from dark to light, a half moon still shining in front of them.

"Drop her?" Sue said. "She's coming along. I couldn't leave her, Libby. I'd never forgive myself."

Libby had swallowed hard, focused on the road ahead of her. "Of course," she said, seeing the logic of that. After all, Sue's husband, Mitch, was dead. "You don't have anyone to take care of her like I do." She'd nodded, talking herself into the idea. "Why, I have Harp. He loves those kids. He'll make sure they're okay." She even laughed. "He's better with them than I am anyway."

"Sure, he is," Sue told her. "If I had Harp . . ."

She didn't finish because she couldn't. It simply wasn't true. Sue would never leave her daughter behind. Never. And that lay between them all morning, as they drove farther and farther from Holly. Until finally Libby said, "Let's go back."

Sue nodded, relieved. "All right," she said.

They never talked about going away again.


*The entire way cross-country* Libby tried not to think about Dana's face receding in her rearview mirror as she drove away. To think about that would be to think about consequences, and Libby knew that train of thought would lead her straight back to Holly. She had tried to leave before, and it was the image of her children that brought her home again.

This time she was determined to go and stay gone. She concentrated on not thinking. Because she hadn't taken the proper time to plan everything out carefully, she only had two tapes with her, and one was Dana's, *The Violent Femmes*. It gave Libby a headache. The other was Simon and Garfunkel's *Greatest Hits*, and how long was a person supposed to listen to that? So she drove, singing along with the radio when she could and singing alone, loud, when she could only get religious stations.

If she'd had the time, she would have mapped out a route that was interesting. She would have really seen America. But the way things had worked out, Libby felt as if someone was right on her tail, chasing her. That if she were to slow down, to stop and look at anything at all, she would go back. It was as if something bigger than herself was right there, breathing down her neck.

So she moved forward, singing loud, pushing out that image of Dana growing smaller and smaller. She slept in Motel 6s, careful to fill out the comment cards, checking off Good or Fair in the boxes beside CLEANLINESS and COURTESY. She ate at Big Boy restaurants, three meals a day so she didn't get run-down, even though she wasn't very hungry. She made sure to eat a balanced meal, to avoid fried foods and too much caffeine. She took the time to figure out a fifteen percent tip after each meal and to fill in those comment cards too. "Add more chicken dishes," she suggested. "And more fresh fish."

Still, at night in the strange motel beds, when she closed her eyes, her family's faces came crashing into her head, and Libby had to press hard on her eyelids to block out what she had left behind.

Mandy Harper Sullivan, like her brother Tom, was a jock. Field hockey, basketball, and powder puff football. She taught gym at the high school now, and her husband, Frank, owned a Bess Eaton Donuts franchise. She was built real solid, all muscle and tanned strong legs. She was like Tom in that everybody liked her. In school, they were the golden pair. A sister and brother who had everything. And somehow, like her brother, Mandy still believed it too.

That first Saturday after Libby left him, Tom showed up at the garage early like always. Except this time when Mandy looked at him she said, "You look like shit."

Unshaven, bleary-eyed, he looked older, like he had aged years in just a few days.

"I feel even worse," he told her.

She poured him a cup of coffee and he added whiskey to it.

"She is not worth doing this to yourself," Mandy said.

"Yes, she is," Tom told her. "She's worth everything."

Since Libby had left, it was as if Tom was seeing everything through new eyes. Even Mandy. She suddenly seemed simpleminded, all happy with her stupid life. She stood before him frowning, dressed in baggy gray shorts and a UMass sweatshirt, a whistle dangling from a red and white cord around her neck. She would leave here to coach the girl's field hockey team. Both of her daughters, Lindsay and Ali, were its star players. Didn't they know anything? Tom thought, watching her arrange the dozens of doughnuts, all glazed and sugary, on a tray.

"First of all," Mandy was saying, "she'll be back. You know it. The woman cannot take care of herself."

Tom laughed. That was another thing Mandy was wrong about. Libby could most certainly take care of herself. Better than anybody. Who did Mandy think she'd been taking care of all these years? Him? The kids? That was a joke. Libby looked after Libby. Period.

"You don't know the first thing about it," he said. He took a chocolate honey-dipped doughnut and finished it off in two bites.

"I know this," Mandy said. "Cathy Communale is divorced. Dee-Dee Winthrop is divorced. These girls used to drool after you. They would not have left you. Not in a million years."

"Cathy Communale," Tom said.

Way back, in junior high, she had been some kind of roller-skating star. She competed, statewide, nationally. Her mother sewed her these costumes, little flared velvet skirts and tight bodysuits. Her thighs were thick and muscled. And once, behind the school, where the kids who couldn't drive yet used to go to make out, she'd parted those thighs and let him slip his fingers between them, inside the bodysuit, right into her. He still remembered how she used to look out there on the rink, how warm and wet she had felt.

"Cathy was one of my best friends," Mandy said. "And you threw her over for Libby."

Did everyone here live in the past like this? Tom thought. They were kids then. Cathy Communale had parted her thick thighs for him twenty years ago. More, even.

People started arriving, all awkward at first. Here sat Tom Harper, whose wife had left him. No one really knew what to say. So they talked cars. That was always safe. And Mandy poured them coffee and let them slap her ass. Tom felt as if he was watching someone else's life go by.

Then Pat O'Malley said, "My kid's trying out for the football team in the fall."

"He's already that old?" somebody said.

Pat nodded. He used to play too. Tom saw streaks of silver throughout his hair and in the chest hairs that poked out of the top of his shirt.

"You know what I was telling him just this morning?" Pat said. "About that game where you threw seventy yards for a touchdown, Harp. I'll never forget how beautiful that was."

"What a day," Jake Fontainbleu piped in. "The leaves were all gold, and we could smell fall. You know the way fall smells?"

"Right, right," Pat said, nodding, looking at Tom still, with great admiration. "And you threw that ball perfectly. Just right. It was like time stopped, and all there was at that moment was you and that ball falling in a perfect arc, and that crisp blue sky, and the smell of fall." Pat shook his head. "Seventy yards."

"And no one's broken the record yet," Mandy said.

They were all looking at him, shaking their heads, wide-eyed and awed, still, after all this time.

*T*roy *was not friends* with any of the jocks, not O'Malley or Kevin or Mike or any of them. His crowd was the guys who went to school early and sat in their cars getting high before classes. The guys who sat in the last row in class and never had their homework done. The ones who were always getting kicked out of assembly, out of class, out of school. The girls in the crowd teased their hair and sprayed it stiff, wore leather jackets, too much makeup, high heels even with jeans.

Since he'd been with Nadine, Troy hadn't seen them much. But the week after his mother left, he drove down to the Dairy Queen, where they hung out on Saturday nights, sitting on the hoods of their cars, drinking and smoking and planning the rest of their night.

"To what do we owe this pleasure?" Gary Cooper said. Like Libby, his

mother had great hopes for him, naming him after an old movie star, thinking he'd be something special.

"Boredom," Troy said. He hopped onto the hood of Gary's car and
pulled out a small plastic bag of pills he'd taken from Nadine's top drawer.
Right now, she was at work filling Dixie Cup dispensers with Dixie Cups
decorated with autumn leaves. What a joke.

A girl he didn't know let out a low whistle. She had pockmarks on her
face which she had tried to cover up with thick makeup, but even in this bad
lighting Troy could see them.

"A buffet," he said, and spilled the pills onto the car.

Everybody took some, and swallowed them with beer. The girl said,
"Who are you anyway?"

Gary threw his arm around Troy's neck. "This here's my old pal Troy
Donahue. We're teen idols, you know."

"I'm Marie," she said, ignoring Gary, pushing closer to Troy.

"Hey," Gary said. "He's taken. He's got a girlfriend who would whip
your ass in a second. She is bad."

"Do you?" Marie said.

Troy shrugged.

"Although," Gary was saying, "Troy is pretty bad himself."

"A lost cause," Troy said.

Gary's girlfriend, Rena, came toward them, carrying a cardboard box
with hamburgers and french fries in it. She looked at them and said, "What
are you guys on?"

Troy leaned toward Marie. "You want to be really bad?" he said. His
voice seemed slowed down, like a record on the wrong speed.

She was chewing peppermint gum. Troy got a good whiff of it when she
answered, "You bet."

The four of them got into Gary's car and took off.

"This car sucks," Troy said. "We should have these ladies in something
really nice." His eyes met Gary's in the rearview mirror.

"Like a BMW?" Gary said.

"That would be good."

On the way, Marie kept nodding out, her head bobbing up and down,
jerking herself awake, then mumbling before she went out again.

Rena turned around. "Uppers," she said, and poured a handful of pills
into Troy's hand. He opened another beer, and shook Marie half awake.

"Take these," he said. "You can't be bad if you're asleep."

He had to help her take them, and to sip the beer. By the time they got to Williams College, she was tapping her feet and talking so fast he could hardly understand her. They walked around the parking lot, "Car shopping," Gary kept saying, until they found a BMW. A red one. Then Marie took off her shoes and with the spiked heel of one broke the passenger window. She climbed in, over all that glass, talking and talking, unlocking the doors, falling into the back seat. Troy followed her, laughing. There was blood all over her hands.

"I've only had sex with three guys, you know. And I loved two of them," she said. "I was always really good at spelling. Give me a word. Really. Give me a word."

"Mississippi," Troy said.

Gary was driving fast, away from the college, toward the quarry.

"That's easy. Give me a hard one. Come on, come on, come on."

Gary and Troy started laughing. They couldn't stop. "She wants a hard one," Gary said.

But Rena was shouting words. "Occupation. Veterinarian. Hypodermic." And Marie was spelling them.

All the way to the quarry. Once they were there, and Troy led her through the woods, she kept spelling everything they passed. "B-I-R-C-H," she said. "M-O-O-N." She didn't stop even when he tore the zipper on her jeans pulling them down, even when he entered her and pushed hard into her. "S-K-Y, and, and, S-H-A-D-O-W-S." He left her there, spelling, her jeans ripped, her shirt bunched up, and walked back through the trees, past the stolen car, down the dirt road, all the way home.


*Sometimes in the morning* Tom could pretend nothing had changed. Libby had always been a late sleeper, so even if she hadn't locked herself in her room she wouldn't be downstairs in the morning. Tom could drink his coffee and read his newspaper while Dana sulked around him, and Troy—if he appeared at all—held his head in his hands and gazed all bleary-eyed at the table. In the morning Tom could glance up and pretend that Libby was upstairs, dressed in one of her long white nightgowns, all lacy and ruffled, asleep.

When Troy stumbled to the table this morning, Tom could still smell old liquor coming from him. Old liquor and smoke. He had tried to talk to Libby about their son but she had only wrinkled her forehead and narrowed her eyes as if she was trying to remember who exactly Troy was. Remembering that, Tom wondered again how he could have missed so many signs. Of course she was getting ready to leave. Her eyes were already searching elsewhere. Of course.

Tom tried to concentrate on the newspaper. When he glanced up again, Troy was resting his head flat on the table.

"Hey," Tom said. "Pick it up."

Troy opened his eyes and looked up at his father.

"Hey," Tom said again. "What are you doing? Huh? You've got to get ahold of yourself, Troy. Come on."

He touched the boy's head lightly but Troy just closed his eyes again.

Tom knew it wasn't fair to compare your children to yourself. But sometimes, especially with Troy, he couldn't help himself. When he was in school, he'd played sports. The feel of a bat in his hand, or the way a football fit into the crook of his arm, those things meant something. Sure he drank some, smoked a little pot, and there were some mornings after victory parties when he felt the way Troy did right now. But this was something different. Something much worse than just a hangover. The boy had nothing, except maybe that worn-out girl from the Dixie Cup plant.

He thought again of Libby. Young this time, and sitting beside him in his car on a summer night. With a mother like her, how could Troy even look at someone like Nadine?

"I heard," Dana was saying, "that some girl had to get her stomach pumped from mixing pills with liquor and they think she even stole some senator's kid's car up at Williams."

Suddenly Troy sat up. "She didn't die or anything," he said. "Did she?"

"Do you know what they do when they pump your stomach?" Dana said. "They stick like a vacuum cleaner hose down your throat and suck everything out."

"I don't think so," Tom told her. He had just been reading about that stolen car, a new BMW 320i convertible. He looked back at the paper and found the article.

"But the girl's all right?" Troy was asking.

"I heard her hands were all cut up and somebody found her wandering down Route 23 bleeding all over the place and acting weird," Dana said. "Of course, this is according to Mike so take it for what it's worth."

"What's wrong with Mike?" Tom said. He liked that kid, even if he was a Yankees fan. At least Mike could talk baseball.

"Oh, please," Dana said, groaning. "He's a philistine."

"Some kids just took that car for a joyride," Tom said. He sighed. A philistine. Where did she come up with this stuff?

41

"I'm sure that girl is fine," Troy said.

Tom looked at him sharply. Pills and liquor and stolen cars, he thought. Troy was gnawing at a callus on his thumb. Tom took a breath. Even if Libby really were upstairs, she would just sigh and wrinkle her forehead. She would shrug and sigh some more. She would not look at him. "I don't know," she'd say. "I really don't know."

Tom stood and tugged on Troy's arm. "Come on," he said. "We're going for a ride."

"No, thanks."

"This isn't optional," Tom said.

Troy stumbled to his feet, and for an instant Tom saw his son as he used to be when he was a toddler, all thick legs and arms with a shock of black hair that stood straight up like a Halloween cat's. This kid's going to be a linebacker, Tom used to say. He'll be the one to save the Patriots at last.

"Come on," Tom said again, gentler this time.


*Troy hated his father's* obsession with sports. It was plain dumb. All of it—trying to toss a ball through a hoop and trying to hit one over a fence or kick a ball over a post. Dumb. But that's what he rattled on and on about that morning. The Red Sox. RBIs and ERAs and the stamina of Dwight Evans. While Troy tried to not get carsick. Pick a focal point and don't shift your gaze from it at all. That's what his mother had taught him when he was a kid and he used to get carsick. He used to pick a spot on the back of her head as his focal point.

But this morning he stared at the center of the visor he'd put down to block some of the bright summer sun. He wished his father would shut up. He wished the car would stop. He wished that crazy girl Marie was all right. Not dead or in a coma or something. What if, he thought, he turned on the news some night and there were her parents all old and sad, trying to get permission to pull the plug on her? His eyes shifted from his focal point and his stomach lurched.

"Are we almost there?" he said.

His father nodded. "It's heartbreaking," he said. "That's what it is. I should have been a Yankees fan, right?"

"Yeah," Troy said. "I guess so."

The car stopped then, in the middle of nowhere.

Troy followed his father out.

"Boy," Tom said, shaking his head. "I had such big plans."

The fresh air felt good and Troy gulped it down. Here in the quiet, in the shade, his stomach settled and his head started to slowly clear.

"What plans?" he asked finally.

His father seemed almost embarrassed. "I thought we'd have a bunch of kids. A big house." He laughed at himself. "There used to be this TV show called *Please Don't Eat the Daisies* and that was the kind of family I imagined Libby and I would have. Kids and a big old sheepdog and a house and lots of laughter."

Tom looked bewildered as he talked, as if the realization that he didn't get what he'd hoped for surprised him somehow. Until Libby left him, he'd felt he had everything he wanted. He had not even known until this very minute how much his happiness, his sense of who he was, had been tied up with his love for Libby.

"You know," Tom said, his voice full of surprise, "I never did get that, did I? Not the sheepdog. Not the laughter."

Troy could remember lots of laughter. But it was always between him and his mom. They used to be able to make each other laugh. He had a way of turning his eyelids practically inside out so he looked like a monster. That used to make her scream and run away from him and when he chased her she would start to laugh. He used to stretch his arms out straight in front of him and act like a zombie. Oh, no, she'd say, it's the creature from the Black Lagoon. And she'd run and giggle. She could wiggle her ears. It's not a talent, she'd explained to him. It's just a muscle that's going extinct and in another generation no one will have it. I'm a dying breed, she used to say. Then she'd wiggle them like crazy and he would laugh until it hurt.

There were other times when just looking at each other could send them both into hysterical laughter. Not lately. But before she got so sad. Before she'd sit in her room day after day and not talk. Not even to him. Sometime last fall he'd even stood in the doorway and made his zombie eyes at her. But she'd hardly smiled. You nut, she'd said. But she said it like it was the saddest thing in the world.

Now his father was saying how he'd always imagined he'd build that big *Please Don't Eat the Daisies* house up here someday.

"But that's never going to happen," Tom said. "Not for me at least."

"Who owns this land?"

"I do. Libby's parents used to. They thought they'd build up here but they never did. They wanted to be in the thick of things. So they gave it to us when Dana was born." Tom took a deep breath. "Now I want you to have it."

Troy laughed. "Me?"

"Sure. What am I going to do with it?"

"What am I going to do with it?" Troy said. He stared out at the foothills of the Berkshires. In the fall, he thought, when the leaves changed, they would look like a crazy quilt.

"I don't know," his father said. "Do whatever you want."

His father walked back to the car, but Troy stayed a few minutes more, breathing the clean pine smell, staring out at a distant point, clearing his head.

*Some nights, when Nadine* was at work, Troy went out to the land alone. He stretched out smack in the center and imagined he was in a house that he'd built, in a bed with crisp sheets and colorful quilts and lots of soft pillows. Or he imagined he was in front of a big fireplace and that it was winter and the hills were covered with snow, like birthday cake frosting. Or he would just lie on his back and stare up at the stars. There seemed to be more up here somehow. He wouldn't want to lose those stars, so he'd imagine that the house had skylights.

The only thing he couldn't imagine there was Nadine. Whenever he tried to, his mind grew completely blank. She somehow had the ability to erase everything—his image of the distant hills covered in colored leaves, his fantasy of being in bed looking up at the sky, she could even erase the stars. So he stopped trying to bring Nadine into his fantasies at all.

Instead, when she left him at night in her cramped sour-smelling bed and went off to stuff Dixie Cups into their dispensers, Troy dressed and drove through the black woods to this spot. Once there, he felt suddenly freer. Sometimes he slept the whole night there, waking with the sun coming up in his eyes. The sun had a way of making the hills seem like they were on fire.

Until his father gave him this land, Troy had no real focus. If someone asked him, he supposed he would say that he would work for his father at the garage when—if—he finished school. He felt that his future was more immediate. It was that very moment with Nadine, or planning how to get high that night. But when his mother left and his father gave him the land, Troy started to feel as if he could make things happen. He read woodworking magazines. He had always liked shop in school. He used to make things for Libby, bookends and once a small wooden jewelry box. Now he went into the basement at home and practiced using the tools again. He was sure that on this very spot he could build something real, something long-lasting.

Sometimes he drew plans for a big house as he sat up there in the early morning light. Then he would stretch out his arms and flip his eyelids and walk zombielike through his imaginary rooms. He pretended he could walk through walls and windows. He moaned and made zombie noises and sent them echoing across the hills. And then he would catch himself, a seventeen-year-old guy pretending he was a zombie, and he would start to laugh.

*he last day of school*, June twenty-fourth, was a half day, as always. Dana and Mike and Caitlin and Kevin all drove to the stone quarry when school was over. The girls had packed a lunch. The guys had brought beer. When they got there, they changed into their bathing suits and stretched out on some rocks. Now Kevin and Mike were diving, showing off.

"They think they're Tarzan," Caitlin said.

"They are so boring," Dana said. She propped herself up on her elbows and watched. The best thing about Mike was his body. He wasn't very tall but he had a great build. "He spends all his free time working out," she told Caitlin. "That is the extent of his life."

"Kevin doesn't even do that," Caitlin said.

Dana looked over at her. She counted Caitlin's ribs, easy as can be.

Caitlin's eyes were hidden behind bright blue sunglasses. "We should make a plan," Caitlin said.

"What kind of plan?"

Caitlin raised her sunglasses above her eyes. In the sunlight, Dana could see her freckles more clearly.

"An escape plan," Caitlin said. "An escape from Holly." She pointed with her chin toward Mike and Kevin. "From boys like them."

Dana nodded. "We could take the SATs," she said. "Go to college." She thought of her promise to God the day her mother left. Maybe if she kept her part of it, Libby would come back.

Caitlin dropped her sunglasses back over her eyes. "College," she laughed. "No way."

"What then?"

"New York," she said.

And by the way she said it, Dana could tell this wasn't a new plan.

They had schemed to do a lot of things together. When they were little, they wanted to be professional roller skaters. They would go to the rink in Lee every Saturday and practice. Caitlin even won some state competitions. For a while, they thought they should become airline stewardesses. Caitlin heard about a school in Florida that trained people for jobs in the travel industry. But then she flew to Atlantic City with her mother and was airsick the whole time.

"New York," Dana said.

"I've been thinking, I could become a model. I'm tall enough," Caitlin said.

Dana stretched out again flat on the rock and closed her eyes. She imagined what it was like in New York. She'd have to go to the library and read up on it. Rent Woody Allen movies. She smiled at the idea of being somewhere so far from Holly.

"You know that play *Cats?*" Caitlin said. She was almost whispering. "I'd like to see that."

Dana nodded. "Yeah," she said. "Me too."

Dana did not really have her own idea about what she wanted to do, or where she wanted to go. She worked more from a negative point of view. She had a long list of what she *didn't* want: to marry Mike, to marry anybody, to work at the Dixie Cup factory, to act like her mother. She supposed she'd have to leave Holly in order to avoid all of these things. If it took roller-skating or serving cocktails in the sky, she'd do it. She could hear Mike and Kevin climbing the rocks toward them.

From above her, Mike shook his curly hair, splashing cold water all over her. She knew she was supposed to jump up, squealing and giggling. She was supposed to yell, "Stop it!"

Instead she opened her eyes and said, "Grow up."

Suddenly, *Holly seemed to* sprout dozens of available women. Everywhere Tom turned there was someone else smiling at him, wiggling past him, flicking their hair or batting their eyes. He felt like an animal, emitting some kind of primal odor. A signal that said *Needs a mate.*

At first, it was easy to ignore them. All he had to do was think of Libby, of their last time together. He was embarrassed at how little sex he needed, at how a memory could keep him going for a long time. But he was sure that was because of love. When you love someone, that was the feeling that supersedes everything else.

On the night he came home and found Dee-Dee Winthrop sitting on the front steps, he didn't suspect a thing. He chalked it up to one more case of this sudden overflow of women. It was so hot that night, he had taken off his shirt in the car, and so he stood barechested in front of Dee-Dee, his T-shirt rolled into a damp ball in his hands.

"I brought you some sloppy joe filling," Dee-Dee said. She pointed to a red pot.

"Thanks," he said.

It was so still that he could hear her breathing, hear her body shift.

"People forget after a while," she said. "Don't they?"

He didn't want to ask her in. He wanted to go up to bed, keep the lights out, and remember Libby.

"I didn't forget," Dee-Dee was saying. "How could she do this to you?"

"You know," Tom said, "I'm not quite myself yet."

Dee-Dee was nodding away.

"I really appreciate the chili—"

Still nodding she said, "Sloppy joes. That's okay."

"—but I need this time to myself. To my own thoughts." It sounded so stupid when he said it out loud. He felt like he was making love to a ghost every night, alone in the dark with just memories.

Dee-Dee stood. "You don't have to explain to me. When you're ready, I'll be here. Meanwhile, have a sandwich. Get yourself together."

"Thanks," he said.

But he was thinking, Ready? Ready for what?

*Dee-Dee was right.* After a few weeks, the people stopped coming. They stopped bringing casseroles and calling up to ask if he needed anything. Tom kind of missed all the company. Now, if he stayed home, he was completely alone. And all he did was think about Libby. He kept expecting her to call. Or to just show up back home. But as each day passed, he realized how unlikely either of those things was.

Whenever things got slow at the garage, he found himself going over the last few months in his mind, like a constant replay of the same game, again and again. For about a year now, Libby had been staying in her room by

47

herself for long stretches of time. Sue brought her magazines and face cream, and stayed up there talking with her. He brought her food up on a fancy white tray he'd bought special. He always put a bud vase on the tray, and one flower in the vase.

Then, after weeks like that, she'd suddenly appear back with the family, all dressed up and smelling good. Her hair done, her makeup on. She'd set the table with the good china, the one with the pattern of raised daisies around the border. She'd buy a bottle of wine, and make a special dinner. She always had a theme when she cooked. Once, autumn was one of her themes. She'd sprinkled fall leaves across the table, all red and gold and orange, and made soup that she served in pumpkin shells.

The last time she'd done this was back around March sometime. She hadn't been doing much since Sue's big New Year's party. Then one rainy day he'd come home from work and found her polishing the furniture with lemon Pledge. She had on a tight gold dress he'd never seen before, and her highest high heels. Her hair was in an upsweep, her earrings long and dangling.

"You look so good," he'd told her. And he'd kissed her and kissed her until she laughed and pulled away.

"Don't muss me up yet," she told him.

He'd looked around at the table, all done with gold candlesticks and a gold tablecloth. He couldn't quite figure out her theme, but he didn't really care.

"Where is everybody?" he'd asked her.

"Caitlin's. And who knows where the son is."

That night he had made love to her for hours, the way they used to out on those country roads, in his Firebird and in the cornfields. He buried his face between her legs and thought he might never leave there. When she came, it was with more fervor, more intensity, then she'd ever come before, squirming and screaming and twisting. After something like that, why would she leave?

E*ven when all of Millie's* hair started to fall out, she remained optimistic. A real *Reader's Digest* kid. The kind who won over all the nurses' hearts and inspired everyone around her to seize life, to be happy. To Renata, Millie's

attitude was maddening. Even eight-year-old children should be angry at
death, Renata thought. Even little girls should feel cheated, robbed. Should
insist on more time.

But Millie took her illness in stride. She was all those Drama in Real
Life children Renata used to read about with fascination. All the ones who
fell down wells or got mangled by farm machinery or submerged in icy
waters; all the ones who suffered from unpronounceable illnesses that left
them aged, crippled, blind. As a young girl, Renata used to read those
stories over and over and try to imagine herself as one of these dying
children. Would she bravely face needles, transfusions, transplants? Would
she be the one to assure family and doctors that all would be well?

In those stories, the last lines were always an image of the parents
walking away from the hospital, heartbroken but infused with the will to
carry on. Little Becky would want it this way, the mother would think. And
she would do something life-affirming, like plan her summer garden as she
walked into the blazing sunlight. Somehow, back then, Renata could not see
herself in the role of smiling, dying child.

And now, watching as her own daughter smiled bravely up at her while
radiation zapped her small body, Renata could not see herself in that other
role either. The role of the mother looking toward a childless future seemed
just as impossible.

"What are you thinking about?" Millie asked her.

This child did not speak in a feeble, fading voice. She did not whisper.
And her glazed eyes were opened wide, their gaze directed right on
Renata's face.

"Flower gardens," Renata said.

"You mean flower boxes?"

They had tried that once, tried to coax geraniums out of a box hung from
their kitchen window. But there was too little sunlight and they'd had to
give up.

Renata sighed. "No, Millie," she said. "I mean gardens. Some people
have yards where they plant beautiful flowers that actually bloom."

"Like the Brooklyn Botanical Garden," Millie said. "Like Daffodil Hill."

Renata did not believe in epiphanies, in moments when suddenly the
world shifted somehow and brought renewed insight. But if she did believe
in that, she would point her finger to this moment when her own realization
hit. Here was her little girl with chalky skin and only a few patches of hair
littered across her bumpy head, smiling and remembering a spring day

when they took the number 2 train out to Brooklyn to see a hill blanketed in daffodils in full bloom.

It was in that moment that Renata leaned her face close to Millie and said, "I think we should move away. I think we should go to Massachusetts."

One of the things that most disturbed Renata was how the treatment had robbed Millie of her smell. She knew that the smell of children had been much romanticized, described as sweet, as powdery, as honey or lavender or milk or spring air. Her child's smell was none of these. Millie's hair sometimes went unwashed. She sometimes stayed indoors too much. She ate spicy food—beef vindaloo and chicken with garlic sauce. The combination made her smell like a foreign country, musky and exotic. It made Renata think of places like Rangoon or Casablanca. Places that had bent streets, strange spices, hot weather.

The radiation had taken away Millie's smell, and left in its place something neutral and antiseptic. The smell of cafeterias and public rest room disinfectant and classrooms.

"What are you sniffing at me for?" Millie said, trying to pull away from her mother.

"They've taken your smell away," Renata told her, more out of surprise than as an answer.

"My smell?" Millie repeated, and laughed. "It does smell like pee in here. Maybe that's what you think is me."

"Listen," Renata said. "Listen to me." She gripped Millie's shoulders a little too hard. "We're going to move back to Massachusetts so you can run around the woods and see people's flower gardens and eat vegetables right from the dirt. I mean tomatoes that are not smooth and perfectly round."

"Like tomatoes from New Jersey," Millie said, using the voice she used when she was trying too hard to please her mother.

Renata loosened her grip. If she believed in poetic license, she would have believed that she was actually feeling her heart ripping, tearing apart. She pressed her face to her daughter's. She thought that with her hair gone like this, Millie looked the way she had as an infant, bald and lovely. Renata tried to remember when she had last cried.

*Renata believed in absolutes.* You got the facts and came to conclusions, figured out solutions. But Dr. Jinx had no solutions. He talked about the

MRI results, and what the biopsy showed. He ordered more radiation. Yet in the end he said, "Treatment of neuroblastoma is always controversial."

"But you took a biopsy," Renata reminded him. "You went inside her head." Then she added, "You have the facts."

Dr. Jinx sighed. He made a church out of his fingers, the way children did in that game, and then he stared at it. "It appears the mass is too close to major blood vessels to operate—"

"Is it malignant?"

He folded his fingers into the steeple. "Neuroblastoma is a tricky one. It's somewhere in between malignant and benign."

He turned his hands around and wiggled his fingers. Renata watched them move. She'd gone for a second opinion with a Dr. Wu who'd said the same thing. The radiation might work. This one, Dr. Wu had said, was a wait-see.

So Renata took Millie for radiation. She watched as the technicians donned the lead aprons and masks. She watched too, through a small window, as Millie got her dosage, her bald head the only part of her body exposed, the rest covered with sheets of lead to protect her. The technicians drew Xs and lines on her head in blue Magic Marker that did not wash off fully but instead left shadowy figures behind. If only those pens really were magic, Renata found herself thinking.


*Many of the children* in the waiting room wore hats to cover their bald heads. On the day of her last treatment, Millie sat slumped on Renata's lap, surveying her options.

"That girl over there," Renata said, nudging Millie toward the right direction. "Very tasteful."

Millie sighed. "She looks very old, Mama."

The word stuck in Renata's throat like a dry bone. Old. The thing was, the girl *did* look old. She sat, slightly hunched, the lids on her eyes heavy and drooped. On her head she wore a colorful silk scarf, decorated with bright dancing horses. Renata guessed she was maybe twelve or thirteen.

"Whatever happened to millinery shops?" Renata said. "Stores devoted entirely to hats." She wondered if there were still millinery shops in places like Los Alamos. Places where people lost their hair, where people needed hats.

A nurse walked out, clutching a clipboard, wearing a worried face. Renata hated the way she recognized all the nurses now. The portly one who looked and sounded like she worked in a beer garden in Munich. The short pregnant one named Tracy. That one had Renata worried. Should a pregnant woman be exposed to so much radiation?

This one, Louise, was the one Renata most disliked seeing. She spoke in earnest, hushed tones. She confided in the parents. A few weeks ago she had admitted to them that she'd had cancer herself. Breast cancer. "I survived a mastectomy," she'd said. "You'd be amazed what a person can live through." She'd sounded more earnest than ever.

But mothers with sick children don't take comfort in survival rates for cervical and breast cancers, for adult diseases. They want to see teenagers graduating from high school, or very young children starting kindergarten. They want survivors like their own children so that at night they could whisper that everything would be all right. So that as they held their little ones' head over the toilet, watching the radiation and drugs ravage their small bodies, they could remind them of the other little girl who had just won the GE Science Award or the boy who now played in a rock band. Survivors of plane crashes or fires or adult cancer did not matter. Only this did.

Louise, the nurse, was walking right toward Renata and Millie, all frowns and concern.

"Renata," she said. "Hi." She patted Millie's arm. "And how's this little one?"

"I've been better," Millie said.

She always seemed to confess these facts to everyone except her mother. Renata said, "Of course you've been better."

Louise lowered her voice. "This is her last treatment," she said. "You know that, right?"

Renata nodded.

The electric doors opened and a young woman came through, holding her whimpering son in her arms. She was not speaking, but instead she made small noises meant to comfort him. It sounded as if she was talking in some ancient forgotten language. Renata tightened her grip on Millie.

The nurse shook her head. "That's a sad story," she said. "Bones."

"Bones?" Renata repeated, then wished she hadn't.

The nurse touched her shoulder. "You don't want to know," she said. With forced enthusiasm, she said, "So, Millie, this is it."

Her words were meant to give hope, but to Renata they seemed even more final.

*"You can be anyone you* want," Renata whispered to Millie. "Wigs are the answer."

Millie was too ill to respond. Her tongue was swollen, her lips chapped. The smell of her vomit clung to everything in the room.

"When I was in junior high," Renata said, "everybody wore these things called falls. They were hairpieces. Ponytails or braids that you bobby-pinned on. Very cool."

One of the scariest things about all this, Renata thought, was the way Millie's skin seemed to be turning translucent. The way her veins stood out against her flesh so that Renata could almost see the blood pulsing through her body. Even the veins in her eyelids were apparent. Renata closed her eyes a minute and tried to imagine all that radiation attacking the tumor in Millie's head. She tried to imagine battles, world wars. She tried to imagine victory.

Finally, the nurse, Louise, returned.

"This was a bad one," she said, staring down at Millie.

Renata could only nod. She felt exhausted from all the fighting.

Louise whispered, "Why put them through this? It's pitiful."

Why? Renata thought. Because you hope it works. Because Dr. Jinx and Dr. Wu got the facts and thought this might be the solution. Because when it's your kid you try absolutely anything. Why did all those sick people board planes to Lourdes and Fatima and Chimayo? Why did they bother to wash themselves in clay or grotto water? Mrs. Ramone had told her just yesterday to sprinkle a silver dollar with holy water, tape it over Millie's heart, and leave it there for thirty-one days. "Trust me," Mrs. Ramone had said.

"I'll get her some ginger ale," Louise was saying.

Renata watched as the woman moved. She tried to see if she could notice the missing breast, the place in her where cancer had once been. But Louise's uniform betrayed nothing. She was, Renata supposed, healed.

*"Tina Turner," Millie said* to the saleswoman.

The saleswoman wore half-glasses attached to a gold rope. The glasses were outlined in fake jewels. She looked out of them, at Renata, as if for permission.

"Anything she wants," Renata said.

The wig store was on a noisy corner of Fourteenth Street. The women inside were serious about their wigs. Most customers crowded around the

Oprah Hair section. One woman sat, head back, while another wove hairpieces into her own black hair. Above her hung a sign in green fancy letters: EXTENSIONS.

"Tina Turner," Millie said again.

She clutched Renata's hand in her own feverish one.

For the walk there, Millie wore an old navy blue bandana over her head. But when the saleswoman brought out the Tina Turner wig, she quickly removed the bandana.

The saleswoman's mouth opened, then closed quickly. Her face softened.

"Tina Turner it is," she said.

Her eyes drifted toward Renata again, but Renata avoided them. She could not stand to see the pity that she'd find there.

Instead, she adjusted the wig on Millie's head, then lifted her up toward the mirror on the counter. Her daughter seemed almost weightless.

Millie giggled. She held a clammy fist to her mouth like a microphone and belted, "What's love got to do with it?"

*Basically, they had nothing.* When it came time to pack, to leave New York, Renata felt they could walk away from everything they owned and it would not matter. The thought seemed liberating. They could start over, shed this life completely. She didn't articulate to herself all that could mean. Snakes shed their skin, she thought. Who knows what else could be molted, left behind.

Since she'd gotten those wigs, Millie spent a lot of time looking at herself. Today she wore the curly bright red one, the one that made her look like Little Orphan Annie.

Renata was holding a pair of candlesticks in her hands, trying to decide if she should bring them or not.

"This year," Millie told Renata, "I think I want a Ninja Turtle lunch box."

"Millie, you don't need a lunch box," she said, then decided to leave the candlesticks behind also. She could use old wine bottles to hold candles. She even knew how to get by with no holders at all. Take a piece of aluminum foil, drip wax onto it, then stick the candle on. That would hold, she knew. She smiled at how simple it was.

"You mean I'll eat in the cafeteria?" Millie said. The thought seemed to upset her.

"No. I mean you're not going to school when we get to Massachusetts."

"But I have to," Millie said, her voice even more hysterical now.

"No, you don't," Renata said.

She knew that sick children always did go to school. She'd watched mothers on television protesting for children with AIDS to be allowed to go. On *60 Minutes* they'd had an entire segment on a little girl with cerebral palsy and how she'd finished at the top of her class.

But Renata had always thought those kids should have stayed at home. They should do whatever they wanted with their days. They should learn the songs of birds, the names of wildflowers. They should have pets, and dolls, and eat only ice cream if they wanted. What good would spelling or arithmetic do them?

"But Mama," Millie was saying, "I'm in third grade. I get to write in cursive this year. On white paper instead of yellow. I have to go."

"Wouldn't you rather stay home all day with me?" Renata said. "I have big plans for us."

Millie looked puzzled. "But kids go to school," she said. "Even in Massachusetts."

Renata looked around at their apartment. She thought that the day she left this place she'd be filled with emotion. But everything had changed. She felt calm and certain. They would go to Holly and watch the autumn leaves burst into color. They would see deer, and porcupines, and all the animals in Millie's picture book, *What Lives in the Woods?*

"In third grade," Millie said sadly, "you get to write cursive."

Renata said, "We've got so much to do, you're not going to want to write cursive. You'll see."

When they finally were ready to go, after Renata lugged all the boxes downstairs and piled them on the street to be taken away, she carried Millie to the car. It was Jack's car, and he'd loaned it to them for as long as they needed it. Tonight they would drive to the beach with him for a bon voyage party, for lobster and champagne. Then they'd be on their way.

"I'm just going to take a last look," Renata told her daughter, buckling the seat belt around her small waist, pulling it tight. "I'll be right back."

At the door to the building, Millie called to her.

"Mama," she said, "is this an adventure?"

Renata hesitated. Then she smiled. "Yes. It is."

Upstairs she walked around the three rooms of their apartment, although she wasn't sure what she was looking for. A friend of Jack's would stay here until the lease ran out in six months. She'd told Jack his friend could do whatever he wanted with the furniture then. You might be back in six months, Jack had told her. You might need this stuff. She knew what he meant, why he looked down at the floor when he said it. But she, unlike the doctors and Louise and Jack, had hope. She was not coming back to New York. Especially not alone. So she'd said, No, I won't need it. He can keep it or sell it or give it away.

After all, she thought now, she was off on an adventure. Furniture was not necessary. It would only get in their way.

When she left the apartment again, she noticed an envelope tucked into the door frame.

Renata peered into the hall. The light bulb was too low a wattage, so the hall was poorly lit, all dark and shadowy.

"Mrs. Ramone?" Renata called.

But no one answered.

She opened the envelope. Inside was a silver dollar. Renata held it in her large hand, closing her fingers over it. This had been blessed, she knew. Someone else had hope too.

"Mrs. Ramone?" she said again.

Still there was no answer. But Renata knew that someone was watching her. Someone she could not see.

D*ee-Dee Winthrop took* off her white tank top and size 38-C bra right in Harper's Garage on a Friday night. She had come to pick up her car, a 1974 Celica that she refused to give up on. It had been ready all day. But Dee-Dee said she couldn't get there until after nine. So Tom had ordered a pizza from Domino's and sat, watching the Red Sox on TV, eating pizza and drinking beer, waiting for her.

He had even thought, as he sat there alone, that there were a few things about Libby being gone that he liked. No one frowned every time he opened another beer. And he could order a pizza with extra cheese and sausage, the way he liked it, instead of her way, which was black olives and green peppers and which always gave him indigestion. She read too many magazines, had too many silly ideas. Before she left she'd been on a new kick: fat intake. She knew how many grams of fat were in everything. Spare ribs, seventy. Potato chips, twenty-five.

He finished off the last piece of pizza and smiled. Extra cheese and sausage pizza must be way up there in fat, he thought. All the things that tasted good were.

"Who's winning?" Dee-Dee said from the door.

"Detroit," Tom said. When he stood, he realized he'd had a few beers too many. He felt a little unsteady, and was grinning foolishly.

Dee-Dee's husband, Gordon, had left her and gone to live in a cabin in Maine, way up near the Canadian border. This had changed her. She used to be the PTA president and an organizer of things like church bazaars and leukemia drives. In high school, she'd been the president of Future Home-makers of America. Thinking of this, Tom laughed out loud. Dee-Dee Win-throp did not look like a homemaker at all. She had on a short tight skirt and a white tank top and she smelled like the entire perfume counter at Jordan Marsh.

"What's funny?" she said. Her lipstick was a bright color. Magenta or fuchsia or one of those other colors whose name he could never remember.

"You," he said. "Future Homemaker of America." That was when he was sure he'd had too much to drink. The thought popped into his head and right out of his mouth.

But Dee-Dee didn't seem to mind. She laughed too.

"You know something I remember about you?" she said, moving closer to him. "Besides all the usual stuff like you being Class Jock and all that. I remember how whenever we studied a new country in social studies you always made the map. And the teacher would hang it up and point to it. You were good at that. I used to think you were really smart."

And that's when she took off her blouse, reached behind her back and unclasped her bra, and let her size 38-C breasts spill out, toward him.

"Whoa," Tom said, and held out his hands as if to keep her back.

"Libby is not coming home," Dee-Dee said. Her voice was firm, serious.

She was unzipping her skirt now, wriggling out of it. Libby was tall and thin. Tom used to like to trace the line of fine golden hairs on the small of her back. Dee-Dee Winthrop was full and round. Not fat exactly. Zaftig. A full-figure girl like that old actress who sold bras and girdles on TV.

"Not bad for someone who's had five kids, am I?" Dee-Dee said. She moved toward him, her hands on her hips, still teetering in high heels.

"Five?" Tom said. He could only remember two. A daughter with a crazy name and the boy who went out with Sue's kid. He backed up as she moved toward him, so that he was now against the television. "Do you have five?" He shook his head. "Wow."

"Xavier, Kevin, Paulina, Kirk, and Connie," she recited. "All Future Homemakers have at least five. It's in the rule book."

He could hear the crack of bats and the crowd cheering. He wondered who had scored, then laughed again. He was alone with a naked woman for the first time since Libby left and he was thinking about baseball.

"Now what's funny?" she asked him.

This time he didn't answer her. He just shrugged.

"I used to sit behind you in algebra," Dee-Dee said, her voice low, "and I could smell you."

"Smell me?"

"You smelled like a real guy. You know? And I'd look at those curly hairs on the back of your neck. The freckles on your arms."

She reached over and touched the sleeve of his shirt.

"You still got freckles?" she whispered.

He could smell cigarettes on her breath. He tried to remember who was the last girl he had kissed, besides Libby. His mind came up blank.

"You know," he said, as her breasts pressed against him, as her hands groped for his zipper, "I love Libby. I mean, I love her."

"Uh-huh," Dee-Dee Winthrop said, kneeling in front of him.

Her thick lipstick felt strange on his penis. He heard himself groan, his knees buckle. Things were getting stranger every day.

*aitlin tried to cut a* mirror with the small diamond chip on Dana's ring, but it didn't work. "Real diamonds," Caitlin said, "can cut glass. They can be pawned for money to put down on a lease for an apartment." She held up the ring. "This will get us nowhere."

That was how Dana felt about Mike, she realized. Being with him would get her nowhere. It was as if taking that ring from him was giving away something of herself. Something big. And now everything he did bothered her even more. The way he guffawed at television shows like *Cheers* and *M*A*S*H* that he'd already seen. The way he showed off by breaking a two-by-four in half with his hand. The way he thought everything was status quo.

She tried to tell him all this one night, sitting across from him in her living room. She watched his jaw muscles tighten, the way they did before he stepped onto the mat before a wrestling match.

"It's just that I have these plans and all," Dana said. "To go to New York with Caitlin. I think it's just easier to do this now before we get any more involved."

Mike stood when she said that. "That's stupid," he said. "I've been with you forever. I mean, we've done everything together. How much more involved could we get? Give me a break, Dana."

In the movies, even after the girl breaks up with the guy, she still calls after him as he leaves. But Dana didn't. She just watched him walk out. It wasn't until she picked up the phone to call Caitlin that she realized she still had the ring.

Caitlin shrieked when she heard. "You're crazy," she said.

That was when Dana started to tremble. "But we don't even like Mike. Or Kevin. They cramp our style, remember?"

"No, no," Caitlin said quickly. "It's good. Great, even."

In the background Dana could hear Kevin's voice, and the theme song to *Cheers*.

"Listen," Caitlin said, "I'll call you later. This is the one when Sam and Diane first sleep together."

"Sam and Diane?" Dana said. "I'm talking about real life. I'm talking about breaking up with the guy who taught me how to drive."

"I know," Caitlin said. "You are the bravest person I know. Seriously."

"Uh-huh," Dana said. "Then how come I'm shaking?" But the phone was already dead.

She dialed Mike's number, but when his sister answered she hung up. Then she dialed the recorded weather message, over and over, listening to the forecast for company.

"Okay," Nadine said, "Ready?"

Troy nodded. He closed his eyes and waited for the now familiar sound of surgical tape tearing from his skin.

"Ooooh," she said, "this is a good one."

He opened his eyes and looked down, but closed them quickly again when he saw blood. He could smell rubbing alcohol, and feel the sting of it on his still tender skin as Nadine rubbed his forearm with it.

They had drunk almost an entire bottle of Wild Turkey before they sat themselves down in the tattoo parlor in Albany again, and he was still a little drunk. Nadine had to drive the whole way home, because he kept throwing up. She was the toughest woman he knew. Nothing bothered her. She sat and watched the needles press the design into her shoulder without even blinking. She drove almost ninety on the New York State Thruway, singing at the top of her lungs and finishing off the restof the Wild Turkey, acting as if she wasn't even a little drunk, as if blood wasn't oozing out through the gauze on her shoulder.

"Okay," she said now. "Look."

Troy opened his eyes and held his arm up in front of his face. It was swollen and red, but even so he could make out the face of John Lennon looking back at him.

"Cool," he said, and smiled.

As calm as anything, Nadine tore the bandage off her shoulder. He saw a flash of red and looked the other way.

"You are such a baby," she said.

"A lot of people can't stand the sight of blood," he said.

She didn't answer him. He waited a few minutes then peeked. The peace sign tattoo was the size of a quarter, sitting right on her shoulder.

"It looks good," he said.

Nadine straddled his lap, facing him. "I want to get more," she said. "I want to cover every inch of my body."

"Then you can join the circus," he said.

"You know, it's illegal to do faces. I wonder why that is."

For some reason, Troy found himself thinking about his mother. He used to be almost afraid of her. She was that beautiful, that remote. He used to feel tongue-tied around her. He used to want her to notice him more than anything. Once he started hanging around with Nadine, Libby started to notice. So he would leave things around for her to find—rubbers, pot, anything to get a reaction from her. He wondered what she was doing right this second, in Los Angeles.

Nadine was talking and talking, about crazy things.

"There was an old movie," she was saying, "where some guy had *Love* tattooed on one hand and *Hate* on the other. Like yin and yang, you know?"

He closed his eyes. His head was throbbing and his arm, where the new tattoo sat, burned.

"And in freak shows you can make lots of money for things like that," he heard Nadine saying. "Thalidomide babies or Siamese twins."

He felt her face close to his.

"The tattooed man," she said.

Suddenly, there was nothing Troy wanted more than to be home, in his own bed where it was quiet.

"That way," she said, "you can see America."

Troy opened his eyes, pushed her away from him, and sat up. "I don't want to see America," he said. "I just want some sleep." He felt tired deep in his bones, as if he hadn't slept for years.

"Well, excuse me," Nadine said.

Her eyes were shining, but otherwise she looked tired too, all pasty and drawn.

"I'll come by later," he said, struggling to his feet.

She pointed at him. "You're bleeding again," she said.

He looked down and saw small beads of blood covering John Lennon's face.

"W*ell,*" *Tom said, clearing* his throat. "I'll call you."

Dee-Dee lit up another cigarette, then put the car into gear. He leaned over and kissed her quickly on the mouth. Then he closed the car door for her. He didn't wait for her to drive away. He turned around and walked right back into the garage instead. He felt terrible. He knew he was not going to call her. He didn't even really like her.

The garage office looked the same. Arsenio Hall was just ending, the pizza box lay open and empty on the table. But just a few minutes ago he had pulled out of Dee-Dee Winthrop right there on the desk. Tom flopped down in the desk chair. Was this what his life was going to be like from now on? Sex with divorcées in the garage late at night? Feeling empty and awful afterward, then going home alone and thinking about Libby? He was thirty-six years old, and he knew there was an entire generation of men his age who had laid every woman they'd ever met. Men who had gone to discos and singles bars, who had lived with women without marrying them, who did not even have children yet.

But Tom didn't miss any of that. He liked what he'd had. And the thought of this other life depressed the hell out of him. His mind raced over all the available women in town. He imagined trysts like the one he'd had tonight. It had felt good, he thought. But he hated the taste of cigarettes. He'd never liked big breasts. And all the other women whose faces he conjured up were wrong too. Tom closed his eyes and forced himself to think about Libby. She wore that expensive perfume—Beautiful. Even now his hands still smelled like that terrible stuff Dee-Dee was wearing. Libby seemed vague, a blur.

He opened his eyes and sighed. "What a mess," he said out loud.

When *Troy pulled into* the driveway, it was almost two in the morning. He turned off the car, but did not move. He had forgotten how quiet it was here, in the woods at night. His head and arm were still throbbing, but somehow the darkness and silence soothed him, seemed to make his pain go away.

Headlights appeared behind him. Startled, Troy threw the car door open, felt his heart pound. He must have fallen asleep for an instant, and the bright lights scared him awake.

"Troy?"

Troy peered into the light. It was his father, walking slowly toward him.

"Where've you been?" Troy said. His voice sounded unusually loud.

Tom sighed. "Don't ask," he said.

Troy nodded. "Okay."

"We haven't seen you around much."

"Well, it's summer. You know."

Tom sighed again.

"It seems weird not having her here," Troy said, lowering his voice this time. "I mean, she wasn't exactly talkative or anything. But she filled up the house anyway. You know."

"Yeah," his father said.

Troy was looking down, at his father's sneakers. There were splashes of grease on the tops and sides. For some reason he did not understand, they made Troy feel sad.

"I guess," he said, faltering, "I guess it's hard on you."

Tom reached out, as if to touch Troy's arm, but he didn't quite make it. Instead, his arm just hung there, in midair.

"Nadine is nuts," Troy said.

Tom laughed. "Another crazy woman," he said.

Troy looked up then. In the light from the car, Tom looked especially young, younger even than Troy. And then Troy saw something else, on the side of his father's face, working its way down to his neck—a streak of bright lipstick.

The front door creaked open and Dana came outside.

"What is this?" she said. "A family picnic?"

"Well," Tom said, "I guess I don't get Father of the Year this year. Two kids, both teenagers, both awake in the middle of the night."

Dana was frowning, as usual. "You have lipstick all over your face," she said. She pointed her finger at Tom. "Everywhere."

His hand shot up to his cheek.

"And you," she said to Troy, pointing to him now, "are bleeding. Your arm is covered with blood."

"A new tattoo," he said. Then he added softly, "John Lennon."

Dana looked like she might start to cry. "I'm moving to New York. I'm growing my hair long and I'm going to read important books and go to the ballet."

"What is that supposed to mean?" Troy said.

Tom looked at his daughter, then at his son.

"We've got to fix this," he said.

Dana narrowed her eyes. "Fix what?"

His arm swept forward. "This," he said. "Everything."

He put his arms around each of them. "Come on," he said, urging them forward. "Let's go to bed."

"And you smell like perfume," Dana said, wriggling in his grasp.

"I know," Tom said, not letting her go. He pulled both of them closer to him. "I know."

"I don't like Massachusetts," Millie said.

"Millie, honey," Renata said, "we've only been here five minutes."

"It's too little," Millie said. She sighed, and steamed up the car window with her breath. Then she drew an M in the spot, and watched it vanish.

In the back seat of Jack's dark blue Oldsmobile were a few boxes of their stuff, and one suitcase of clothes each. It's like starting fresh, Renata had said when they left New York three hours earlier. Now, heading down Route 23, catching sight of familiar things from long ago, it didn't feel like something fresh and new at all.

"Right now," Millie was saying, "they're getting their new spelling words. Hard words," she added. "Third grade words."

"I'll give you new words," Renata told her. "How's that for a great idea?"

Millie shrugged. She breathed on the window again and drew a broken heart.

"Today your word is agriculture," Renata said. They were passing a few scraggly farms now. Poor-looking farms, with a few cows and dilapidated barns, some corn and pumpkin patches here and there.

"I bet you thought pumpkins grew from sidewalks," Renata said.

But Millie wouldn't laugh. She hadn't even smiled since they got in the car. As they drove away, Jack waving goodbye from the sidewalk, Millie had yelled to him, "We'll be back!"

"It's not the same if *you* give me words," Millie mumbled.

"What do you want from me, Millie?" They were passing the church now. On Friday nights in junior high Renata used to go to dances there. She sat on a folding chair and watched as all the pretty girls like Libby Holliday and Sue O'Hara danced with the jocks. Remembering, she could suddenly smell the musty cellar smell mixed with candles and incense burning. The songs they played were by Bobby Vinton and the Supremes, "Blue Velvet" and "I Hear a Symphony." And the chaperones would stick yardsticks between the couples dancing, to make sure no one was pressed too close.

Renata used to sit right up front and watch. She did not expect to be asked to dance. She wasn't even sure why she went, delegated to a group of girls who were doomed to be wallflowers—fat Teresa Harvey, and Wanda Gallucci, who wore thick glasses and had a dark mustache that everyone used to make fun of. *Heil Hitler!* the boys would say when she walked by them in school.

"I don't know why you want to go to school so bad anyway," Renata said under her breath. Now they were passing familiar houses. Not houses Renata had been inside, but the ones where other girls gathered for slumber parties and postprom breakfasts. She felt a lump in her throat. Why was she back here? This town held no good memories for her, just feelings of being an outcast, of being lonely.

"Is this the town?" Millie said. She was starting to whine.

The car stopped, right in the street. Renata pumped the gas pedal. Nothing.

"Is it?" Millie whined.

Renata glanced around. Holly looked like any New England town. Not the postcard-perfect ones. She wasn't sure those existed anywhere. But it had a little village green with a gazebo in the middle, where on summer days bridal parties gathered for pictures. There was a well-kept World War II monument with carefully tended red and white flowers and small American flags. That's where they were now, in front of the monument. Ahead of them, Renata could see the diner shining silver and bright in the afternoon sun, and the cheap Italian restaurant that served wine in straw-covered bottles.

"Now what?" Millie was saying.

"Now we get out and walk to a garage," Renata said. She stepped out of the car, into the bright day, and held her breath for an instant. Down the road, across from the Friendly's and the pizza parlor, stood the movie theater where everyone used to go on Saturday afternoons to make out. It was all boarded up now, its marquee shouting FOR RENT.

"Let's go already," Millie said.

"That's where I got my first kiss," Renata said. "The Palace Theater."

Millie looked down the road. "Looks like a real hot spot," she said.

They started walking again, past the Cumberland Farms and the drug-store where Renata used to buy her mother Jean Naté sets for Christmas.

"In New York," Millie said, "movie theaters stay in business. People go to them."

Renata paused. The used-furniture store looked even more like a junk shop than it used to. There were a few new stores, but even they looked empty and sad. Renata was starting to feel pretty depressed too.

"What are we doing here?" Millie said. She looked at Renata solemnly. "Since we left New York, everything has gone wrong."

"Millie, nothing has gone wrong until this very minute."

She took Millie's hand roughly and led her toward the garage. Harper's. Renata frowned. Tom Harper owned a garage? That seemed impossible. She tried to picture him, but saw only a blur of him running bases, or twirling Libby Holliday in a dance. "Here," Renata said, handing Millie a handful of change. "Get a soda from the machine and I'll be right back."

When Renata stepped into the office, though, she knew immediately that the handsome guy behind the desk was Tom Harper. The blurry image took shape then. He looked up and smiled. It was still the smile of a golden boy, a boy who had everything at his fingertips. Nothing in Holly ever changed.

Tom *was on the phone making* up excuses to Dee-Dee Winthrop when the door to the office opened and a big, familiar-looking woman walked in. "Customer," he blurted to Dee-Dee. Relieved, he hung up, fast.

"My car's broken," she said.

She was almost six feet tall, with long wild hair all salt and pepper.

She pushed her face real close to his. "Tom?" she said.

That took him by surprise. He was so used to being called Harp that the sound of his own name startled him.

She laughed, a deep loud laugh. "Well, how about that? I'm in town five minutes and already I see someone I know. Things never change in Holly, do they?"

Oh yes they do, he thought. But he smiled and told her, "I guess not."

"We went to school together," she said, and she thrust her hand in his and shook it, hard. "Renata Handy."

Her high school face floated into his mind. Renata Handy was the school weirdo. She used to dress like a gypsy. She claimed she could tell fortunes. She disagreed with everything everyone said. She tried to get the school cafeteria to stop serving meat, then lettuce, then grapes. She burned her bra in front of the school one day and got expelled. Renata Handy used to frighten him, she was that strange. And by the looks of her, she hadn't changed much herself.

"Well, hi," he said.

"Hello yourself, Tom Harper." The door opened again and a little girl wearing a Tina Turner wig came in.

"Mama," she said, "what's so funny?"

Tom tried not to look surprised that Renata Handy was this little girl's mother. He bent down and said, "I used to go to school with your mama."

"The School of Visual Arts?" the girl said.

Tom looked up at Renata. She must have weighed close to 180, he figured.

"No, Millie," she was saying. "Way before that. High school."

The girl nodded solemnly. "Oh."

Tom straightened up again. "So," he said, "your car?"

"I think it's the muffler," Renata told him. "My friend just had a new one put in, too. About a month ago at Midas."

Tom swallowed hard. Midas. That night back in March with Libby, that had been her theme. The Midas touch. He thought it had something to do with mufflers; she intended for it to have something to do with turning plain things into gold.

The house Renata and Millie rented was on the outskirts of town, beside some of those farms they had passed when they came in. It was not in very good shape. The old man who had lived there had been a pack rat. Old bundles of newspapers were stacked everywhere. There was a shelf full of odd teacups in the kitchen and another of thimbles in the living room. But mostly there were boxes—small wooden ones, broken music boxes, tin and plastic ones. Everywhere Renata looked she found more boxes.

The old man had died, and his grandchildren were renting the house as it was. You just have to put up with the junk, they had told Renata. Someday, they would come and clean the place out. But they lived in Florida and Arizona and California, and they didn't know when they could get back East.

"Well," Renata said, "isn't this place something?"

The top of one bundle of newspapers read WE LIKE IKE!

Millie was scrunching her face up, the way she did right before she started to cry.

"I guess he had cats," Renata said.

She started to open windows. The place had land. Lots of land. In a fantasy of hers, she and Millie were running across a meadow littered with buttercups. The fantasy was actually an old shampoo commercial for Herbal Essence. But she'd made it one of her own. There were no buttercups though, just weeds and overgrown grass as far as she could see.

Renata swallowed hard. She was thinking of the city too. Of the way the lights looked at this time of evening, slowly blinking on.

"I hate it here," Millie said. And she started to cry.

"What do you want from me, Millie? Huh? What?" Renata wanted to cry too.

"A family," Millie said.

"A what?"

"A family. One that lives in a real house. A sister and a father and a dog. And a better car."

Renata dropped onto the magenta couch. It felt damp. A sister? Where had this idea come from?

"Honey, you don't just go and get a ready-made family. It doesn't work that way. Look at the Ramones. They don't have those things."

But Millie wasn't listening. "And I want to go to school. I want spelling words."

"Okay, okay," Renata said. She closed her eyes and tried to think of what to do. She tried to remember why this had seemed like such a good idea in the first place.

*ibby prided herself on being* practical. She got a job right away, and a small efficiency apartment in West Hollywood. The job was at Von's, a supermarket chain that just happened to be where Michelle Pfeiffer used to work. There was, Libby admitted, the teeniest part of her that liked that connection, a very small voice that said, If it could happen to her, then just maybe.

After her first paycheck, she enrolled in acting classes. But she did not pretend she was going to become a star. Once, Libby had read that Marilyn Monroe always went to her classes at the Actors' Studio dressed down, so for her class Libby wore black leggings and an oversize white shirt. When she walked into that class, the teacher looked at her and shouted, "House-wife!"

Another woman might have fallen apart at that. But Libby put on her best smile and accepted it. They were after types here. She'd read all about it in a book at the library called *How to Make It in Hollywood: A Realistic Guide.* Of course she couldn't help but think if she had dressed up, worn that electric blue spandex dress and high heels, the teacher might have seen her as something very different. Somewhere deep down she was a little disappointed he hadn't looked at her and shouted "Star!" But she was after all a thirty-six-year-old woman with two teenage children and a husband with the beginnings of a beer belly. At least, she told herself as she took her place in class, at least she was here. Finally.

*After that time she tried* to leave with Sue, Libby had never actually attempted to run away again, not physically at least. Instead, she concentrated on making it big right there in Holly. She went to the library and got books like *How to Become a Millionaire Without Ever Leaving Your Living Room* and *Get Rich Now.* She was a firm believer in the library system. She had written letters to her senator when they cut library hours, and signed a petition at her branch to open on Sundays. When Dana and Troy were small, she used to take them to the library once a week, even though the books remained on the kitchen counter, unread.

The first thing Libby taught herself was calligraphy. People were always wanting a professional-looking envelope for wedding invitations. Tom bought her a set of pens, and different-colored inks, gold and silver, purple and pink. The colors most often chosen for celebrations. She hung signs in the Price Chopper, written in perfect calligraphy. Only one person called, but Libby knew that word of mouth was an important part on the road to success.

The customer was named Sherri, and she was getting married. Libby listened patiently to Sherri's story. She was seventeen years old and worked at GE. Her fiancé, whose name coincidentally was Tom, had been laid off for seven months and collected unemployment. Libby frowned. What way was that to start a new life? she thought. Sherri told her that their color scheme was lilac. Her aunt was making all the dresses, including her own wedding gown.

Libby looked at Sherri, who still had a smattering of acne on her forehead and chin, and said, "I can't do these for you."

"I got the money," Sherri said. As if to prove it, she took out a roll of what seemed to be all five-dollar bills, held together with a rubber band.

The invitations were lilac, with two teddy bears dressed like a bride and groom and a big poem about true love. Libby was starting to feel nauseous. "It's not that," she told Sherri.

"What then?"

"It's against my principles," Libby said.

"Huh?"

"I don't think you and Tom should get married," Libby said. "You should wait until he gets a new job. Maybe you should go back to school. Get your diploma. Think about a career." Libby could see this girl in a white uniform, her hair pinned back, the acne gone. "Maybe you could be an X-ray technician. Or a dental hygienist."

"Look," Sherri said, "all I want is these envelopes done fancy. That's all. I don't want to go to school. I don't want to be cleaning some strange guy's teeth. Or getting zapped with radiation. I just want this." She slapped her hand down on the stack of invitations.

She wasn't unattractive exactly, Libby thought, studying her. She wore her pants too tight, and her eye makeup was all wrong. "You should wear earth tones," Libby told her. "It would give you a softer look."

Sherri started to scoop her invitations into her bag. "Hey," she said, "fuck you. I mean, who do you think you are?"

"I'm sorry," Libby said. "I just can't do them."

Her next venture was giving home parties to sell sexy lingerie. The brochures said she could earn as much as ten thousand dollars a month. There were drawings of pyramids, placing her at the top and all the women who would start to work for her at the bottom. She read a book called *How to Sell Anything At All to Anybody*, ordered her stock, then invited five women to a party.

Libby set the mood by burning candles and rubbing perfume on her light bulbs. She made tiny cucumber and watercress sandwiches, cut off all the crusts and cut them into shapes, triangles and circles. She filled bowls with fruit and bought jugs of Glen Ellen white wine. The stereo volume was set low, and Libby selected mood music—Donna Summer and Al Green, albums from the midseventies when disco was big.

They ate all the food and drank all the wine, but all they did was laugh at the merchandise.

"Harem outfits?" Dee-Dee had said. "Puh—leeze." And she'd rolled her eyes and pretended to gag.

They all giggled at the corsets and teddies and crotchless underpants, even when Libby recited her sales pitch. "Need a little spice in your love life? Tired of your certain someone snoring beside you? Then it's time for you to enter the world of La Magique."

Someone had brought some pot and they all smoked it, laughing even harder, making crude jokes about the lingerie. Alice Rose spilled her wine on a French maid outfit, and Sue, to be polite, bought some flutter-kinis, the cheapest item available. Libby gave each of them a party favor, a small vial of strawberry-flavored lotion, and sent them home.

Tom came in when he heard them leave. "Are we rich?" he said.

"The idea is to get them to have home parties too. Then I get a commission off what they sell." She looked around at the dirty wineglasses, the empty plates, the sexy lingerie strewn around the room. "It's a pyramid. It can't fail."

Tom picked up a garter belt. "I'll buy this if you'll wear it."

"You already bought it, you jerk. We're stuck with all this junk!"

He tried to put his arms around her. "I don't mind being stuck with it," he said. "Hell, let's use it."

She pushed away from him and started to pick up all the bras and panties. "All you can think about is sex. You don't understand what I'm trying to do here."

"No," Tom said, sighing, as he bent to pick up the harem outfit, "I guess I don't."


*For her second acting class,* Libby wore the electric blue spandex dress. An actress has to be versatile, she'd read. She wanted her teacher, Carl, to see every side of her, how much of a chameleon she could be. When she walked in, the two young blondes in the class glanced at each other. She hated them. They weren't even twenty-one, and they always wore tight black things. They had too much hair, gobs of it. And smooth flawless skin. Their names were Heather and Ashley. Libby decided, as she took her place, that they looked like everybody else, nothing special, just two more California girls. In a way, she thought, she felt bad for them.

Acting class made her feel very self-conscious. They had to do things that seemed irrelevant. Like breathe in a particular way that reminded her of her childbirth classes. Then Carl made them say "Ha." Then, "Ha ha." He kept making them add Has until they were laughing like crazy people. To Libby, it didn't make any sense. Heather and Ashley really got into it, laughing like mad. Libby watched them. Were they really laughing? Or were they acting? Was that the point?

In the high school drama club, acting had been so simple. Everyone had told her she was a natural. They certainly hadn't stood around doing this kind of thing, pretending to laugh.

"Close your eyes," Carl was saying. "Focus on your center."

Libby closed her eyes. Her center? she thought. What was that supposed to mean? She tried to imagine Michelle Pfeiffer doing this. She was sure she never had. Even though Carl's credentials were impressive, episodes of *Kojak, Columbo, Barney Miller* and parts in lots of big movies, Libby couldn't help but wonder if maybe she had chosen a bad acting class.

"Are you there?" Carl was saying, his voice hypnotic. "Are you in your center yet?"

Libby opened her eyes and looked around. Everyone else was doing the proper deep breathing, their eyes closed. One guy, George, had even taken off his shoes and socks and was sitting there like a yogi, fingertips pressed together, legs folded like a pretzel.

"Now," Carl said, "we'll go around the room and I'd like you to find a sound that describes your center."

Carl's eyes were closed too. He started by giving a big grunt, as if he was going to the bathroom. Libby tried to think of a sound that wouldn't embarrass her. She thought of a hiccup, a sigh, a clearing of her throat.

Heather and Ashley sounded as if they were having orgasms, sighing and moaning and licking their lips. George hummed, one long note that he held for quite some time. And then it was Libby's turn. She hadn't found her center. She was sweaty, panicked. Maybe she had no center. Maybe she was completely hollow, not even a housewife, certainly not a star. The very air in the room seemed to be waiting for her sound. She felt as if someone had ripped out her voice box. Nothing would come out.

From beside her George farted.

"Good!" Carl said.

Heather and Ashley giggled.

"Wait!" Libby shouted.

But they were already on to the next exercise. Carl was talking in that slow hypnotic voice. Everyone thought she had farted publicly, that her center was that low and ridiculous. Libby wanted more than anything, in that moment, to be back home in Holly.

They were going around the circle again, this time shouting one word that described their center.

"Fuck me!" Heather shouted.

No one bothered to tell her that was two words. Libby felt like crying.

"Mom!" George shouted.

They were waiting for her again. She didn't have time to think. She just opened her mouth and screamed, "Tom!"

Autumn

In *Massachusetts, Renata* and Millie's routine changed. Now it was Renata who woke Millie every morning, who tugged on her hand and pulled her into the world from her bed. No more Froot Loops for breakfast. No more late nights. They were a mother and daughter living in Holly, Massachusetts —fresh air, long walks, and apple cider.

Millie was miserable.

"There's no noise here," she said, opening her arms and indicating the autumn foliage, leaves bursting with bright yellow and red. The smell of wood burning in fireplaces filled the air. "There's no sirens. No people on the streets. No nothing."

"This," Renata told her, "is how most Americans live." She banged on her chest, Tarzan style. "Smell this good clean air, Millie."

Millie's face crumpled. "It smells like things rotting."

She was right. Under all the other smells, hidden almost, was the smell of earth, of rotting apples and dead leaves.

Millie dropped to the ground and spread her arms, sweeping them back and forth as if she was making a snow angel in the fallen leaves.

"Remember how our street used to smell?" she said, her voice dreamy. "First it smelled like espresso from that coffee shop? Then it smelled like cats from that one building. And then it smelled like—"

"Millie," Renata said, "kids should be raised in the country." She looked off toward the horizon where the foothills of the Berkshires rose a smoky blue in the afternoon light.

Millie sat up. "Remember how at night the boys stood around and played their radios? Real loud? And Mrs. Ramone would lean out her window and yell at them and then they'd put it up louder? Remember how they used to break-dance in the middle of the street and not let cars go by?"

"You'll get used to it here," Renata told her. "Wait and see."

———

*Renata got a job as* assistant manager of a Waldenbooks at the mall. She wore a name tag that said *Ms. Handy* and kept a blue pencil tucked behind her ear. Hardly anyone ever came into the store. It was the most boring job she'd ever had. She found herself missing the late night crowds at Goldilox, the teenagers with pierced noses and black leather clothes, the old gray-haired hippies who sat reading poetry to themselves at the counter, the disheveled couples who had stumbled from their beds for challah french toast, the women with their belongings spilling from shopping bags who ordered tea and took their tea bags with them when they left.

One day Renata even called Liz, forgetting it was the lunch rush at Goldilox. There was no rush at the mall, just a senior citizens group, all dressed in jogging suits, who walked the loop of the mall every day for exercise and waved to Renata as they passed the bookstore.

"What?" Liz yelled when she finally came to the phone.

"I was just calling to say hi," Renata said. She yelled too, her voice exploding in the empty store.

"Okay," Liz said. "Hi." Then to someone in the restaurant she screamed, "Do not put two people at a fourtop! What is the matter with you?"

"Mall people are weirder than East Village people," Renata said, dropping her voice. "There are women who still have hair like Farrah Fawcett. Men with gold chains. Young men with gold chains. Millie is miserable and I forgot why the hell this was such a good idea in the first place."

"Lentil!" Liz yelled. "The soup today is lentil! Not gazpacho!"

Renata hung up.

The senior citizens passed the store and waved. Renata waved back to them, a big enthusiastic wave. Maybe, she thought, she should open a restaurant. A health food restaurant with sandwiches on thick multigrain bread and lentil soup and soba noodles. That's what this town needed. The people were health-conscious, weren't they? Didn't these senior citizens come here every day to walk?

"My God," a female voice said, "you're Renata Handy."

Renata looked up and saw a vaguely familiar face. The woman had on magenta lipstick, false eyelashes, and a pink sweatsuit.

"When on earth did you move back to town?" the woman said.

Renata studied the face. Suddenly, worse than an LSD flashback, she could see that magenta mouth laughing, smoking in the girls' room at Holly High, whispering when Renata walked in to pee.

"Dee-Dee," Renata said.

"Renata Handy. I can't believe it." Dee-Dee shook her head for emphasis.

Renata smiled.

"Look at you," Dee-Dee said. "You haven't changed a bit. What have you been up to all this time?"

"I had an art career, you know," Renata said, the lie feeling like an egg in her throat. "In New York."

"I remember you always were drawing. Like Peter Max." Dee-Dee rolled her eyes. "You would sit in geometry class and draw instead of paying attention. Swirls and squiggles in bright colors."

Renata nodded. "Yes," she said. "That's right."

"Well, did you get married? Did you have babies?"

Renata kept nodding. "Yes," she said. "But he died in the war."

Dee-Dee's eyes widened. "In the Gulf? Why, you poor thing. I sure had a yellow ribbon on my front door. And so you came home to recover?"

This part at least was true. "Yes," Renata said. "And to open a health food restaurant."

"How brave," Dee-Dee said. She hesitated. "Listen. I have a support group, you know? For divorcées and widows? We have a great time. We go ballroom dancing in Albany and we hostess parties where divorced and widowed men come for cocktails and canapés. We would love to have you. I'm divorced myself, you know? I know what it's like to be alone, believe me."

Renata kept nodding and saying yes. She heard herself agree to go to one of their meetings. Dee-Dee wrote her address and phone number on a Waldenbooks bookmark. Her press-on nails were painted pink.

"So we'll see you at the meeting, right?" Dee-Dee said.

"Definitely," Renata told her.

By the time Dee-Dee left, Renata was so drained, she could hardly wave when the senior citizens passed her again.

"A *small with pineapple,* black olives, and Canadian bacon," the customer said to Dana. He smiled, flashing two deep dimples. "Please," he added.

"Pineapple. Black olives. Canadian bacon," Dana said.

One of the rules at Pizza Pizzazz was to repeat the customer's toppings. Another was to say, "Ten minutes," even if there were fifty orders ahead of theirs.

Dana handed the customer his order slip. "Ten minutes," she mumbled, knowing it would be more like twenty.

She hated Pizza Pizzazz. PIZZA THE WAY YOU LIKE IT. They had over a hundred toppings to choose from and Dana thought that at least ninety of them were disgusting. But this job, three nights a week and all day Saturday, was her ticket to New York. Caitlin worked at Pizza Pizzazz too. It was Caitlin who always reminded Dana every Saturday that these one hundred toppings were their ticket out.

They had to wear khaki safari shorts and Hawaiian shirts as uniforms. One more humiliation, Dana thought, tugging at her turquoise high-tops and watching the pineapple, black olive, Canadian bacon guy. He was very cute. Those dimples. Sky blue eyes.

Caitlin said, "Jalapeño, avocado, mango. Ten minutes." Then she looked at Dana and crossed her eyes. "An L.A. pizza," she mumbled.

Dana had a flash, a quick image like a scene on MTV, of her mother in Ray-Bans sitting on a beach eating a jalapeño, avocado, and mango pizza. Her nails were long and pink, her skin tanned, her lips curled in a smile. Dana blinked her eyes real quick to erase it.

When she opened them again, she thought she saw the cute guy smile at her. He had on a gray T-shirt that said WILLIAMS. A college boy. Someone smart. Someone who came from somewhere else. Every now and then, after work, she still went out with Mike, but only if Caitlin and Kevin went too. Sometimes, and this was what made her sick to her stomach, she still had sex with him. It was easier than fighting. All she had to do was close her eyes and imagine other places—Fifth Avenue, the Empire State Building, the Statue of Liberty.

It was funny how you could just separate yourself from what was happening, Dana thought. How you could transpose yourself to a sidewalk cafe while a boy you've known since you were seven pushed into you, grunting. How you could zap yourself onto Fifth Avenue, give yourself high heels, a zebra-striped coat, two Afghans on silver leashes, while someone you've never seen before looked at you and said, "Cottage cheese, hamburger, tomato, and chives."

*"I don't want to make a* habit of this," Dana told Caitlin as they walked out of Pizza Pizzazz toward Kevin's Camaro.

"Saturday nights with these Neanderthals will make for very funny reading someday," Caitlin said. "You know, in our memoirs."

Caitlin wore two different-colored high-tops—one raspberry, one lemon yellow. Dana's eyes followed those shoes across the street. She didn't even look up when one of the guys whistled like a sailor.

"I can't make a habit of this," she said again.

Caitlin blew a big bubble with her gum, then popped it. Dana could smell grape in the air.

"Think of it as an adventure," Caitlin said.

Dana laughed. "An adventure is something unexpected. Something you don't know anything about." She stopped walking, still several yards from the car. "I know every single thing that will happen when we get in that car. Mike will put his thick arm around my shoulders and say, 'Hey, babe.' When Kevin takes a curve too fast they'll laugh and say. 'An SOB. Slide Over Babe.' They'll have two six-packs of Coors Light and they'll take us someplace to drink them and then pull our pants off and screw us, which will take about seven minutes."

Caitlin had moved close to her. She tried to cover Dana's mouth with her hand. She was giggling. "Dana," she whispered, "did you time it? Seven minutes?"

Dana sighed.

"What is this?" Kevin said, hanging out of the car window. "Let's party already."

Caitlin squeezed Dana's arm, right below the sleeve of the Pizza Pizzazz Hawaiian shirt, where palm trees and parrots danced crookedly. "Come on," she said. "It's better than nothing."

Dana nodded. But she thought that nothing would be much, much better.


Nadine told Troy the ocean was better than woods or mountains.

She cited reasons. "No bugs. No humidity. When you sweat, you can jump in the water and cool right off."

That was why they should leave. That was why they should go to Florida. He should get a motorcycle and fix it up. Then off they'd go.

"Into the sunset," Nadine said.

Ever since his mother left, Troy felt he was getting younger and younger. He couldn't make decisions. He wanted to be fed, to be taken care of. He missed things like homework and study hall and the way the rope felt against his skin when he had to shimmy up it in gym class. At first, when he was sure Libby would come back, he didn't feel like much of anything. But when it hit him she was gone for good, he felt something ooze out of him, like air from a balloon.

"In Florida," Nadine said, "you can sleep on the beach. You can make money picking citrus fruit. Lemons. Oranges. Grapefruit."

Troy knew that if his mother was here, he'd maybe do it. Fix up a motorcycle and take off to Florida, with crazy Nadine clutching his waist, screaming into the wind. Instead, he bought a three-pack of new white Fruit of the Loom T-shirts at Caldor's, a three-subject spiral notebook with a bright blue cover, and a fat pack of Bic pens, fine point.

Nadine eyed his purchases suspiciously.

"Stuff for school," he told her.

That really made her flip out. She started screaming and beating on his chest with her fists.

"School? I'm talking about a life here. I'm talking about the fucking Atlantic Ocean. And you're buying stuff for algebra? For fucking American history?"

He didn't say anything. He didn't even try to stop her from punching his chest. He just watched her and wondered how he had ended up here, in this tiny messy apartment with Nadine.

"We could have a life," Nadine was shouting. "No snow. No Dixie Cups. All the fucking oranges we can eat."

He grabbed both of her wrists in one of his big hands. He could really throw a football with these hands. Somehow he'd stopped doing that too.

"Listen," he told her, his voice soft and calm. "I can't just drop out of school—"

"You already did," she said, twisting her hands, trying to break free.

"Not officially. I can talk to the guidance counselor—"

"I don't want to hear this!" Nadine said. Then she opened her mouth and screamed as loud as she could.

Troy stepped back, away from her, letting her hands drop, and just watched her. All he saw was a girl who looked as if she'd had a hard life, as if she'd seen things someone her age shouldn't have seen yet. Her breasts were flattened weirdly inside her tube top, and her latest tattoo—a sea horse on her ankle—still looked all red and raw. Her hair needed cutting too. Her bangs hung too low across her eyes and the ends kind of fishtailed. All of it made Troy want to run away, fast.

But he waited until she stopped screaming.

Then he said, "Maybe, if you feel this strongly about it, we should cool it for a while."

Now she stepped back, as if he'd hit her. She even put both hands on her stomach.

"I'm sorry," she said. She seemed to consider what she was going to say next very carefully. "Education is very important," she said finally.

Troy nodded.

"Please stay," Nadine said. Now her voice was real squeaky, the way it sometimes got in bed.

"Yeah," Troy said. "Of course." Even though his greatest desire right then was to go home. He wanted to flop down on the couch in the living room and watch *Saturday Afternoon at the Movies*. Or call some of his buddies and throw a ball around. He wanted to take long gulps of milk, straight from the carton.

"I get carried away," Nadine was saying. "I'd die if you left me."

"You wouldn't die," he said, feeling suddenly bad. Not just for Nadine, but for himself. He pulled her over to him. "Come on," he said. "I'm not going anywhere."

"Promise?" she said in that squeaky voice.

"Promise," he lied.

*Mr. Burns, the guidance* counselor, thought he was real cool, like one of the kids. He thought everybody loved him. But really they all laughed at him and his bright shirts with the alligators on the chest and his fat stomach that jiggled when he walked and his mustache that seemed to collect things—cat hair, lint, pieces of food.

Today, Troy saw what looked like cookie crumbs clinging there. Maybe Oreos. And Mr. Burns's shirt was a deep red, with the collar standing straight up as if he'd ironed it that way. Mr. Burns had a habit of always running his fingers through his thinning hair. Troy supposed it was to make sure the bald spot way in the back was covered.

"Hey, buddy," Mr. Burns was saying. "Where've you been? Huh?" He slapped Troy on the arm playfully.

Troy had his whole sad story all thought out. "We've had a real tough time at home, Mr. Burns," he said.

Mr. Burns nodded. His face filled with great sympathy and understanding. "I heard," he said. "What can I tell you? I wish I had all the answers. But I don't. You know, I was in school with them. With your parents. Your dad's a great guy." His face brightened. "And what an athlete, huh?"

Troy nodded.

There was an awkward silence then. Troy glanced around the room. On one wall was an antidrug poster of an egg frying. On another was a navy recruiting poster of a happy sailor. Outside, Troy saw the cheerleaders practicing. They looked beautiful, he thought. They had shiny hair pulled back in ponytails, tanned faces, smiles like girls in toothpaste commercials.

"I want to make it all up," he said. "I missed so much last year—"

"You should have gone to summer school, Troy," Mr. Burns said, shaking his head, reading a file that said in black letters TROY T. HARPER. Under his name someone had scrawled *Dropout????*

"I didn't have any plans or anything then," Troy said. "I do now, though. Really." He looked back out the window, at those girls jumping in unison.

"Don't worry, you can come back. We can fix it so you can do your senior year, graduate with your class, then do some make-up classes in the summer."

Mr. Burns gave Troy one of his good buddy smiles. "Maybe your sister can help you catch up."

Troy shrugged. He doubted that Dana would help him at all.

"Hey," Mr. Burns said, "don't look so grim, we'll work something out."

*The hallways in the high* school were each painted a different color. Baby blue or bright orange or sea green over cinder block. Mr. Burns's office was on the blue hall, and once Troy finally got out of there, he leaned against the blue cinder blocks and took big deep breaths. No more pot, he told himself. Then he amended the vow. Except on weekends. And he would work at his father's garage on Saturdays. He would find a nice sweet girlfriend with shiny hair and a bright smile. He took another deep breath. He would show his mother.

He smiled to himself, imagining his new routine. Getting up early, never missing classes, doing homework. Dumping Nadine. Another deep breath. Then he stepped outside, into the bright sunshine.

The cheerleaders had finished practice and were starting to disperse into small groups. They were beautiful, Troy thought. Every one of them. He passed a group of three and waved. They waved back and whispered. He had a reputation, he knew. He was bad. Wild.

At the end of the drive that led onto the road, Troy saw two girls part.

"I'll call you when I get home," one of them called to the other.

Jessica Tremont, Troy thought. A real snob. But the other girl was unfamiliar. Blond blond hair. Big blue eyes. Braces on her teeth. Freckles on her nose. She looked like she'd stepped right out of a Norman Rockwell picture of an American teenager.

"Hi," Troy said, walking up beside her.

She looked down at the ground.

He did too. His heart soared. She was wearing pure white Keds! And white ankle socks! Her calves were tanned and firm, her knees were beautiful.

"What are you looking at?" she said. She stopped walking and waited for his answer.

He couldn't say, Your legs. That would be all wrong. "You're wearing Keds," he said. He smiled at her.

"Ugh," she said, and started walking again. "You have a tattoo."

"Yeah," he said. He laughed. "I actually have a few. Stupid, huh?"

Again she stopped walking. She faced him, hands on her hips. She had slender hips, small breasts under her navy blue and white cheerleading sweater. The sweater had a big H on it. And a husky that seemed to be running out of the H, right at you.

"I think tattoos are disgusting," she said.

He wondered if the sweater was what made her eyes seem so blue.

"They are," he agreed. "I went through this weird time." He shook his head. "I don't know."

He was glad he was wearing one of the new T-shirts. It was pure white too.

"Can I see it?" she asked him.

"See it?"

She pointed at his arm, where Yosemite Sam was poking out from under his sleeve.

Her eyebrows were so pale, he could hardly make them out. She was a real blonde. A natural. Not like Jessica Tremont.

"Sure," he said. He lifted his sleeve and she lightly touched the tattoo, tracing the dark outline.

"What is it?" she said.

"Yosemite Sam."

"I don't know who that is." She looked up at him. "I know who you are, though. Jessica told me. She said you are wild. Bad news."

"I'm not." He smiled at her. "I'm good news."

She started to walk again. She seemed to be deciding something. "You look a little bit like Matt Dillon," she said. "Don't let it go to your head, though."

"I won't."

"We just moved here," she said. "From Minnesota."

"Wow," he said. "Minnesota." He knew nothing about Minnesota, except where it was on the map. He thought about that, then said, "It must get pretty cold there."

She smiled at him, all shiny and silver. "Yes," she said happily. "Very cold. There are places in Minnesota where you can die just from breathing the bitter cold air. It freezes your lungs. But we lived in Minneapolis."

"It's okay to breathe in Minneapolis?"

She laughed. "Yes."

They had stopped walking again. "I think you're very pretty," Troy said. He didn't look at her when he said it.

"My father would kill me if I went out with someone who had tattoos."

Troy nodded.

"He would absolutely murder me."

Troy almost said, I didn't ask you out. But he wanted to do this just right. "I could wear long sleeves," he said.

She looked past him, down the road, but didn't say anything.

"Would he kill you if you told me your name?"

She glanced at him, then away again. He could see that she was smiling. "It's Jenny. Anderson."

Jenny, he thought. What an absolutely perfect name. Jenny.

"And I know you're Troy."

He waited, considering before he said, "Would he kill you if I called you?"

"Probably," Jenny said. She searched inside her red-flowered backpack, then pulled out a pen. "Do you have any paper?"

Troy shook his head. Then he extended his arm.

Jenny hesitated, then wrote her phone number below his elbow, pressing hard on his skin.

Tuesday night, *Renata drove* to Dee-Dee Winthrop's house. She told herself that she wanted a normal life for Millie, that going to Dee-Dee's meeting was a way of doing that, even though it felt anything but normal. It was funny, she thought as she stopped the car in front of Dee-Dee's white Cape with the black shutters and Hondas and Nissans crowded into the driveway, in a way returning to Holly was therapeutic for her too. A way to confront the old ghosts of teenage girls whispering about her in the girls' room at school. She had returned, a hero's widow, a member of a group.

Renata had tried not to dress funny. She wore jeans and clogs and a paint-splattered T-shirt for authenticity—after all, she was an artist as well as a hero's widow, wasn't she?

Giggling spilled out of the house and froze Renata before she got to the front door with the big brass W and a droopy yellow ribbon hanging on it. It was the same terror that used to strike her before she entered the smoky high school girls' room or the locker room at the gym. She could already identify Dee-Dee's voice above all the others. Like a burglar, Renata crept behind the hedges and flattened herself against the wall, creeping toward the window.

Renata could just see into the living room, all colonial furniture in autumn colors, studio portraits of children on one wall.

"I can't believe she was married to a soldier," another voice was saying. It was a voice that was both familiar and strange to Renata.

"I can't believe she was married to anyone," someone else said.

And then yet another voice said, "Remember that time she did her oral report on astrology? She said she could read the stars?"

Everyone started laughing again.

"Sure," Dee-Dee said. "She got up there and started talking about her moon being in Sagittarius . . ."

Renata stepped out of her hiding place, crushing chrysanthemums and asters. She walked across Dee-Dee Winthrop's front lawn and back to her car. She didn't know if they saw her and she didn't care.

When she got home, Millie was sitting in the yard, staring up at the night sky.

"Back already?" she said.

Renata sat down beside her. "I didn't go," she said. "I never liked those girls in school and I don't like them now."

"There are more stars here," Millie said.

"Not more," Renata said. "You can just see them better here. The lights in the city dim them."

"Oh," Millie said.

And the two of them sat there for a while more, watching the stars, not talking.

*roy stopped calling Nadine.* He could not even believe that he had wasted so much time with her. Lately he felt that he'd spent the last few years in a fog that was starting, finally, to lift. He imagined that he was like this guy he saw in a movie once, who was wrapped up like a mummy for ages, then slowly had all the bandages removed and saw the world differently than he used to.

It was not easy to explain this to anyone. Especially not Nadine. At home, the phone would ring and ring and when someone finally answered she'd hang up. She called all night, until his father took the phone off the hook. Troy knew she was following him, even though he never actually saw her. He felt her, those crazy eyes of hers on him, watching.

The first week of school he called Jenny Anderson every evening after dinner. They talked for hours, until her father yelled for her to hang up already. The second week he started to sit with her at lunch, and wait for her after cheerleading practice, then walk with her almost all the way to her house.

On the afternoon that he heard Jessica Tremont call to her, "Be careful" as soon as he appeared, Troy decided he would ask her out. Fuck Jessica Tremont, he thought.

"What did Jessica say about me?" he asked Jenny.

She hesitated. "She said I shouldn't be talking to you. She said you had dropped out of school and lived with some drug addict or something."

That afternoon, the cheerleaders had made their pom-poms out of blue and white paper, shredding it and gluing it together. Jenny held hers gently in her arms. Without saying anything, Troy took her backpack from her.

"I think you're nice," Jenny said. She leaned against a stone wall on the corner where they usually parted.

"I like you so much," Troy said softly. "I even dream about you." He had been having dreams about her. But they were not the kind of dreams you told a girl you had.

"You do?" she said.

"Practically every night."

"I don't really care what Jessica says about you."

"I did date a girl for a while," Troy said. "But she wasn't a drug addict."

Somehow this information seemed to be a relief to Jenny. She stepped closer to him. He could smell her perfume. It was light and flowery.

"So then do you think maybe I could take you out Saturday night?" he said.

She swallowed hard. "Yes."

He touched her chin with his fingertips, very lightly. "Yes?" he said. "Really?"

She nodded.

"Great." He removed his hand and he thought that maybe she even looked a tiny bit disappointed. Like maybe she thought he was going to kiss her.

"Great," he said again.


*Troy wanted everything perfect.* He washed his car. He ironed his shirt. He went right up to her front door and rang the doorbell. He shook Mr. Anderson's hand and said they had a lovely home. It wasn't really so lovely but when he said that Mrs. Anderson smiled. He stood when Jenny walked in the room. He promised to have her home by eleven thirty.

Jenny had on that flowery perfume and baggy jeans with a white blouse. He could see the outline of her bra underneath, a tiny rosebud nestled in the center. He made himself look away.

They went to the movies in Pittsfield and then to Elizabeth's for pizza.

He told her, "I'm crazy about you."

She blushed and said, "Me too."

When they left the restaurant he held her hand. She had short nails with clear polish on them and a gold ring with a heart in the middle. She was so perfect.

He didn't take her to the quarry. He drove her straight home. In front of her house he kept the radio on real low. For a while they just sat there.

"I like this song," Jenny said.

He didn't even know what it was but he said, "Me too."

"Now when it comes on I'll think about you," she said.

He leaned over, close to her. "Can I kiss you?" he whispered.

She tasted like fruit, like berries and oranges.

Her voice was nervous when she spoke. "Wilson Phillips," she said. "The group that's singing. Wilson Phillips. Their parents were all famous in the sixties. The Beach Boys and the Mamas and the Papas."

He kissed her again. He wanted to really kiss her, to put his tongue inside her mouth, to press her close to him. But he didn't. He just kissed her again, then shut the ignition off. He walked her to the door where they stood holding hands for a while. Her parents had left the outside light on for her and he felt conspicuous standing there under it. So he leaned over and kissed her again, on the cheek this time, then watched as she opened the door.

Before she went inside she turned toward him.

"Will you call me tomorrow?" she said. She looked like a little girl.

He nodded.

When she smiled at him, her braces flashed, all silver and shiny in the light. He stood there for a moment longer. He wished his mother could see him now. She wouldn't believe it.

"I know," *Dana said to the* boy with the dimples. "Pineapple, black olives, and Canadian bacon."

He smiled, showed her those dimples again. "Right," he said.

"Ten minutes," she told him, but he didn't leave the counter.

"What's the weirdest order you ever got?"

He had on that gray T-shirt again. The one that said WILLIAMS in purple across his chest.

She smiled back at him. "Pineapple," she said. "Black olives—"

"And Canadian bacon," he finished.

"Pretty disgusting," she said. She had started to sweat. She hoped he wouldn't notice.

He scanned the list of one hundred toppings. "More disgusting than tofu and goat cheese? Or cherry and jalapeño?"

Dana leaned toward him. She could feel the sharp edge of the counter digging into her hip. "My idea of a pizza is pepperoni and mushroom from Elizabeth's. Or their sausage and pepper." She spoke in a low voice. "That's pizza."

"Where's Elizabeth's?" he asked her.

"Pittsfield." For a crazy minute Dana almost thought he was going to ask her if she wanted to go there. With him.

But then a tall girl with straight blond hair appeared. A girl who looked as if she played field hockey, who knew Mozart from Bach, who went to college.

"Do you think I could order here?" the girl said to Dana. "A small pineapple, black olives, and Canadian bacon."

Dana felt the boy's eyes on her face. But she didn't meet them with hers. Instead, she repeated the girl's order.

The girl was saying, "Hi, Billy. Did you already finish reading *Hamlet?*"

"Not yet," the boy with the dimples said. "I'm still working on that paper for Matthews' class."

Billy, Dana thought. What a dumb name.

"Ten minutes," she said. Then she put the girl's order all the way at the end of the row.


"*Did you know that in this* area alone there are over twenty-five different kinds of apples?" Caitlin said.

"That's fascinating," Kevin said. "Isn't that fascinating?"

He looked back at Dana and Mike in the rearview mirror.

"Fascinating," Mike said.

They took a curve too fast.

"Whoa," Mike said. "An SOB."

Dana focused on the darkness outside the window. She tried to make out animals in the woods. Just a few years ago they had been able to see deer on this road. Once, her father even saw a bear.

"We should go to a movie or something," Caitlin was saying. "Wouldn't you like to see a movie, Dana?"

"Six bucks," Kevin said, "when you can see it free on HBO in like a month."

"You can't see it on HBO in a month," Caitlin said.

"Whatever."

Mike pressed his lips against Dana's ear. "Why so quiet?" he whispered.

She couldn't think of a good reason, so she said, "Once my father saw a bear on this road."

Mike squeezed her close to him. "Are you afraid of bears?"

Dana tried to pull herself free. But he was too strong. All that wrestling training.

They finally reached the quarry, and Dana was the first one out of the car. She shivered, feeling the beginning of autumn in the cool air.

"Frat boys," Kevin said, pointing.

There, on a rock, were four guys, in WILLIAMS sweatshirts, drinking beer and singing songs. One of them had a guitar. And Dana could tell by the size and color of their beer bottles that it was imported beer, Beck's or Saint Pauli Girl. Beer from a country where people spoke a different language.

Caitlin nudged Dana in the ribs, her elbow sharp.

"Isn't that your boyfriend?" she whispered. "With the guitar?"

Dana nodded. She imagined that he could see her too, that he recognized her, and she felt suddenly embarrassed to be here with Mike, clutching a six-pack and a ratty old blanket. She was afraid he could see right through her, that he knew exactly why she was here, and what she was feeling. Dana bent her head and walked away quickly, her sneakers slipping in the moist dirt.

Behind her, Mike was laughing. "Yeah," he said, "she can hardly wait to get her hands on me."

Dana bit hard on her bottom lip, hoping that boy, Billy, couldn't hear. Mike ran to her and caught her arm too hard, sending them both tumbling to the ground. She smelled the beer on his breath. In the distance she heard the other boys singing some kind of folk song, by Simon and Garfunkel or someone like them.

Mike was kissing her, big wet kisses that left her feeling dirty. Already she could feel him, hard, pressing against her.

"I have my period," she lied.

"I don't care," he said.

That song was one her mother liked.

"Well, I care," she told him.

It was something about being a rock.

"Please," he said. He unzipped his pants, took her hand in his and wrapped it around his penis.

About being all alone.

Dana squeezed her eyes shut and moved her hand up the length of Mike's penis. She felt his body shift, heard him exhale hard. Zap, she thought, and she was on that rock with Billy. She was on that rock sipping imported beer. And she knew all the words to the songs he was playing.

$C$*arl told Libby that originally* he saw her as feature film material. "But you said 'Housewife,'" she reminded him.

"Yes, yes," he said. "But feature film wife slash mother. Think Jo Beth Williams."

Libby struggled to conjure the face of Jo Beth Williams. She couldn't.

"But," Carl said, "I was wrong. Forget Jo Beth Williams."

Despite herself, Libby started to feel excited. He was wrong. She wasn't housewife material after all. She had made a point of dressing up for every class. Not that she imitated Heather and Ashley, but she took a cue from them. They showed up in their short black outfits, all long legs and blond hair and Carl always gave them interesting roles to read. Libby didn't get angry when those two got to do a scene from *A Streetcar Named Desire,* or when he cast Ashley as Laura in *The Glass Menagerie* and she was stuck being the mother. Instead, she tried harder to look sexy. Last week she had worn tube tops from breasts to thighs, just those bright bands of color. Now here was Carl changing his mind about what she could become.

"Commercials," he said. "A housewife on commercials."

"Commercials," she repeated.

"You don't have that big-screen presence."

Libby looked down at her feet. They were killing her from standing at Von's all day and then being pushed into the stiletto heels she had on.

"There's a lot of money to be made in commercials," Carl told her. He did not sound unkind.

Libby took a breath. In high school she had played the second lead in *Fiddler on the Roof.* Tzeitel, the oldest daughter. Everyone told her she stole the show.

"I have stage experience," she said, trying to sound bright and determined. "Perhaps I should try theater." Then she added, "Again."

Carl handed her a card. "Be at this address at ten o'clock tomorrow. They're auditioning women for a floor wax commercial."

"Floor wax?" Libby said. It was funny how after all these years she still remembered her lines in *Fiddler*. Her very first one was, "Mama, you know that Papa works hard." The girl who had played the lead, Golde, was not nearly as good as she was. "You know," Libby said, "I can sing too."

"Yes," Carl said. "You mentioned that at some point." He was standing, ready for her to leave.

Libby tried to be professional. He had given her a lead on an acting job. She certainly didn't see Ashley or Heather in here. Besides, Farrah Fawcett had started in commercials. For shampoo, of all things. That had led to *Charlie's Angels*, to marrying Lee Majors. To a full-fledged career, for God's sake. Maybe she was on her way, after all.

She put on her best smile and shook Carl's hand, firmly. A handshake was very important. It gave a real message as to who a person really was. Carl seemed startled. His handshake was limp, like a boneless chicken breast. As she walked away, Libby sang "Matchmaker," softly, just in case he was still listening.

*Libby was practical. She* prided herself on that part of her personality. Sometimes, back in Holly, when she was depressed, she wrote down all of her positive attributes. It made her feel better. Practical was always way at the top of that list, even before pretty and slender.

That was why she did what she did. Because she was practical. Because she knew from her research that Hollywood was corrupt, that you had to play their game. When she walked into the waiting room for that audition and saw twenty other women, all pretty and slender, all her age, she realized she had to do something to get that commercial.

Suddenly, standing there surrounded by women who looked just like her, Libby decided that getting chosen for this floor wax ad was the most important thing in the world. It was what she had come all this way for, what she had risked everything for, why she had left her husband and children. When her name was called and she walked into the room for the audition, her only hope was that the man she was about to meet wasn't too disgusting.

He wasn't. He wasn't her type, either, but he wasn't the worst person she'd ever seen. He was a little short. He could lose ten or fifteen pounds. He was a bit older than she expected, close to sixty, she figured.

Libby had had an affair once, with a man named William Monroe. If one afternoon constituted an affair. That was five years ago, at the Marriott in

Boston. She had seen an ad in the paper that said a major airline would be in Boston recruiting flight attendants. Maybe, she thought, that was the job for her. She imagined herself flying around the world, jetting into Paris and Rome, sipping champagne.

Tom hadn't liked the idea. "But it says here you'll have to relocate," he told her. Ever so slightly, he moved his lips when he read. Not enough for anyone to really notice, although she always did.

"So we'll relocate," she told him, pretending that she would take him along.

"I don't know, Libby," he said. He looked frightened.

She went anyway, dressed in red, white and blue, trying to look like a flight attendant right from the start. But at the interview, they didn't even ask her questions. They just sat there, waiting for her to say something. After a few minutes they thanked her and showed her out. Later she realized that they wanted someone who would just talk, someone friendly and cheerful. Probably she seemed much too professional for that kind of job, too mature. But at that moment when they didn't want her, before she figured out why, she had gone down to the bar and ordered a drink. Libby wasn't used to being rejected.

That was where she met William Monroe. He was in Boston on a job interview too, a handsome man a few years younger than Libby. He thought he'd gotten the job he'd come for and felt like celebrating. They drank too much and then she went back to his room with him. After they'd made love, she threw up. "Too much to drink," she told him.

But really she wasn't sure if that were true. It was, she thought, just too much. Blowing the interview, having sex with a stranger, all of it. And life itself, this feeling of being trapped, of not knowing which way to turn. Sitting on that cold bathroom floor of William Monroe's hotel room, Libby had remembered a guidance counselor in high school named Mr. Polaski. She had tried to explain to him her need to do something big, something away from Holly. Mr. Polaski had been in the Peace Corps. He had a thick mustache and long sideburns. She thought she could trust him. But he said, "Pretty girls like you should get married and make their husbands happy." "But I want more than that," she told him. He thought a long while. "You could be a teacher," he said finally. Somewhere out there women were burning their bras, demanding things, but in Holly women were still just pretty future wives.

That was how Libby still felt—confused, trapped. Magazines were always writing about successful women. They showed proof, pictures of women in suits with briefcases and running shoes, waving goodbye to their husbands and children, going to an office where they made important decisions. Libby always studied those pictures carefully. The women seemed to be the same age as she was. Yet somehow they had found out something that she hadn't. They had houses that overlooked the ocean, or town houses in historic parts of cities. They had jobs and nice clothes and children who understood them. She had nothing.

A few years ago she had tried to start a book club. She had read in the newspaper about how they were popular in cities everywhere. Women got together and made fancy dinners and discussed important books. But at the very first meeting they couldn't decide on what book to read, Jackie Collins or Judith Krantz. No one would listen to Libby's suggestions. No one liked the risotto it had taken her so long to make. Alice Rose spilled her wine on Libby's personal copy of *The Women's Room.*

When they finally left, Tom helped her clean up. "You know," he said, "I like to read. If you want, we can read the same book and then I'll talk to you about it."

He hadn't read a book since high school and she knew it. Although she supposed his offer was sweet, that someone else would think she had the best husband in the world, it only made Libby even sadder.

Now, here she was up against twenty other women. She was not special here. All she wanted was this one thing, to mop a floor on national television. Other than that one afternoon with William Monroe, the only man she had ever had sex with was Tom. Still, she faced the man who maybe could finally change her life and said, "I want this part more than anything in the world and I will do anything for it." Then slowly, staring past his gaze and out the window at the skyscrapers of Los Angeles, Libby unbuttoned her blouse.

Dana knew something was up when Caitlin walked into Dana's study hall, her face all creased with worry. Study hall was first period for Dana, and all around her everyone was hurrying to finish homework due next period. Usually, Dana wrote lyrics to rock songs in the back of her Spanish notebook. For these forty-five minutes every morning, she pretended her songs were good. She could imagine herself on MTV, surrounded by men in tuxedos, dancing and spinning, her latest hit playing in the background.

In her fantasy, she looked a little like China Phillips from the group Wilson Phillips. Her mother had told her that China Phillips's mother used to be in the Mamas and the Papas. "I laughed when I read they named their kid China," her mother had said. "I mean China?" And then her mother had gone into all the weird names the old rock stars gave their kids, God and America and Zowie.

Now she watched as Caitlin whispered to Mr. Ross and they both glanced over at Dana, their eyes all sneaky. Mr. Ross taught chemistry and always smelled like one of his experiments, sickly sweet or slightly eggy. He crooked his finger at Dana.

"Ms. Harper," he said. He insisted on calling everybody Mr. or Ms. His big joke was to say on the first day, "Do we have any Mrs. here?" Last year Dorrie Flagg got pregnant and married some guy in the marines over the summer. She'd come back to school wearing a baby blue maternity dress covered with faded bunnies, and when Mr. Harper asked that stupid question she'd raised her hand. "I'm Mrs. Bay now," she'd said, and everyone giggled.

Dana walked past all the tables filled with microscopes and test tubes toward Caitlin and Mr. Ross. Caitlin's jeans were too big for her, and they were bunched up funny by an old beaded belt that said HOLLYWOOD across the back, except now it said HYWOO because Caitlin was so skinny she had to almost double it up.

"Ms. Mitchell has to talk to you," Mr. Ross said. "She has exactly three minutes and only because it's an extreme emergency. Right, Ms. Mitchell?"

Caitlin nodded. She took Dana's arm and practically dragged her into the hall. Even through the closed door they could hear Mr. Ross saying, "Don't you people have anything to study?"

"What a jerk," Caitlin said.

"He smells like Dr Pepper or something today," Dana said.

"Listen, I wanted to tell you first. In case anybody mentions it even though I don't know how they'd ever find out, but you never can tell in this one-horse town who knows what." Caitlin looked around and sighed. "Man," she said, "what I would give for a cigarette."

Dana leaned against the wall. It was painted dull yellow and lined with army green lockers. With a red felt-tip pen someone had made a row of peace signs in a crack between two cinder blocks. Dana spit on her finger and rubbed them off.

"Are you listening?" Caitlin said. She sounded annoyed.

"Yes."

"Your mother called last night. She called my mother at like two a.m. or something. Scared the hell out of her."

Dana felt her whole body stiffen. Even her toes seemed to be rigid.

"She called to tell her," Caitlin was saying, "she's going to be on television Monday night. In a floor wax commercial."

Dana wondered if she could walk if she tried. That's how stiff she felt. Like a board. Like one of these cinder blocks behind her.

"I figured it was better to tell you. I mean, what if you watched TV and saw her."

Dana nodded. She felt like the Tin Man in *The Wizard of Oz*, all stiff and creaky.

"I hope I did the right thing," Caitlin said.

Dana managed to nod again.

"I didn't know what else to do," Caitlin said, looking down the hall. "God, do I wish I had a cig right now." She turned back to Dana. "I should get back to English. *Beowolf.*"

Dana wanted to say thanks, or to at least tell her she'd done the right thing, but all she could do was walk on her stiff legs, robotlike, back to study hall.

*Dana hardly ever went into* Troy's room. It smelled weird, like pot and socks and sweat. But today, when she heard him come in from school and climb the stairs and close his bedroom door, she decided to go in there and tell him. Since she had gotten home, all she had done was lie on her bed and think, Oil can, oil can, just like the Tin Man. He had needed a heart, and Dana felt as if hers was missing too. Hers was in a red convertible, driving down Hollywood Boulevard.

She knocked on Troy's door and hesitated before opening it, even after he yelled "Come in." She never knew what she'd find Troy doing.

But he was just sitting on his bed reading *The Scarlet Letter*.

"Why are you walking so weird?" he said. "You look like those Iraqi soldiers when they march down the streets of Baghdad."

His room didn't smell too bad. It just had a guy smell, that was all. Dana sat on the very edge of his bed. She saw he had a bandage over his John Lennon tattoo, to hide it.

"Well," she said, "Mom is in a TV commercial. It's airing Monday night." Then she said, "Floor wax."

Troy's thick eyebrows bunched together so they looked like a caterpillar creeping across his face.

"A floor wax commercial?" he said.

Dana watched his Adam's apple bob up and down real quick. "She called Sue," Dana said.

Troy nodded slowly. One finger held his place in *The Scarlet Letter*, and Dana saw that he was pressing real hard, crinkling the cover.

"Sue," Troy said. "Figures."

It did figure, Dana thought. It was always Sue whom their mother let in to her room when she hid up there for days on end, and Sue whom they'd find her on the phone with when she should have been talking to them, asking them how school was that day.

Dana looked at the wallpaper on Troy's walls. It was old, put up when he was a kid. There were Revolutionary War soldiers and cannons and Redcoats, but they had discolored so that nothing was red or blue or black anymore. Instead, everything was some shade of gray, battleship or silver or blue-gray. Except the Redcoats. They had turned a strange orange.

Dana didn't know what else to say, so she just sat there for a while longer.

*Neither of them told their father.* But Monday night after dinner he said, "So? Should we watch her or not?"

Dana supposed Sue had told him. She tried to imagine being in love, the way her father was with her mother, and having that person leave you. She had never really thought about it that way before, but now that she did, she saw her father a little differently. He was a tragic figure suddenly. He'd been abandoned by his wife! What did he think about alone in bed every night? Dana wondered.

"Do you want to watch her?" Dana asked him, her voice so gentle that he looked at her startled.

"It's going to break my heart," he said after a minute.

How much can a heart break? Dana wondered. Was there some cut-off point where it couldn't hurt any more than it already did?

"But I would sort of like to see her," her father said softly.

Troy swallowed so hard that Dana heard him do it. "Me too," he said.

"I feel like I have no heart at all," Dana told them. "Like I'm stiff and cold and my chest is empty. Like the Tin Man."

Her father put his arms around her and hugged. He hadn't done that since she was a little girl. "Oh baby," he said. "I am so sorry."

"I hate her," Troy said. Dana heard him swallow real hard again.

Their father said, "I feel like my heart is one of those ones you get on Valentine's Day when you're a kid. And it keeps getting ripped up. And ripped up some more."

"Still," Troy said, "watching her would be better than not."

Their father nodded too enthusiastically. "Definitely. And maybe it would help in a funny kind of way."

They settled in front of the television. Tom lined up three bottles of beer beside him. He drank the first one very fast, his eyes glued to the set even though Libby wasn't supposed to be on until halfway through the Monday movie.

*Jeopardy!* was almost over, the contestants busy trying to write down their questions for the Final Jeopardy answer: "He was the only president ever to wear a Nazi uniform."

Dana tried to figure out the question but she was getting that old stiff feeling again. Everything felt paralyzed, even her tongue and brain.

Troy muttered, "Ronald Reagan. Who else could it be? He probably was in some stupid movie."

No one else said anything until the movie started. Then Tom said, "A goddamn commercial." And then they were silent again.

When she appeared on their television, Dana leaned forward. They all did. The seats creaked and rustled. Their breathing changed. There she was, all blond and beautiful being beamed into living rooms everywhere, waxing a floor until stars shot out of it.

Dana thought about how some family in Kansas had just seen her mother, someone in Hawaii and Texas.

"You okay?" their father asked. He didn't sound okay.

"She seemed like a stranger," Troy said. He walked out of the room, and Dana could hear him making a telephone call in the kitchen.

"She did a good job, I think," Tom said. "Don't you think so?"

Dana shrugged. She was waiting to feel something.

"Still feel like the Tin Man?" he asked her.

"Yeah."

Troy didn't come back after the commercial. But Dana and Tom stayed and watched the movie. Dana heard her father make a strange noise, almost like a choked sob, but she didn't look over at him. She was afraid he'd feel too embarrassed.

Finally, Dana turned off the television.

"I guess she'll never come back now," Tom said.

The room was very dark without the light from the set. But Dana could see that his head was bent.

"I guess she's gone for good," he said, and he made that strange sound again.

Dana stood in the middle of the living room, trying to figure out what to do. She could hear Troy, still on the phone, his voice low. Tom was still looking down, peeling the label off the beer bottle. He had it almost off in one piece, but then it ripped.

"No one loves me," he said. He looked up finally and she saw that his face was wet. "That's what we used to say when we were kids. If you can't rip it off in one piece, it means no one loves you."

Dana thought, I love you. But she didn't say anything. She stood there a moment longer, and then went to bed.

In the morning, she found something from her father sitting beside her bed, on the crowded night table. It was an oil can, from his garage. She could still smell oil on it. She picked it up and held it in both her hands. He must have driven to the garage to get it, then driven all the way back home and left it here for her to find when she woke up.

She got up quickly, wishing she had said or done something last night, standing there with him after the movie. But when she ran downstairs to find him, to say something to him, he was already gone.

*Sue was small and thin.* Not like her kid, Caitlin, but scrawny and small-boned. She reminded Tom of a homeless cat, or a lost child. She had never once cut her hair, so that it grew all wild and ragged to her hips. Seeing her now, pressing her face against the screen door of her house, Tom thought that if he didn't know better, he would guess her to be a teenager instead of a grown woman.

"Harp," she said. "Hi."

It was the morning after he had watched Libby on that commercial, and Tom had not slept at all. Instead, he'd sat in front of the television as if she might appear again and step from the screen into the living room. Even two six-packs of beer had not made that fantasy come true.

"You look awful," Sue was saying. She opened the door for him and stepped aside. She was wearing a worn dark green cardigan that was too big for her, and she kept hugging it close around her chest.

"And you smell," she said when he passed her.

Tom pulled up a chair and sat on it backward.

"Let's see," Sue said, "you need black coffee."

He didn't watch her as she moved about the small kitchen. Tom always felt slightly embarrassed in Sue's presence. He knew too much. Back when Mitch was alive, they used to tell each other everything. Tom knew that Sue had a crooked scar on her inner thigh from jumping a fence when she was a kid. He knew that during sex, she liked to rake her fingers across a man's back, leaving a red path behind. He knew everything, all the intimate details.

Sue was close to him now, putting a cup of coffee in front of him. The mug said *Happy Holidays* and was covered with red and green snowflakes. Tom stared at the cup so as not to look at Sue. He tried to make more words out of *Holidays*. There were *day* and *days*, of course. And *say*, and *lay*.

"I know it was hard," Sue said. "Last night."

Tom kept staring. *Hay. Sad.*

"I watched," she said. "I kept thinking about how much she wants this. How much she always wanted this."

*Lad. Had.*

"Harp? Say something."

Tom looked up at her. "Do you have any beer?" he said finally.

*When he opened his eyes,* Tom could not figure out where he was. He didn't feel frightened. Just confused. He tried to lick his lips, but his mouth was too dry. It made a little popping sound when he opened it. From somewhere far off he heard voices. Women's voices, hushed and excited.

"I mean I'm really just a kid. Is this what I'm supposed to be doing?" That was Dana.

"When I was your age, I had a dead husband and a baby." That was Sue.

Tom closed his eyes again and thought. He was on Sue's couch, an old thing with busted springs digging into his back. She kept a fringed bedspread over it to hide all the tears and holes. But the bedspread was all bunched up and Tom could feel the scratchy upholstery underneath. He had sat at Sue's kitchen table all day, drinking all her beer and then some Jack Daniel's. He had cried.

Sue told him that was a good thing. The crying. Get it out, she'd said. He hadn't really talked to her. There were no words for heartbreak, no vocabulary that really captured what it felt like. But Sue had been right. The tears had helped.

"She is the most selfish person on this planet," Dana was saying. "I hate her. I really do."

"Someday," Sue said, "you are going to have to make a choice between what you want and what everyone else needs and then you won't be thinking about what's selfish and what's not."

"I would never hurt so many people," Dana said. "Never."

Tom sat up, unsteadily. It was dark outside, and dark in the room. He followed the light from the kitchen, pressing the palms of his hands to the wall as he walked. They all looked up when he stumbled in. Dana, Sue, Caitlin.

"Hi," he said.

Dana was frowning at him. She had done something else with her hair, something new, but he couldn't tell what.

Tom cleared his throat. "I could use that coffee," he said.

"Let's just forget her," Dana said, her voice more intense than he could ever remember it being. "Let's just start new."

Tom reached out, touched his daughter's head lightly. He was surprised how hard her hair felt, like armor. That was what was different, he realized. She had dyed one side bright orange, the side that used to have a peace symbol shaved on it.

He smiled at her. "Let's go home," he said.


*Dana drove.*

When they pulled into the driveway, Tom said, "I thought I saw somebody in the trees. Back there."

"Nadine."

The name sounded vaguely familiar to him. "Nadine?" he repeated.

"Troy's old girlfriend," Dana said. "She follows him around."

"Uh-huh," Tom said.

They stepped out of the car, into the darkness. The smell of rotting leaves was strong and there was a hint of frost in the air.

"Daddy," Dana said.

This startled him. She had not called him that in a very long time.

Tom took a step closer to her. He still felt unsteady on his feet, so he placed one hand on the hood of the car.

"Thank you for the present," she said. "The oil can."

She didn't wait for him to answer. Instead, she slipped into the house quickly, so he couldn't see her face.

*"I know,"* Dana said. "Pineapple—"

The college boy shook his head. "No," he said.

She thought. BillyBillyBillyBillyBillyBillyBilly.

"Andouille, shrimp, and hot pepper," he told her.

"Oh. Now you're going Cajun," Dana said. Then repeated his order. "Andouille, shrimp, and hot pepper. Ten minutes."

He smiled but he didn't walk away.

"Something else?" she asked him, forcing her voice into nonchalance.

"What happened to peace and love?" he said. He pointed at her newly dyed hair.

Dana shrugged. "I like orange now," she told her. She was trying for sassy.

"Well," he said, "it's certainly orange."

She narrowed her eyes at him, trying to decide if he was making fun of her.

But then he said, "Want to go out later? There's this thing at school."

She didn't answer right away. She had to wait for her heart to slip back into place.

"What kind of thing?" she said. She started to wipe the counter in front of her.

"A dance. There's a band and some kegs." He was smiling, showing off his dimples.

Dana felt Caitlin watching her. They were supposed to go out with Mike and Kevin after work. She tried to imagine a college dance, but kept picturing scenes from *Animal House,* crazy guys in togas rolling on the floor to "Shout."

It seemed as if everyone was waiting for her to say something.

She shrugged. "Okay," she said, as if it really didn't matter at all.

*There was an employees'* locker room at Pizza Pizzazz, where they could change their clothes or go during breaks for a cigarette. Dana was back there, getting out of her uniform, when Caitlin came in with a small pizza. Sausage, tomato, and fresh basil.

"A mistake," she said, holding the pizza up for Dana to see. "With normal ingredients for a change."

Caitlin sat on one of the long wooden benches that lined one wall, put her feet up, and bit into a piece of pizza.

Dana tried to smooth out the wrinkles on her shirt. She could feel her hands tremble. She thought, BillyBillyBillyBillyBillyBillyBilly.

"Maybe you could tell me what I'm supposed to say to Mike," Caitlin said. She finished her first piece and started on a second.

"Tell him I got sick," Dana said. Then she added, "Of him."

"Ha ha."

Dana wished she had worn something different. She had on a sea green bowling shirt that said *Roy* in black script above the pocket and PAULIE'S BAR AND GRILL across the back. She'd bought it at the Goodwill store along with a maroon and white letter jacket. She'd thought both things were hilarious when she bought them, but now, when she put on the jacket she knew that neither thing was funny at all. She looked completely stupid. She looked like exactly what she was—a townie.

Caitlin kept eating pizza, watching Dana look at herself in the mirror.

"You think this guy can save you or something?" Caitlin said. "You think he's going to whisk you away to Westport, Connecticut?"

"I think maybe I can talk to him using three-syllable words. I think maybe he knows the capital of New Mexico. Who wrote *Oliver Twist.*"

Caitlin laughed. "I get it," she said. "You love him for his mind."

Dana turned to her. "Do I look awful?" she said.

Caitlin shook her head. "You look great. Those college jerks won't know what hit them. You look hip. Totally hip."

Dana took a breath. "Really?"

"Yes." Caitlin rolled her eyes. "Now go before the Neanderthals arrive."

"You going to stay back here?"

Caitlin nodded. There was grease on her chin.

"Have fun!" she called to Dana. "Be good!"

*Dana had grown up eighteen* miles from Williams College but she had never been on the campus except for once, in fifth grade, when the music teacher took the entire class to hear the Boston Symphony play there. Now she was arriving on campus in a red sports car that still smelled new.

She expected the dorm to look more like a hotel inside. But it reminded her of high school—cinder blocks, cheap indoor-outdoor carpeting, bulletin boards. Billy took her hand and led her through a maze of hallways. Every room had different music blaring from it. David Byrne, the Beatles, Patsy Cline. Dana was glad it was so noisy. That way she was sure Billy couldn't hear her heart pounding.

Finally he said, "Here we are" and opened the door into a kind of rec room. The room was dark and smelled like old beer. A band was playing some song from the fifties, like "Runaround Sue" or "The Wanderer," and everywhere Dana looked there were people—dancing, talking, kissing in corners. She took a deep breath, decided she didn't look too out of place. Even though most of them were totally prepped out, all Ralph Lauren and Pappagallo.

Billy did not let go of her hand.

"Want a beer?" he said.

She nodded, and let him lead her to a keg.

While he poured the beers into plastic cups, a girl that looked vaguely familiar came over to Dana.

"Don't you work in Pizza Pizzazz?" she said.

Dana considered lying, but then changed her mind and nodded.

"They have the best pizza," the girl said. "I always get roasted pepper and fontina."

Dana nodded again. "That's a good combo."

Other people were joining them around the keg.

"Do you go here?" someone asked her.

"No," Dana said.

Billy was holding her hand again.

"She's from town," he said, acting cool.

Suddenly, Dana hated everyone in that room. She knew they were laughing at her. A townie who sells pizza. She was sure that's what they were thinking. The hell with them, she thought, feeling calmer.

"I grew up in town," she said. She made it sound special, important. "Our house is a real dump because my mother went sort of loony." She crossed her eyes and stuck out her tongue. "She decided she wanted to be a movie star. But first she went to bed and thought about it for about ten years. Then she up and left." She added, "She's in a TV commercial." And when she said that the band stopped and her voice echoed through the room. But she refused to feel embarrassed.

A few people moved closer.

Dana sipped her beer. "My loony tune mother. Of course in the meantime we're all going to pot. My father's practically drinking himself to death and my brother has completely mutilated his body by getting like a dozen tattoos." She pointed to her own body as she explained, "John Lennon, yin and yang, Yosemite Sam."

"Really?" the first girl said, the one who liked pizza with roasted pepper and fontina. "That's really tragic. Like that Flannery O'Connor story."

Dana nodded. " 'Parker's Back,' " she said, happy that she'd just read it in English class.

Be outrageous, Dana told herself when she felt her heart do that jump again. Fuck them all.


*No one had ever sat Dana* down and explained the birds and the bees. Except Caitlin, and her information had been all wrong. "Sperm is like Superman," Caitlin had told her. "It can leap through pants, through water, anything. You can get pregnant like this." She'd snapped her fingers, fast and loud. In ninth grade health class they'd been given a pink booklet that said otherwise; the boys were given a blue one and a sample condom. That was it.

Every month Caitlin and Dana thought they were pregnant. The booklet hadn't explained enough and they were never sure. They had sex on the same night for the first time, in tenth grade, at the quarry. They both thought it was completely boring. Kevin, Caitlin had said, sounded like the Amtrak train leaving Springfield just before he came. Dana said Mike sounded like a pig. Sometimes, when they got really bored with the guys, they made fun of them right in front of them and Mike and Kevin never caught on. Amtrak is not leaving tonight, Caitlin would say. And then she and Dana would start to laugh and not be able to stop. Isn't that fucking funny? Kevin would say, and they'd laugh even more.

Caitlin was sure love would change all of that. Even though last year she'd had sex twice with an exchange student from Finland she had a big crush on, and it was just as dull. No train sounds, but he got there even faster, she'd said. It was over before it even began. They decided that Finland was such a cold country that people didn't want to stay naked too long—they might freeze. And for a while, Dana and Caitlin had a new joke. Another Nordic winter, they'd say, and then they'd start to laugh. What's that supposed to mean? Mike had said and Dana had looked at him completely straight-faced and said, "It gets very cold in Nordic countries. That's all."

Caitlin followed rules that Dana did not quite trust. You couldn't get pregnant if you did it standing up or if you did it when you had your period. You couldn't get pregnant if you did it in the shower or the lake. But Dana made Mike wear a rubber no matter what. You can't get pregnant in the water, Caitlin insisted. But something seemed wrong about that to Dana. Mike said she was crazy. So you get pregnant? he'd say. Big fucking deal.

Once, last winter, Dana had masturbated. She did it by accident, when she was taking a bath. And something happened that felt much better than when Mike was on top of her, huffing and puffing. She didn't tell Caitlin and, even though she wanted to, she didn't do it again.

Just last week, Caitlin had seen her mother with some guy who tended bar at Tiny's Tavern in town. Caitlin hated that her mother went there every Friday and Saturday night, but she also supposed that her mother was lonely so she pretended she didn't care. What she hadn't known was that while she was at Pizza Pizzazz, Sue brought guys home. They were always gone before Caitlin got home.

But last week, Kevin's car was in the garage and Mike couldn't get one so Caitlin had come straight home from work. She'd seen a motorcycle in front of the house, and a light on in her mother's room. Instead of going inside, she'd crept around to the bedroom window and peeked and there was her mother with this guy who she knew was the bartender at Tiny's. His name was Marty and he was a Vietnam vet who everybody said was fucked up over the war. But what Marty and her mother were doing looked nothing like what she and Mike did. This looked like something out of a movie, all slow motion and erotic.

The next night she watched the same scene except with a different guy. This one, who wore a gold wedding band, looked unfamiliar. Caitlin told Dana every detail, even though Dana did not want to hear and kept covering her ears. This is your mother, Dana kept saying, but somehow Sue had seemed like a stranger on those nights, like someone else, this sad little woman with too long hair who still talked about Mitch like he'd died yesterday instead of eighteen years ago. Sue was not a person who looked and acted like a porno star.

Anyway, now Caitlin had very romantic notions about sex. When we move to New York, she said, we'll find out. Meanwhile, that same old Amtrak train kept leaving Springfield.

---

*Billy's room was small and messy.* Dana couldn't believe that this was what college was like. The furniture was worse than hers at home.

"You read a lot," he said.

Dana shrugged. "For school and stuff."

"You're a . . . diamond in the rough," he said, and he stroked her cheek lightly with the back of his hand.

Dana was sure that was an insult. But something had happened. She had played this role back there, a tough townie. And she had liked it. Billy had liked it too, she thought.

She studied his pale face in the soft light from the desk lamp. Every time her heart leaped the way it just did again, she had to get control. She couldn't like him too much. She couldn't fall for those dimples. She had to be the boss, to act like nothing mattered.

So this time, when he leaned over and kissed her on the lips, and her heart flip-flopped, she decided to really show him. She pulled back and laughed.

"What do you want, Mr. College Boy?" she said.

"I like you, Dana. A lot."

There it went. A belly flop.

"Oh, really?" she said, and made herself laugh again.

"I never met anybody like you," he said.

And another one, this time like her heart dropped from a high diving board.

She didn't think it through until later. Right then, all she did was unbutton the shirt that said *Roy* above the pocket and wiggle out of her faded jeans until she was standing there in her white Jockey underwear. When she told Caitlin about it later, she said she wanted to keep him surprised. She wanted to make him fall for her, make his heart do some of those high dives. That's all.

She wasn't ready for what came next. It was like all that stuff Caitlin had been trying to tell her last week. The slow motion, the tongue, the carefulness of it. Not at all like Mike. This was something else. Real soft he whispered to her, "Are you protected?" and when she shook her head he reached for a condom in his desk drawer, real smooth. Nothing like Mike, who thought birth control was silly, who tried to convince her that rubbers reduced his pleasure.

"Is that what you learn in college?" she whispered to Billy afterward. It was hard to keep her tough-girl attitude.

Billy laughed. "No," he said, "they teach me this." And they started all over again.

*There was something wrong* in the silence the next day when Billy drove Dana home. She pretended everything was fine. She thought, If two people do all those things together at night, there must be something special between them. Not love exactly. But something like love.

Still, when she tried to sit close to Billy in the car, he seemed to tense up. And when she asked him what he was doing that night, he snapped at her.

For the rest of the way, Dana gazed out the window, at the foothills of the Berkshires and the trees still tipped with bright autumn colors. When they drove through Lee she said, "You know that guy in the Dunkin' Donuts commercial? The guy who says, 'Time to make the donuts'?"

Billy shook his head. "No."

"Well, I saw him in there once," Dana said. She pointed to the drugstore, but Billy didn't look. "I guess he has a weekend house here or something," she added. Then she looked out the window again.

Billy's room had had some posters hanging on the wall—Bette Davis in black and white and Jim Morrison and a sexy woman in a bathing suit. While he showered that morning, Dana had studied them, and the books on the small row of shelves. They were mostly textbooks, and books like *Slaughterhouse Five* and *Rabbit Run.* The room looked like any boy's room. It could have been Troy's. It could have been Mike's. On the desk there was a fancy matchbox car, a Ferrari, and Dana just knew that someone had given it to him as a joke. "I got you a car for your birthday," someone said. And there it was, six inches long, all shiny and red and important-looking. The oldest joke around.

What bothered Dana were the neatly framed photographs of Billy and a girl with a heart-shaped face and dark brown hair neatly held back in a headband. There were three pictures in all, including one tucked into the edge of the mirror. That one was the kind you take in a Woolworth's photo booth, small and black and white with the faces slightly exaggerated. If somebody had a girlfriend somewhere, they would not—could not—take another girl to their room and do such intimate things with her.

On the way home, while she looked out the window, Dana tried to think of ways to phrase a question about the girl. She could start it by saying, "I noticed some pictures in your room . . ." She could ask, "Do you have a girlfriend or something?" She could laugh when she said it, so he wouldn't know it mattered.

They reached the dirt road that led to her house. She lived three miles down.

"Sometimes," Dana said, "around this time of year we see deer on this road."

"Yeah?" Billy said.

She tried to think of something else to say but couldn't.

"This is real rural," Billy said.

His voice startled her. She looked around at all the bright yellow construction machinery, the pink ropes that marked off land that had recently been sold.

"People from out of town are buying it all up and building on it," Dana said. That was the wrong thing to say. *He* was from out of town, after all. "You can stop here," she said.

They were still about a mile from her house, but Dana did not want him to see where she lived, to see the dull green chipped paint, the lopsided roof.

Quietly, she asked, "Where do you live?"

When she said it, she felt slightly sick to her stomach. This boy was a stranger. She knew nothing about him.

He drummed his fingers on the steering wheel. He looked straight ahead.

"Chappaqua," he said. "New York."

"Oh."

He looked at her. "You know it?" He seemed almost hopeful.

"No," Dana said. She tried to revive her role from last night. "Are you kidding? I've never been farther than Albany. We don't go anywhere."

He nodded.

She felt almost desperate. Something was very wrong here. "Do you have a pen?" she said. Her eyes darted around the small car. "I'll give you my phone number."

"I don't," he said.

"That's okay," she said too quickly. "We're in the book." She fumbled with the door handle. She kept thinking about the way she had felt last night, twelve short hours ago. How he had been able to give her that feeling she'd had in the bathtub, how he had whispered things to her. He had said her skin was soft. Like silk, he'd said.

She was out of the car now. She stepped back, away from it, while he smoothly shifted into reverse.

And then Dana remembered something.

"Hey," she said. She grabbed at the hood of the car as it lurched backward.

"Harper," she said. "My last name. It's Harper."

H*ere in Massachusetts,* things grew. Old fruit trees in the yard that had seemed at first to be past their ability to bear fruit, suddenly bloomed with apples and pears. A grapevine that twisted along the back fence developed fat Concord grapes. Renata felt inspired by all the productivity that surrounded her and she started a window box of herbs. That too began to grow, and the smells of fresh rosemary and sage filled the kitchen now.

Even Millie was impressed. As much as she did not want to like Massachusetts, the burst of nature that surrounded them there got to her. She tended the herbs, plucking the fragrant stalks to top homemade pizzas and salads.

"See, Millie?" Renata told her. "Anything is possible."

Millie's face was smeared with juice from the grapes, dark purple smears that ran down her chin and neck.

"Maybe this is where you'll meet Prince Charming," Millie said. She had a system for eating those grapes—she sucked the insides from the skin first, then ate the rest.

"Not that again," Renata said. She was planting bulbs—tulips and crocuses. They had to be put into the ground before the first frost. Then in spring they would be the first to bloom, the first signs of warm weather, of life.

She remembered going to the Brooklyn Botanical Garden on a cold March day and being greeted by a hill alive with daffodils, their bright bursts of yellow and white the only vibrant sign around. The trees were still bare, the grass not even beginning to show green.

"Wait'll you see these babies," Renata said. "In March they'll poke their heads out and then we'll know warm weather is on its way."

"I thought the groundhog did that," Millie said.

Renata concentrated on her planting, on the feel of cold earth against her hands. She could already imagine the shock of pink and purple against dried dirt, the spray of color along this edge of the yard.

"Mister Russo," Millie was saying, "he teaches ESL, he's very handsome. He's not married."

"How do you know?"

Millie shrugged. "Maybe I asked him."

"Millie, don't do that. Honey, aren't you happy like this? Just the two of us?"

Millie plucked another grape, sucked its insides into her mouth. "Sometimes fathers come and pick up their children at school. Like there's this girl named Brie Conan and sometimes her father is waiting for her outside. He wears plaid shirts and faded jeans and if it's cold he wears a red down vest. Sometimes he has her baby sister in a caboose on his back."

"A caboose," Renata said, "is part of a train."

Millie sighed. "Then they drive off in their van. Home. Like a family."

"A papoose is what I think you mean," Renata said. She stood and studied her work. "This is going to be great. Just you wait until spring."

Millie didn't answer. Renata turned toward her daughter, who sat cross-legged on the grass, as if she had a secret.


*Monday morning Millie said,* "Brie Conan is the most beautiful girl in the whole world. She has long straight hair like people in Sweden and she wears light blue sweaters with snowflakes right here." She pointed to her collar.

"Brie is the silliest name I ever heard," Renata said.

"It's French! Why do you have to ruin everything?"

"It's cheese. What's her sister's name, Camembert?"

Millie stood and stiffly put on her coat. "Sometimes," she said, "I hate you."

"Hey!" Renata said. But Millie was gone, closing the door with a loud smack.

Renata sat in the quiet kitchen. She could smell rosemary, and a trace of mint. The furnace hummed and banged, then the house was completely silent. How quiet it was without Millie, Renata thought. How unbearably quiet. Suddenly, she was gripped with fear. What if something really happened to Millie? What if something happened to her today?

She rushed to the door, opened it, and called, "Millie!" But the bus had come and gone. Renata had heard terrible stories about buses filled with children, Girl Scouts or Little League teams. How foolish to think school buses were safe. What did she know about the driver of that bus? She tried to remember if Millie had ever mentioned who it was. Then it came to her. It was a man with a name like Butch or Spike, and Millie had said he was simpleminded. Like a big overgrown kid, she'd said.

Renata glanced at the clock. They wouldn't be at school yet. She imagined Butch stopping for a new group of children. It seemed someone like that could be so easily distracted. A rabbit darting along the road, a child singing off-key. How could they have hired this man to drive children around? She waited as long as she could, then dialed the school.

"This is Renata Handy," she said, "I just wondered if bus number twelve is there okay?"

"All the buses are," the secretary said. She had a bright peppy voice that Renata found annoying.

"Number twelve is there?" Renata said.

"They're all in their places with bright shining faces," the woman said, practically chirping.

"Well," Renata said, feeling suddenly foolish. "Thanks."


*She could pick out Brie* Conan's father immediately—red plaid shirt, faded jeans bleached white at the crotch and knees. He had a beard, worn boots, the red down vest and a baby asleep in the carrier on his back. She guessed that he worked outdoors from the color in his cheeks and the way his hair seemed to have sun highlights in it. If this man had an indoor job, Renata speculated, he wouldn't have so much gold in his beard, he would look as pale as all the other New Englanders did this time of year.

She went over to him. He leaned against the back of his van. The van was black and dusty.

"Hi," she said. "You must be Brie's father."

He nodded. He was good-looking in a rugged kind of way. She guessed he wasn't very smart. Conan the Barbarian, she thought, and smiled.

"I'm Millie's mother," she said. "Renata." She was glad she was still dressed from work, that she looked nice.

"Millie," he said, rolling the name around on his tongue. "Was she at the party Saturday?"

Renata tried not to look surprised. "No," she said. "She wasn't."

"What a zoo that was," he said, smiling. When he smiled, nice crinkles appeared around his eyes. "A dozen little girls. M and M's everywhere. All these tiny little Barbie shoes." He held his thumb and forefinger up to show just how tiny. "You know how it is."

"Yes," Renata said.

But she didn't. Millie had never had a birthday party like that, with a cake shaped like the Cookie Monster and kids playing Pin the Tail on the Donkey. Last year they had gone for Indian food on East Sixth Street and she'd let Millie order anything she wanted. They'd had red snapper tandoori and extra nan.

"I'm sorry," Brie's father was saying, "I can't place Millie."

"We just moved here," Renata said. She hated this man. She hated his little blond daughter with the Barbies and the snowflake sweaters.

"We did too," he said. "Well, in July. From Boston. I was working in advertising and needed to quit the rat race." He held up his calloused hands. "So here we are."

He wasn't dumb after all. She hated him even more. He had slid closer to her and she got a whiff of the baby, soapy and powdered. The school doors opened and a flood of children spilled out, pushing and shouting.

"What do you do out here in the boondocks?" Renata asked him. She didn't look at him. She was making a plan.

"I own a nursery," he said. He laughed again. "The tree kind."

Renata caught sight of Millie, walking alone, head bent, her wig bobbing as if it had a life of its own.

"I just planted some bulbs," Renata said. "My first time. Usually I kill everything I touch." She looked him full in the eyes. His were dark green. "Maybe you could stop by and check them out?"

He shrugged, then looked toward the children approaching.

"I make a mean martini," Renata said.

He nodded. Renata turned back toward the children. Millie was lagging behind, dragging her school bag on the ground. Renata gave him directions to the house. Then Brie was there, surrounded by other little girls, all giggling and pigtailed. She was the leader of this group, that was clear.

"Who wants a ride?" her father shouted.

He picked up his daughter and spun her around. One big happy family, Renata thought. Then went to meet Millie.

*He made a pretense of* checking her bulbs, bending and examining what she'd done. Then he pronounced them "just fine."

"Good," Renata said. She wore a T-shirt and no bra, knowing the cold air would make her nipples hard against the thin cotton. Knowing this man would see them. She wasn't sure why she was doing this, she just knew she had to.

Last night Millie had told her, "I saw you talking to Mr. Conan. I wish they weren't quite such a happy family. Then maybe he'd be your Prince Charming and Brie could be my sister. And we'd all live happily ever after."

"There are no Cleavers," Renata said.

"What are Cleavers?"

"They're like Huxtables," she told Millie. "Make-believe."

Standing here now, trying not to shiver, Renata wondered if she had to prove that to Millie, or to herself.

"I've got those martinis," she said.

"I hardly earned them," he said, showing those crinkles around his eyes. But he followed her inside.

His name was Joe. Renata asked him, "Now that's a nice straightforward name. How did you ever settle on Brie?"

He shrugged and laughed again. "The baby's Star," he told her. "Does that make you feel better?"

She refilled his glass, making sure to brush against him. It had been a long time and she was surprised how easily it all came back to her.

"They're both awful," she said.

Joe grabbed her around the waist. His hands were big.

"Here you have this little baby," Renata said, "this beautiful child, a wife. What are you doing here?"

"Checking your bulbs," he said.


*It had proven nothing* except that she did, in a way, miss sex. Joe Conan cheated on his wife. This wasn't the first time, Renata was sure of that. And he would keep doing it. She was sure of that too. All along she had believed that there were really no happy families, that things were not what they seemed. And she was right.

Three days earlier Joe Conan had been serving cake at his daughter's birthday party. This afternoon he'd been making love to her right on the kitchen floor. Right now, she thought, he was probably standing in front of the school, his baby on his back, waiting like a good father for his little girl. Being with him here had made her feel good for a couple of hours. But now she felt like hell.

Millie practically danced through the door. Renata was still in her bathrobe, sipping tea. She had stayed under a hot shower for a very long time.

"Mama, guess what happened?" Millie said. She jumped onto Renata's lap.

"You won the lottery?"

"Brie Conan's father gave me a ride home. And they invited me over on Saturday."

"That is news," Renata said.

"I wish I wish I wish they were not such a big happy family. Oh, Mama," she said, resting her head on Renata's shoulder, "I know that's an awful wish, but I wish it anyway."

*D*ana felt dreamy, foggy, confused.

"That," Caitlin told her, "is love." Caitlin produced evidence. Books with a woman wearing a torn dress on the cover, her breasts almost completely exposed. A fire raged behind her. A man rushed toward the woman. " 'When Lamont was away from her, Cassandra could not think straight,' " Caitlin read. " 'She couldn't remember even the simple things—how to bake bread, how to cut back the rose bushes.' "

Dana looked out her bedroom window, at the messy piles of dead leaves, the tangle of weeds. "Rose bushes," she said. She imagined that Billy's house in Chappaqua, New York, was lined with tall dark green hedges, perfectly shaped and trimmed. That there was a colorful garden where flowers and bushes grew in an interesting geometric shape. She made the house brick with ivy climbing one side.

" 'With Lamont,' " Caitlin was reading, " 'nothing else mattered. Cassandra could forget the war that raged in the real world, the world outside his arms. She smiled, remembering the pressure of his manhood against her thigh, his mouth on her breasts . . .' "

Dana flopped back on her bed and groaned. "Please," she said, closing her eyes. No, she thought. Billy's house would be large and white, with black shutters and big columns in the front. She gave him two sheepdogs, a gazebo in back. She made his mother look like a young Katharine Hepburn in baggy trousers and a straw hat to protect her fair skin from the sun. She added long gloves, to protect her arms from the thorns when she had to cut back the roses.

" 'No, Cassandra reminded herself. The real world was Lamont's arms.' " Caitlin sighed and tossed the book at Dana. "Chapter twelve," she said. " 'Love.' "

*Every time the door at* Pizza Pizzazz opened, Dana looked up, expecting to see Billy. He would come in late, she decided, and drive her back to Williams with him. They would go to another party. In her backpack, she'd put her toothbrush and the apricot soap she used to wash her face. She'd put a pair of clean underwear and extra socks.

Two girls walked up to the counter.

"Hi," one of them said. She had very straight, very long brown hair. "Danielle, right?"

Dana frowned and shook her head.

"From the party?" the girl said. "Last week?"

Caitlin moved closer to Dana, pretending not to listen but pressing her leg against Dana's.

"Oh," Dana said. "Right."

"You were with Billy. You told all those wild stories about tattoos and a crazy mother."

"Is Billy here?" Dana said.

The girl looked puzzled. "I don't know. But could I have a goat cheese and shrimp pizza with extra garlic?"

Caitlin repeated the order. "Goat cheese and shrimp with extra garlic. Ten minutes."

The girl laughed. "What are you? A team or something?"

The door opened and Dana looked past the girl. Three guys walked in, smelling like beer.

"See ya," the girl said.

"Danielle," Dana said softly.

"She's nobody," Caitlin said. "He'll be in. Don't worry."

Dana saw the girl, waiting for her Diet Coke from the drink person, watching.

She made herself smile. "I'm not worried," she said.

The girl whispered something to her friend. Their eyes flitted toward Dana, then away.

———

*"You could come out with* Kevin and Mike and me," Caitlin said in the locker room.

"No thank you," Dana said. She pressed her hand against her chest to feel her heart beat. It was still thumping away in a slow perfect rhythm. "Remember, in ninth grade when we told Stephanie Masciarotte that we french kissed and she said we could get pregnant from that? She said we'd never get married. 'Don't buy the cow if you can get the milk free.' Remember?"

"I remember," Caitlin said. "But I never understood it. I figured it was some weird Catholic thing. She went to Saint Agnes's until eighth grade, you know."

"It means a guy won't call if you sleep with him. That's what it means."

Caitlin laughed. "That is so stupid. What are Mike and Kevin doing? Driving us nuts, that's what. We can't shake them. Stephanie wanted to become a nun. She like cleaned the altar at St. Agnes's every Saturday before mass. This is not a normal person."

Dana made up a list of reasons why Billy hadn't come in. Maybe he went home to New York. Maybe he had to study, or write a paper. She thought of the photograph of the girl in his room. Maybe, he had a girlfriend. A real girlfriend who didn't give him the milk for free.


*Her father decided that* Sunday was family day. They would eat a nice lunch together. They would go on some sort of an outing.

Today he made Hamburger Helper with a side of pork and beans.

"So," he said. "What should we do today?"

Troy shrugged. Even in the house now he always wore long sleeves to hide his tattoos. Still, Dana could make out John Lennon's chin at his cuff.

"We could drive somewhere," their father said. "To Bennington, maybe. We could go and see that war monument they have up there."

"Sure," Troy said. "That sounds great."

Dana said, "Hamburger Helper tastes like chemicals or something."

"You," Tom told her, "are a grump. Who's that boy who called this morning?"

Dana looked up. "What boy?" Her heart was pounding now. She didn't even need to search for the sound.

"I wrote it down somewhere," he said.

"Where?"

Tom looked startled. "I don't know. By the phone, I guess. In the kitchen."

She was already up, walking as fast as she could. "Why didn't you come and get me? What's wrong with you?"

"You were asleep," he said.

But she just waved him away, like an annoying fly or something. On a pad lined with little red hearts she found the note. Justin, it said, and then a number. She brought the whole pad back out to the dining room with her.

"We could drive up there and maybe have dinner out," her father was saying.

"Who is this?" Dana said, pointing to the note. "Justin? What does that mean?" She felt as if she couldn't control herself. As if she would start screaming any minute.

"It's his name, I guess," Tom said.

"What exactly did he say? Exactly?"

Troy and Tom looked at each other.

"What?" Dana said, her voice rising.

"He said could he speak to you—"

"To Dana?"

Her father rolled his eyes. "Of course to Dana. 'May I speak to Dana?' he said and I told him you were still asleep and he left his name and number. The whole conversation lasted about thirty seconds. Maximum."

She threw the pad down on the table. "He must have said Billy. Not Justin. I don't know anybody named Justin."

She didn't wait for him to answer. Instead, she stormed out of the room and up the stairs.


*The war monument was closed.*

" 'Winter hours,' " Tom read from the sign. "It's not winter yet."

Dana sat slumped in the back seat. She was sure it was Billy who had called. Her father was dumb. Family day was dumb.

"Let's go home then," she said.

Tom tossed the car keys back and forth, from one hand to the other. Back and forth, back and forth until Dana thought she would lose her mind.

"We could eat somewhere," Troy said.

"We just had lunch like two hours ago," Dana muttered. "This is so stupid."

Her father and Troy were outside, leaning against the car.

"There's this museum or something at Williams," Troy said. He sounded almost shy about it. "This girl I know told me about it."

"A museum?" Tom said. "With what? Paintings?"

Troy shrugged. "I guess."

"You are both such philistines." Dana said. "What else would be in a museum?"

Her father poked his head in the car. "Dinosaurs," he said.

"Let's just go home," she said.

Troy said, "Yeah. I think the museum's closed on Sundays anyway."

They got back in the car.

"In Boston," Tom said, looking in the rearview mirror at Dana, "there's a museum that has these see-through mannequins. You can watch all the body systems at work. Digestion. Respiratory. Different parts light up. The kidneys. The heart."

"Fine," Dana said. Her feet were tapping as if they could get her home sooner.

"And the mannequins talk. 'This is my heart. It beats so many times a minute. It pumps this much blood.'"

Dana rolled her eyes.

"Not all museums," Tom said, "have paintings."

*I met you at a party* last week," Justin said on the phone. "At Williams? I was the one who told you that my mother was nuts too."

Dana frowned. She didn't remember anything like that.

"Now she takes lithium though, so she's better," Justin said.

"Uh-huh."

"I was wondering if you were free Thursday night. There's this party here. At school."

Dana touched the little holes in the mouthpiece of the phone, tracing them in a circle.

"There's going to be that same band. They play at just about every party," he added.

She thought about Billy and her heart started to go crazy. Something else too. She got this liquidy feeling in her thighs that spread upward and made her feel warm, like she had a fever.

"I might be going with Billy," Dana said. You don't do those things like that with someone you don't like, she wanted to say. He likes me.

119

"Gee, I don't think so," Justin said. He had a slight accent, like he was from somewhere south, but not too far south. "He suggested I call."

Dana swallowed hard. She could feel her face getting red and hot.

"I even think Melissa is going to be here for the weekend."

Melissa, she repeated to herself. Melissa.

"What do you say?" Justin asked her. He didn't sound at all impatient. His voice was smooth and polite with that touch of an accent. A gentleman.

"Okay," Dana said. She was afraid her voice would crack if she said anything more.

*Dana called Billy from* the pay phone in the parking lot of Pizza Pizzazz. The phone rang for a very long time. She listened to it, trying to imagine that dorm, the long hallway that smelled of incense and socks and soap. Caitlin had told her about something called creative visualization. You had to close your eyes and picture the thing happening, as if it were a movie in your brain. If you could really visualize it, then it would definitely happen.

There were warm-up exercises, like imagining a lemon until the picture is so real your lips actually pucker, but Dana felt pressed for time. So she just pictured the dorm, the long hallway with the phone at the end, and hoped for the best. Finally someone answered, all out of breath, and when she asked for Billy the boy just let the phone drop. Dana heard it bang against the wall. She heard voices, doors slamming, footsteps. She held for so long that she had to feed more change into the pay phone. While she waited, the sign that said PIZZA PIZZAZZ in red and green lights went off, leaving the parking lot dark.

When Billy came to the phone, he was out of breath too.

"Hi," Dana said, all phony, trying to sound nonchalant. "It's Dana." She almost added Harper, but stopped herself.

"Hey," Billy said. "How's it going?"

"Good. How about you?"

"Great, but we're in the middle of Oktoberfest? It's this big festival? And I'm in the keg race."

Dana swallowed hard. "Oh. What's that? A bunch of guys running with a keg?"

"Basically, yeah. So I've sort of got to go. But it was great talking to you. And I'll see you soon, right?"

Dana tried to say something fast. About Justin. About the girl in the picture. About how she'd had the same boyfriend since seventh grade and they'd just broken up really. I am not what you think, she wanted to say.

"Did I tell you how my best friend . . . her name's Caitlin . . . how we're going to New York—" This was not what she meant to say at all, but it seemed important suddenly that Billy knew her, knew that she mattered.

But Billy was talking to someone else. He was saying, "No shit! No shit! This I've got to see."

"Hello?" Dana said, even though she knew her voice was just shooting into that long hallway, that no one was listening. "Hello?"

*Billy was there with the* girl from the picture. He kept his hand resting on the small of her back. She had a way of tilting her head and looking up at him and almost smiling that made Dana uncomfortable, even from across the room. It wasn't a full smile. Instead, just the corners of her mouth turned up, as if she was slightly amused. She went to Sarah Lawrence, a fancy school somewhere in New York. To go there, Dana figured from the way everyone talked about it, you had to be very smart and very rich.

Justin was not bad-looking. He was from Washington, D.C. "Not many people are actually from there," he'd told her. She didn't care. His manners bothered her. They seemed too planned, too purposeful. All she wanted was to watch Billy and his girlfriend.

"They've gone out since they were like fourteen," Justin told her.

"I had a boyfriend like that," she said, trying to sound as if she was beyond all that. "Eventually you outgrow each other."

She looked back toward them again. His hand had not moved. Her smile had not widened. They were like a Barbie and Ken doll, posed there for everyone to see.

Justin told her he wanted to be president.

She was hardly listening. "Of what?" she asked him.

He rolled his eyes. "Of the United States," he said. He wore small round glasses like someone in a picture from the 1920s. Behind them his eyes were a light amber.

When he went to get them some more beer from the kegs in the corner, Dana drifted toward Billy. She saw when he noticed her standing there. Her mouth went all dry and cottony.

"Dana," he said, as calm as can be. "Are you here with Justin?"

Close up, his girlfriend looked even more doll-like. Smooth skin, like porcelain. Eyes clear and shiny. Glossy hair. Dana had an urge to muss it all up somehow.

"Melissa," he was saying, "this is Dana . . . I'm sorry. I forgot your last name."

"Harper," she managed to say. If she blinked she would cry. She felt the tears right there, ready to fall. "I have something in my eye," she said.

"Here," Melissa said, holding out a napkin. "Contact lenses, right?" She smiled now, a full sweet one.

Dana looked up, into those clear eyes. "Right," she said.

*Dana told Caitlin all* about it after work on Saturday night. She did not think she had ever felt so miserable.

"Listen," Caitlin said, "there is no reason to be so upset. A, the girlfriend is the one who looks like an asshole. B, he couldn't be nice to you with her right there. C, this guy Justin wants to be the president of the United States. You could be the first lady. And D, we're leaving this town in a mere six months and will never see any of these people again anyway." She smiled.

Dana was lying flat on one of the long benches in front of the lockers, staring up at the ceiling with its cracked paint and fluorescent lighting.

"I don't know what to do," she moaned. "I feel so awful."

"Billy will call you," Caitlin said. "I just know he will."

Dana closed her eyes. She had put on her tough-girl act. She had laughed too loud and said outrageous things. She had made sure Billy could see her and hear her the whole time. She had made sure that he saw her leave the party a little too early with Justin's arm around her. She had acted like a total jerk, done everything wrong.

"Are you upset because you slept with Justin?" Caitlin was saying. "Big deal. We need experience. We need excitement."

Justin had not even driven her home in the morning. Lacrosse practice, he'd said, all polite and apologetic. She was not even quite sure what lacrosse was. He'd walked her to the bus stop and very carefully written down her telephone number and the nights she worked. He would make a very good president, she thought. He seemed so sincere.

Dana did not open her eyes. All college boys, she decided, were smooth. They knew how to get you all heated up and it had nothing to do with love at all. It had nothing to do with anything. They told you your skin was soft as silk or velvet, they whispered "Are you protected?" and produced birth control like magic. It was as if they'd all taken the same course on sex. At this moment, she hated herself.

"You can't just lie there forever," Caitlin told her. "It isn't the end of the world."

"I know."

This was what a girl needed a mother for, she thought. When a boy breaks your heart and you sleep with his friend to get even when really it doesn't even matter and your life makes no sense at all. Not even a little. A mother was supposed to hold you in her arms. She was supposed to give you advice. She was supposed to tell you that you weren't such a bad person. A mother would fix everything. A mother would make her daughter feel like she mattered, like she was something even though she felt like nothing.

To Libby, it seemed as if everyone in L.A. was in the business, one way or another. Even Von's was filled with would-be stuntmen and screenwriters, actors and composers. Back in Holly, Libby was always special. She was the prettiest, the smartest, the best dressed. Here, she started to feel ordinary. Everywhere she looked she saw someone who seemed to sparkle more than she did.

She believed the floor wax commercial might change that. As she stood at the checkout line, ringing up produce she'd never even heard of before, things like arugula and shiitake mushrooms, she half expected a customer to recognize her, to shout, "Hey! Aren't you the woman who makes stars fly out of floors?"

But no one ever did. Instead, they passed through her line, smiling blank smiles, flashing too perfect teeth and too enthusiastic wishes for a good day. She weighed their asparagus and bananas like a robot. Sometimes, as she stood there working, a flash of that day came to her—the man's bulging stomach hanging over small black bikini underpants, the sunlight glistening on the glass skyscraper, the hot pressure of his hand on her head. She had walked out of there triumphant, expecting something more than the part, although she wasn't sure what exactly.

Her friend Janice at Von's had made a comment about the myth of the casting couch. "Do you believe," Janice had said to her over drinks at El Torito, "that some idiots believe a blow job will get them somewhere?"

"Well," Libby said, "it could. It could get someone a part or something."

Janice stared at her over the salted rim of her margarita. "Yes," she said. "Or something."

*A girl named Tammy* who used to work on lane six got a big part in a Steven Spielberg film. Tammy was twenty-two and everyone said she looked like a young Susan Sarandon. Her last day at work they threw her a party in the back room. Libby watched as Tammy stood there, not even trying to act modest, just gushing and nodding and looking all superior. Really, Libby thought, Tammy looked nothing like Susan Sarandon. Not at all.

She left the party early and took her place back behind the cash register. Her first customer was another bright-eyed tanned woman in shorts and running shoes, the kind who doesn't stop running even in the supermarket, her feet moving up and down in rhythm, a Walkman playing in her ears. She bought seven kinds of lettuce and three bottles of Evian. Libby did not even know there were so many different kinds of lettuce until she got this job. Lettuce had started to irritate her.

The woman jogged away, and Libby started to ring up the next customer's groceries. It was funny how she could tell a lot about someone by what they bought. This guy, for example, was just moving in to a new place —toilet bowl brush and cleaner, dishwasher detergent, laundry soap, light bulbs, and floor wax. *Her* floor wax. Behind her, Libby could hear Tammy shouting her goodbyes. "I'll give Steven a big hug from everyone," she said.

Libby gripped the bright blue container of floor wax.

"I did this commercial," she said. "I'm the woman who mops the floor and stars shoot from it."

The man had one of those mustaches, a Fu Manchu, and shaggy brown hair in need of a trim. He smiled, and Libby was happy to see his teeth were not perfect.

"Maybe you saw it?" she said. "On TV?"

He shook his head. "Sorry."

She kept ringing up his items. Eggs and milk and bread, the basics. She noticed it was normal bread too, no special grains, just good old Wonder. Tammy passed in front of the windows, on her way to her car and success. Libby had never noticed before that Tammy was swaybacked. That would be a definite minus.

"I've been really disappointed in Spielberg movies lately," Libby said. "He's slipping, in my opinion."

Mentally she started to construct a letter to him. *Dear Mr. Spielberg, You have brought my family and me many hours of joy. However—*

"Well," the man said, "he's never been one of my favorites anyway."

"Is that right?" Libby said, and she nodded. "Interesting."

"As a screenwriter, I'm trying to achieve something else. Something more. A deeper level of understanding of the human condition."

She nodded again. "What a treat," she said. "I've only been out here a little while and it just seems that everyone is so materialistic. Kind of shallow, though I hate to stereotype."

*Perhaps, Mr. Spielberg, instead of hiring swaybacked young girls for your films, you should try to better understand the human condition.*

He was buying an awful lot of wine, she noticed. Beer was always Tom's drink. She had grown to hate the smell of it. There was something special about a man who bought wine. Ten-dollar bottles, no less.

"That'll be eighty-three seventy," Libby said.

She watched as he pulled a hundred-dollar bill from his wallet.

"Do you like Kurosawa?" he asked her.

"Mmmmm," she said.

"Because his new film is playing tonight and I thought you might like to go." Then he added, "With me."

"Why, yes," Libby said. She looked around to see if anyone was seeing this screenwriter ask her on a date, to see the new Kurosawa, whoever that was. No one seemed to notice.

She could still remember the day Tom Harper walked up to her in front of everyone and asked her out. Those girls had almost fallen over. That was to a movie too. *Butterflies Are Free.* Goldie Hawn and Ingrid Bergman. Libby smiled. She felt she had come far after all.

*He wasn't a real screenwriter.* Or at least he'd never sold anything. "Because Hollywood doesn't want to hear the truth," he told Libby. He worked building sets. That was why he had such strong arms, she thought, trying not to stare at the thick biceps peeking out from the sleeves of his black T-shirt.

She loved that his name was Jeremy. "Like from that old TV show," she told him. "Those three brothers up in Seattle? They're all lumberjacks and they have these great names. Jeremy, Jason, and Joshua. What was the name of that show anyway?"

Jeremy didn't know what she was talking about. He had no sense of pop culture at all. "Where did you grow up?" she asked him. "Mars?" "Close," he said. "Here."

Libby was glad that she had time to go to the library and read up on Kurosawa. Then she raced to the video store and rented *Ran.* She got to watch half of it while she got ready for the date. This guy, she thought, was a real artist. So she wore her black tights and an oversize black sweater, like Audrey Hepburn in *Funny Face.*

It had been hard to stay awake during the movie. Reading those subtitles was just awful. But she'd managed, and now they were eating dinner in Santa Monica and through the big restaurant windows Libby could see the waves and an almost full moon.

Sometimes things turn around in a flash. It already seemed a million years ago that she had been watching Tammy flaunt her success, feeling like a failure herself. Now here she was with this deep, smart man, sharing a plate of calamari and looking at a full moon. And, she reminded herself, she had done a floor wax commercial. People back home had probably seen her. She smiled imagining it.

"What?" Jeremy said. He covered her hands with his.

"I was just thinking," she said. She took a breath and hoped she'd gotten it right. "Kurosawa said that *Ran* was human deeds as viewed from heaven. That's kind of what you're after, isn't it? In your writing, I mean."

He looked at her across the table, then leaned over and kissed her, right on the lips. "You're amazing," he said.

Libby smiled at him. Thank God for that Pauline Kael book. People really should use the public library more, she thought. Maybe she'd write a Letter to the Editor about that. Jeremy was talking about *King Lear*. Libby tried to concentrate. She nodded and smiled some more. Then it popped into her head. The name of that show with those three brothers in Seattle. It was *Here Come the Brides*. She would keep that to herself.

On Saturday nights, Tom started going to Tiny's Tavern. A place he used to think only desperate people went to. Now he knew it was where people went on the nights Arsenio Hall wasn't on. When there was nothing keeping them at home.

Whenever he saw Sue there, she ignored him.

So did Dee-Dee Winthrop.

Except the first time when she'd grabbed the new roll of fat around his middle and said, "Putting a little on, asshole." She'd pinched hard too.

What Tom did on Saturday nights was sit on the last bar stool, way in the corner, and methodically drink dollar drafts. He had no opinions. People around him would scream about the Patriots, the Red Sox, Saddam Hussein.

They'd complain about taxes, the school superintendent, their kids. And Tom had nothing to say about any of it.

Then one Saturday night, working on his ninth or tenth beer, he happened to glance up at the television. Usually it was tuned to ESPN here, but tonight it was on a regular channel and he looked up and saw his wife smiling down at him while she mopped a fucking floor.

Someone behind him said, "Harp, that's your wife." And the guy's voice was filled with awe. As if it was something good, something special, having your wife walk out on you and mop floors on TV.

It was the same one: She has moved into a new house and finds a grimy kitchen floor. The family is devastated. They stop everything and just stare at that dirty floor. But Libby knows exactly what to do. She grabs a mop and some floor cleaner and suddenly fucking stars are leaping off the floor. It's that shiny. And the family is happy. And Libby leans close to the camera and smiles right at him. See? she seems to be saying. See?

It seemed to Tom that Tiny's got completely silent. But he did not look around. He just finished his beer and the bartender, a guy named Marty, put another one down in front of him and a shot of tequila next to it.

"Here, man," Marty said. "On me. On the house."

This guy had some terrible past. Got screwed up in Vietnam. All sorts of problems.

"Thanks," Tom said.

Sue came and sat next to him. "You're drinking too much," she said.

Tom motioned for another shot. Tequila, unlike beer, burned all the way down your throat, right into your gut.

"I work. I feed my kids. I watch television," he told her. "I deserve a little something."

He didn't look at her. He was thinking about Mitch. How, during sex, Mitch could pick her up by the waist with both hands, she was that little.

"That sounds like a bad movie," Sue was saying.

Tom shrugged. He could get to like tequila, he thought as he downed the second shot.

"I watch a lot of bad movies," he said. Then he added, "We've got cable."

"Come on," Sue said. "Let me drive you home now."

Tom turned toward her. "Did you know all along?" he asked her. "Did you know she was planning on leaving?"

Sue said, "Yes."

Marty had a long ponytail streaked with gray. "I'll make sure he gets home all right," he told Sue.

Tom was glad to see her go.

"You can't trust anybody," he told Marty.


*Waldenbooks was nestled* between Filene's and CVS at the mall. Walking into that bookstore made Tom feel strange. He wasn't even sure what he was looking for. He walked up one aisle and read the titles of the books there. They were the kinds of books he had to read in school. That wasn't what he needed.

He stood in the middle of the store and tried to figure out a plan. That's when he saw her. Renata Handy. She was standing behind the cash register, reading a book, looking a little bored. He did not want her to see him. But no sooner did he think that than she looked up and right into his eyes.

She looked startled.

Tom smiled at her. How could he tell her that he was here for help? That people who had written certain books were always on *Oprah* and *Donahue*, telling the audience that their books could save you. How could he tell Renata Handy that he drank too much? That he fucked a Future Homemaker of America right on his desk? That his wife sold floor wax that made stars shoot out from the kitchen floor?

"You look confused," Renata said.

She was wearing an African print tent dress that made her seem even more exotic.

"I am," Tom said. He glanced around the store. "I'm looking for . . ." He looked at Renata again. One of those writers on *Oprah* had a book about healing a broken heart. He couldn't tell Renata that. "A book," he said.

"Well," she laughed. "You've come to the right place."

His eyes settled on the rack of books in front of him. They were travel books. *Let's Go Spain. Let's Go Italy. Let's Go Great Britain.*

"Are you going somewhere?" Renata said.

He looked at her, puzzled.

"Oh," she said, and she laughed again. "You were looking at the travel books."

"Yes," he said. "I thought maybe I'd go to Spain."

Renata brightened. "Spain. I've heard Barcelona is something else."

"Me too," he said. He picked up *Let's Go Spain.* "This should be helpful."

Renata started to walk back to the cash register. He watched her big feet. She had on those sandals that Libby used to call granola sandals. And red knee socks.

"Anything else?" Renata said.

There was another book, written by a rabbi, that was supposed to give new meaning to your life. It was an inspirational book.

Tom sighed. "No," he said.

"How about a bookmark?" Renata asked him.

"Sure," Tom said. "Why not?"


*Even though it wasn't* yet Thanksgiving, the mall was decorated for Christmas. Santa's Toyland was built, the little mechanical elves continuously hammering and sawing. Renata decided to make this Christmas the best one yet. Not, she reminded herself, because it might be Millie's last one, but because they were here, in New England, and because in the past she had practically ignored the holiday, claiming atheism or commercialization as the reason.

Already, on her lunch breaks from the bookstore, Renata shopped for Christmas gifts for Millie. She hid them in her bedroom closet when she got home, all professionally wrapped in shiny foil paper with perfect bows. Sometimes, when she and Millie were sitting together watching television, Renata would break into a smile imagining Millie's face as she opened package after package on Christmas morning. It was that image that led Renata through department stores and toy stores searching for the best stuffed animal, the brightest fingerpaints, the happiest puzzles and coloring books.

Today, she was buying miniature ponies with hot pink and lime green manes when she saw Tom Harper again. Renata started to wave like crazy. Ever since she had walked away from Dee-Dee Winthrop's, she felt braver somehow. From time to time, someone she'd known in high school came into the bookstore for a new Jackie Collins or Danielle Steel book. They always wore too much hairspray and bright lipstick. They mumbled something about her brave dead husband. And Renata looked them right in the eye, knowing they would not meet her gaze. Sometimes she'd say something especially weird so they'd have something to talk about at their next meeting.

And now here was Tom Harper, back from Spain, she figured. She imagined him with Libby topless beside him on a beach on the Costa del

Sol. Or sipping sangria at a sidewalk cafe. It was hard even now not to think of them without seeing a kind of glow around them, a special aura that assured them their place in the world.

Tom seemed to look right at her then.

She gave him a big smile. After all, she had a place in the world too, didn't she?

And then, Tom Harper walked away. No hello, no wave, nothing. As if she didn't exist. Suddenly, Renata was at every basement church dance, every school lunch, every horrible embarrassing moment of her life in Holly when boys like Tom Harper passed her by, ignored her, ridiculed her, and took girls like Libby Holliday and Dee-Dee Winthrop and Cathy Communale into their arms and hearts. In that moment Renata realized with an awful sharp pain in her chest, right where she assumed her heart nestled, that you really never do get over those hurtful days, when every hour, every moment of smiles not returned and insults whispered and giggles covered with hands and downcast eyes cut into you, left scars that do not go away, even years and years—lifetimes, really—later.

Even as she walked slowly back to work the feeling remained. In New York, she had blended into the scenery. She had been as anonymous as a nondescript building. She had almost forgotten what it was like to have someone look away, pretend not to see you.

The mall was not a big one. Renata was sure if she looked hard enough she could find Tom Harper and tell him to grow up. She would walk right up to him and tell him exactly what she thought about him. She would tell him he was getting fat.


*Millie attended the same* elementary school Renata had gone to, an old two-story building with wooden floors and walls lined with bulletin boards decorated for the season—construction paper leaves falling, smiling witches on broomsticks, turkeys shaped from children's hands. Already Millie had been elected the blackboard monitor, in charge of washing the blackboards at the end of each day and going out to the playground to clap the erasers clean.

All of the teachers there were young. They dressed in pastel jumpers and wore sensible shoes and white blouses with Peter Pan collars. The old, blue-haired, droopy-breasted teachers from Renata's childhood had all retired, taking their smell of lilac talc with them. For this, Renata was especially happy. No one would be comparing Millie to her mother's terrible schoolchild days.

One of the teachers, Mrs. Donahue, stayed after school to watch the children whose mothers worked. She gave them craft projects to keep them busy. She fed them graham crackers and apple juice. Mrs. Donahue, who was ten years younger than Renata and less than half her size, made Renata want to sit down in one of the child-size chairs and be taken care of—read to and fed and taught to make wreaths out of elbow macaroni.

When Millie saw Renata at the classroom door, she waved excitedly. She was wearing a new wig, from the Oprah wig line. It was big and fluffy and jet black.

"Millie," Mrs. Donahue said, "why don't you finish gluing the macaroni to that plate while I talk to your mother a minute." Her voice sounded like a cartoon character's, all high and squeaky.

She motioned for Renata to walk down the hall a little way with her. Renata could smell the shampoo Mrs. Donahue used. It smelled like piña coladas. Her hair was shiny, some of it held back with a bright red barrette.

"Mrs. Handy," Mrs. Donahue said.

Renata shook her head. "Renata."

Tiny creases appeared on the teacher's forehead, then disappeared. "It's about Millie," she said. Quickly she added, "Everyone loves her. She's darling."

"But?"

Mrs. Donahue considered what she was about to say very carefully. Her eyes were rimmed in bright blue liner, her lips covered with clear gloss.

"Those wigs," she said finally, raising her eyes to Renata. "Why does she wear them?" Then, softer, she added, "Some of the children make fun of her."

Renata looked right into Mrs. Donahue's blue-rimmed eyes and said, "She got a bad haircut and she's embarrassed."

Those creases reappeared in the teacher's forehead. "A bad haircut," she repeated, rolling the words around in her mouth like marbles. Again she seemed to be considering her words. "I thought she was sick," Mrs. Donahue said. "A few years ago, it was my first year teaching in fact, we had this darling little girl named Christie who had leukemia and lost all her hair from chemotherapy. She used to wear a hat. A beret. It was the saddest thing."

Renata laughed, too loud. "Millie," she said, "is terrific. She's fine. I mean, I'm really sorry about this other little girl, this—"

"Christie."

"Yes. Christie. But Millie isn't sick." Renata held up her shopping bag. "I just bought her these Christmas gifts," she said.

Mrs. Donahue did not look relieved. Her forehead was bunched and wrinkled. But she slowly nodded. "Well," she said. "I'm glad it's just a haircut."

"Astor Barbers," Renata said again, laughing. "One of these punk haircut places in New York."

Mrs. Donahue nodded again. "What a relief," she said. She smiled. Her teeth, Renata thought, were as small as a kitten's.

*"Then," Millie explained in* the car, "when all the glue dries, we'll spray-paint the macaroni gold." She leaned back and sighed, happy.

"Millie? Have the kids at this school been nice to you?"

Millie nodded.

"Have they asked you about your wigs?"

Millie smiled at her. The radiation had turned a few of her teeth black. When you grow up, Renata had promised, we'll have your teeth bonded. You'll have an Ultra-Brite smile. "They like the Tina Turner one," Millie was saying.

"Good," Renata told her.

"But I was thinking in a few weeks, maybe I'd stop wearing them. I'll look like Sinead O'Connor."

Renata did not ever want people to laugh at Millie. Thinking that now, she remembered the way Tom Harper had looked away from her at the mall. How he had averted her eyes and hurried past.

She turned the car suddenly down the old dirt road where she had heard he used to live. The tires squealed and Millie giggled.

"Sometimes," Renata said, "you've just got to give people a piece of your mind. Somebody is mean to you, you have to go up to them and say, 'What's your problem?'"

"They're not mean, Mama," Millie said. "They just don't understand."

"Who?"

"The other children. At school."

"They did make fun of you, didn't they?" Renata said. She slowed down as she passed mailboxes so she could read the names on them.

"Only Boyce Franklin." Millie's eyes widened. "Are we going to Boyce Franklin's house?"

"No," Renata said. HARPER, she read. She jerked the car into reverse and slammed on the brakes. "You wait right here."

The place was a disaster. Whatever Libby Holliday was doing with herself these days, keeping up her house was not part of it.

Renata banged on the door, hard.

Tom Harper himself opened it. He looked past her, to the car, then back to her face. "Car trouble again?" he said.

"Why did you pretend you didn't see me today?" she asked him. "At the mall. I was going to say hello and you looked away. Just like in school. I am not a thing, you know. I have feelings."

"I—"

"Out of this dumb town you would be nothing. Do you know that?" She took a breath. "Nothing," she said again. She turned and walked back to the car.

"Who lives there?" Millie said. "Boyce?"

Renata shook her head. As soon as she was out of sight of the Harper house, she pulled over. She imagined Libby in there, laughing at her. Both of them having a good laugh over weird Renata Handy. Renata rested her head on the steering wheel and tried not to cry.

*Tom Harper appeared on* Renata's doorstep the very next morning, while she was getting ready for work.

"You," he said, "are not an easy person to find."

She had not yet finished dressing. She had tucked her nightgown into her jeans and she felt ridiculous.

"I saw you," he said. "You were buying toys or something."

She frowned. "I guess you and Libby had a big laugh over me coming over like that yesterday. But you deserved it."

He seemed startled. "Oh," he said. "Oh. Yeah. Well, I came to say I'm sorry. It's just that after I saw you in that bookstore I felt so stupid—"

"What?"

"Give me a car that needs to be fixed and I feel great. Even a foreign car. Put me in a bookstore . . ." He raised his hands as if he were surrendering.

Renata tried to figure out if what he was saying was true. *He* was embarrassed? she thought.

Tom blushed a little. "So," he said. "I'm sorry. You misunderstood, I think."

She nodded.

When he turned to leave she called after him. "Hey! How was Spain?"
"Spain?"
"You bought a travel book," she said. "Spain."
He laughed. "Oh. That's right. It was for my daughter."
Renata remembered that in high school, Tom Harper had been voted Best Looking and Cutest Smile. She used to think that was stupid but looking at him now, she could see it wasn't stupid at all.

Tom *did not know why* he kept thinking about Renata Handy. She looked stranger than ever. And she was not one of those women who age well. Renata Handy had crow's-feet and lines like parentheses enclosing her mouth. It looked as if she never combed her hair but just left it all tangled and confused. Still, he kept thinking about her, wondering why she'd moved back, where she'd been all this time.

In school, it used to be everyone's favorite pastime to make fun of her. Guys would hunch their shoulders forward and walk like an ape. "Guess who I am?" they'd say. The girls always had strange stories about her. She used to read fortunes in the ladies' room, they said. She did not shave under her arms. In the showers after gym class, she would walk around all hairy, broad-hipped and thick-thighed. There had been a rumor that she'd slept with dozens of men, all older. There had been a rumor that she'd given blow jobs to an entire motorcycle gang from Vermont who had passed through town. Tom himself used to call her Renata Putana. Italian for whore. He would walk like an ape and say, "Guess who I am?" Libby gave him details about Renata's strange musky smell, of her body covered with thick dark hair that she refused to shave, and her strange habits like wearing a gold ring on her big toe or painting her breasts paisley.

Maybe seeing her again, having her confront him as she did, had made him guilty. She still looked strange to him. When she'd stood at her front door, he had smelled a musky animal odor coming from her. Like the smell of something wild and unwashed. On the ride back home, he'd found himself wondering if she still had that famous dense thatch of pubic hair, that thick growth under her arms. But it was a different kind of wondering than it used to be. Now there was something exciting about her. She still seemed slightly scary, but in a good way.

And here it was November, almost Thanksgiving. The air in Holly this time of year took on something special. Anticipation of good things to come. Already the post office had hired holiday employees to stamp the Holly postmark on letters from all over the country. The red and green garland and the bells made of red and green lights were strung downtown. A sign in front of the drugstore counted down the days until Santa's arrival in Holly. Tom could not help but be infected with the holiday spirit. With good cheer.

He kept thinking of Renata Handy coming up to his front door and telling him off like that. Hell, he probably deserved it. He had certainly done his share of laughing at her. She was brave and unusual. That wild smell of hers seemed to be all around him, mingling in the air with the smell of winter, of snow, of anticipation. And, like him, she was alone.

So on the morning before Thanksgiving, Tom again went to the old house she rented. This time the little girl answered the door. In the steel gray morning light, the kid looked even stranger than she had that day at the garage. She was too small and skinny and she had a haircut that made her look like a punk rock singer, all spotted with peach fuzz. Her skin was a funny color, not unlike that morning's sky. An iron gray that made him think of war, of battleships.

"I know you," she said right off. "You fixed Jack's car."

"I guess so," he said. "I thought it was your car, though."

Millie was wearing a thin T-shirt from the 1986 World Series, so faded that the writing was almost impossible to make out. Underneath, her collarbone jutted against the fabric and her shoulders poked out like doorknobs. The kid was definitely creepy.

"What do you want?" she asked him. "I have to get to school."

"I wanted to see your mother."

She didn't seem surprised. She seemed, in fact, almost bored and as he followed the little girl through the cluttered foyer, past piles of old newspapers and *National Geographics,* Tom wondered if she was used to ushering men in to see her mother. He thought briefly of the old rumor about the motorcycle gang from Vermont. Satan's Assistants, they'd been called.

Renata was making sandwiches, cutting up bananas and laying the slices on top of grainy bread thick with peanut butter. She didn't look quite so fat in the loose print dress she was wearing. And with her hair pulled back into a girlish ponytail, she seemed younger, almost sweet.

She looked up, surprised.

"What happened?" she said. "The check bounce or something?"

"What check?"

"For fixing the car."

The little girl perched on a stool between them.

"Millie," Renata said, still looking at Tom, "you didn't finish your health shake or your french toast." Then she added, "I'm trying to fatten her up."

Tom glanced down at Millie and nodded.

"This shake," Millie told him, "has brewer's yeast in it." She wrinkled her face in disgust.

A few weeks ago Sally Jessy Raphael had on these children who suffered from a strange disease that made them age prematurely. By the time they were seven or eight, they looked ten times their age. He wondered if Millie had that disease.

He was aware of a loud silence, of both Millie and Renata staring at him, waiting.

Tom cleared his throat. "I figured since you just got back to town and everything that maybe you didn't have any plans yet for Thanksgiving."

"We bought Cornish game hens," Millie told him. "Little birds with their legs all tied up. Want to see?"

She started to get off the stool.

"No," he said, resting his hand on her bony shoulder to stop her. "I thought you might want to come to my house."

Renata frowned. "Does Libby want us to come over?"

He had forgotten to tell her about Libby leaving. He had said everything backward. He had imagined a different scenario—no little girl, just him and Renata sitting on the couch, a whiff of that wild smell of hers, a story about both of them being alone, needing a family. But this scene was completely different. It was the ponytail that threw him. And the smell of maple syrup and peanut butter.

The paper bag that Renata was putting the sandwiches in was decorated with little yellow ducks. The ducks had bright orange feet and bills.

He cleared his throat again. "Uh . . . Libby and I split up," he said.

If Renata was surprised she didn't show it. Instead, she put an apple in the lunch bag and carefully folded over the top.

"It's just me and my kids."

"How many kids do you have?" she asked him. Her voice was different, softer.

"Two. A girl and a boy."

"Are they little or big?" Millie asked him. Her lips and chin were glossed with maple syrup.

He picked up a napkin from the counter and wiped her face. "Big," he said. "Teenagers."

Millie let him clean her hands too. "What about our Cornish game hens?" she said, looking at her mother.

The tops of Millie's hands were dotted with pale bruises. Tom gently finished wiping them.

"We could bring pies," Renata said. When she smiled, the parentheses deepened.

"Pies would be good," he said.

They *each had a duty.* Dana was making the vegetables. Tom had to stuff and cook the turkey. Troy was in charge of salad and appetizers. But Troy knew that wasn't enough. A real dinner had a fancy tablecloth, linen napkins, candles. He looked through his mother's old hope chest, the one his father had given her back when they were in high school. She hardly ever used the stuff inside.

He sat in the attic on the night before Thanksgiving searching for the things he needed. The hope chest still smelled faintly of a flowery scented sachet that his mother had long ago placed in it. The sachet was filled with pale pink and yellow dried petals, covered in lace that had once been white, and tied with a pink ribbon.

Outside, the wind rattled the attic windows. There were no storm windows up here, and Troy could feel a draft. It reminded him of a ghost, watching him, ruffling his hair. He knew that somewhere outside, Nadine was huddled, waiting. Thinking of her made him tug on his shirtsleeve. Lately, he found himself remembering movies like *Fatal Attraction* or *Play Misty for Me,* movies where old girlfriends came back for revenge, wielding knives. Sometimes when he stepped outside in the dark he called to Nadine. "I know you're out there," he'd shout. "Leave me alone. Go away." But she never answered.

He shivered in the cold room, tugged on his sleeves again, and began to pull things from the chest. There was an unfinished quality to what his mother had put in there, as if her enthusiasm had left her at some point and she'd given up.

"Hey," Dana said.

Troy jumped. "You scared the shit out of me," he said. "Damn."

"What are you doing up here?" she said, kneeling beside him on the dusty floor. She wore jeans torn at the knees and thigh.

"I need some stuff," he said. "For tomorrow."

"You're in charge of salad," she said. "What are you looking for? Some old lettuce or something?" She lifted the old sachet to her nose and sniffed. "Yuck."

"Real families have real dinners," Troy said. "They lay out the silverware in a special order. They use cloth napkins instead of paper towels torn in half. They make things look nice."

"Cloth napkins?" Dana said. "Aren't you fancy?"

Every Saturday night for almost two months now Troy had taken Jenny out. Each time, he rang her doorbell and listened to the soft chiming. It played a tune that he could not identify. He listened to her mother's high heels moving across the floor toward him. Her mother always smiled when she saw him. She led him down a hallway that smelled like floor wax and furniture polish to the family room, a large room with plaid sofas and dark red leather chairs. He shook her father's hand, sipped a soda from a tall glass rimmed in dark blue while her mother went off upstairs somewhere to get Jenny. He sat there, talking about baseball with her father and thinking, This is how real people live. The cat always climbed onto his lap and went to sleep, purring loudly. This is a family, Troy would think. This is a home.

Then, two weeks ago, Jenny invited him to her house for dinner. Until then, their dates had remained the same, chaste and quiet. A movie, ice cream at Friendly's afterward. They sometimes sat parked in front of her house and kissed for a while before she went inside. Jenny called it necking and somehow that made Troy think she was limiting him to just that—her neck and above. It was when they were sitting there like that, after a lot of kissing, that she asked him to dinner. After making out with her, it always took Troy time to control his breathing again, to stop thinking about what lay underneath her pastel snowflake sweaters and smooth khaki pants. He had to work hard to not think of all those days and nights with Nadine.

So that when Jenny asked him, he couldn't even answer. He was concentrating too hard on not thinking about what kind of underwear she wore, or on the hardness inside his own pants, or on Nadine all skinny and tattooed straddling him, tossing her head back, closing her eyes.

Jenny was saying something about an aunt and uncle visiting from Minnesota and coq au vin and a lot of other things that he could not focus on.

Her face floated in front of his. "Are you listening to me?" she said. Her lips were a little swollen from so much kissing.

"Of course," he said. "Coq au vin." He pronounced it slowly, carefully. Wrong.

She giggled. "Coq," she said. "Like Coke, you know. Oh. Vin. It means chicken with wine. It's my mother's specialty. She always makes it for company."

He nodded. He wondered if she was a virgin. She'd had a boyfriend back in Minnesota for a couple of years. Could two people just neck for two whole years?

"My uncle is a pilot for Northwest," she said, settling back in the seat. "They travel everywhere and bring us exotic presents. And my aunt is from Denmark. She's gorgeous."

Troy nodded again. An old song by Van Morrison was playing on the radio. That image of Nadine flashed through his mind again. Nadine would try absolutely anything. He felt himself growing hard again. Shit, he thought, fidgeting in the seat, trying to rearrange his hard-on.

"You are so antsy," Jenny said.

She moved closer to him again and kissed him. Her lips always tasted like berries, like summer. "I could kiss you forever," she said.

But she didn't. She stopped almost right away. "So you'll come to dinner next week?"

"Sure," he said, and started to kiss her again. He thought he might die from wanting her.

She spoke inside his mouth. "Dress nice," she said. "Bring flowers."

Necking, he thought. He let his fingers trace her neck, to the collarbone. Once, when he'd first been with Nadine, she had taken his hand in hers and slowly made him trace every part of her body. Even her feet. Light, she'd told him. And slow. Over Jenny's sweater he moved his fingers slowly, lightly, down. Past the collarbone, to her right breast. He did not hesitate. He drew careful circles until he felt her nipple harden under the wool. He could hear her breathing now.

"Troy," she said.

He waited for the next word. Stop. Or no. When it didn't come, he moved to her left breast and did the same motion. He had never felt anything so wonderful as those sweater-covered breasts under his hand. He thought he might explode from the feeling of her hardening nipples.

Jenny did not move his hand away, but she stopped kissing him and looked at him very intensely. The windows were steamed up. She lifted her finger to the windshield and wrote in the mist. An I, then she drew a heart, and then the letter U.

*Troy could not believe* it when Jenny said she'd spend Thanksgiving at his house. Really? he'd kept asking her. Really? But that night, when he got home and looked around at the house, at its fading wallpaper and the stacks of mail and magazines everywhere and the stale smell of beer from the cans that sat in the garbage bag by the door, Troy wanted to take back the invitation. How could Jenny come here? It was too embarrassing.

And then he thought of their plates with the chipped edges, their odd assortment of glasses and silverware and he felt even worse. Jenny's house was like a palace, everything ordered and perfect. Troy tried to imagine what his mother would do if she were here, if she came out of her room and organized a special Thanksgiving dinner, like the special meals she'd sometimes made for them. Troy could even remember tea parties with miniature cookies sprinkled with colored toppings and birthday parties when she baked him elaborate cakes, coconut-covered snowmen with licorice smiles or bright yellow Big Birds. Somewhere, he thought, his mother had all the accouterments for family life.

That was why he'd gone up to the attic and peeked into boxes filled with old winter clothes that no one wore anymore and extra blankets and camping equipment for family weekend trips that never happened. And there, underneath some of the boxes, dusty and almost hidden, was his mother's hope chest. When Troy opened the lid a fine layer of dust swarmed around him. Inside he found a white tablecloth with matching napkins that had never even been taken out of the package. They were bordered in embroidered tulips, pink and purple and yellow. It was exactly what he needed to show Jenny a real Thanksgiving.

"Perfect," he said.

"And what's going to happen when somebody spills gravy all over it?" Dana said.

She was chewing bubble gum very loudly, snapping it as if to punctuate each point she made.

"We'll wash it," he said. "It's a new invention. Washing machines. Driers."

"Very funny."

Jenny's parents had a lace tablecloth her uncle had brought them from Ireland. And heavy silver napkin rings with a big A engraved on them.

"Napkin rings," he said out loud, and rummaged through the chest.

"Napkin rings?" Dana said, and snapped her gum again.

"That is a disgusting habit you have," Troy told her.

She snapped it once more, even louder. "Is all this for the new girl-friend?" she said. Caitlin had told her that this girl walked like she had a stick up her ass.

"It's for us. We're supposed to be pulling together. Making a family."

"Uh-huh," Dana said.

She pulled her old cardigan tighter around her and walked to the window. Her knees were dirty through the rips in her jeans. It was too dark to see anything, but still she peered out.

"Do you still think about her?" Dana said. "Out there somewhere?"

For a minute he thought she meant Nadine. But then he realized she was talking about their mother. He felt the draft again. The hairs on his arms shot up. His skin got all bumpy. Troy could see John Lennon's chin peeking out, and he tugged on his shirtsleeve again.

"Sometimes," he said. "Yes."

*Millie wore her* Annie *wig* on Thanksgiving. Renata pretended that her daughter's face was not growing thinner, that she did not look even smaller and more lost under the tangle of bright orange curls.

"We could just stay home," Millie said. "Eat our Cornish game hens. Watch the parade."

Last year, in New York, Jack had taken Millie uptown to really watch the parade. They had left at dawn, eaten breakfast at a diner somewhere, then shivered through the whole Macy's Thanksgiving Day extravaganza. When they got home, Millie had told Renata about every float, every Broadway star, in great detail. It seemed a lifetime ago now.

"This will be better," Renata told her. "We'll get out. Get fresh air. Be with people." She arranged walnut halves in a circle on top of a pumpkin cheesecake.

Millie groaned. "I am so sick of fresh air," she said.

Every day, Renata made Millie take a long walk with her. She brought books about birds and trees of New England. They stood together in the woods, trying to identify nature. But nothing looked like the glossy pictures in the books, and so far the notebook Renata had started to record sightings only had chickadee, birch, and pine in it.

Renata dusted the crust of an apple pie with brown sugar and cinnamon. "Are these gorgeous or what?" she said.

Millie shrugged. "They're pies," she said.

"I've got to tell you," Renata said. "This guy. Tom. He was the hunk of high school."

"*Him?*" Millie started to laugh.

Renata examined the lattice crust on top of the harvest pie, looking for any imperfections. She'd stayed up all night baking. She wanted everything perfect.

Suddenly, she started to laugh too. Who would ever have imagined that she, Renata Handy, would be bringing pies to a Thanksgiving dinner at Tom Harper's? Tom Harper, who used to make wisecracks at her when she passed. Who had married the class beauty. Who had grown, through these twenty years since she'd last seen him leaning against the radiator at the end of the corridor in school, slightly paunchy and somehow more appealing.

"What's funny?" Millie said. She stood on tiptoe and studied the pies.

"Everything," Renata said. "All these things people tell you are going to happen, really do."

"Like?"

"Like, I don't know. The prom queen gets fat. The ugly duckling turns into a lovely swan. The class hunk invites you to dinner."

"Mama," Millie said. "I don't know what you're talking about. But your pies are beautiful." She took a small grimy finger and poked it right into the pumpkin cheesecake. Then licked it clean and smiled. "And delicious."

*Renata expected Tom Harper's* children to be beautiful, replicas of their parents. She'd imagined a blond frosty daughter, a tall athletic son. Instead, here were two scrawny teenagers who looked like ragamuffins. The word waif kept running through her mind. She kept thinking about a movie she'd seen about street kids in Seattle. That's what they looked like. Or the teenagers that used to try to hustle her in Grand Central Station.

The girl, Dana, kept eyeing her suspiciously. She had a bad haircut that looked like one of Millie's wigs. She wore ripped jeans and a shirt that could have belonged to Tom. She looked slightly tough, like a girl who already knew too much. And the son, Troy, looked like a juvenile delinquent dressed to see his probation officer. The edges of a tattoo were visible under the frayed cuff of his pale blue dress shirt.

The house was a mess. Run-down, neglected. It looked like a house someone had once loved but had given up on. In fact, Renata thought as she put her pies on the kitchen counter, that was exactly how the kids looked too.

"I never cooked a turkey before," Tom told her. He blushed a little, and shrugged. "Usually we have Thanksgiving at my sister's. Mandy? Do you remember Mandy?"

Renata shook her head.

"She's younger," he said. Then peered through the smudged oven door at his turkey.

Someone had set the dining room table beautifully, with linen and silver and candles. It looked ridiculous against everything around it, like a mirage.

"The pies look great," Tom told her.

She had placed a walnut over Millie's finger hole. Now it seemed silly to have worried so much. This was not at all what she had expected. She thought that Tom Harper would have everything under control, clean and polished. She thought she would be stepping into a glossy photograph, like the ones in *Gourmet* magazine.

He was standing close enough to her that she could smell the soap on him. "It's so hard," he said. "Doing everything alone."

She realized then that he saw the two of them as kindred spirits. The thought surprised her.

"It's like, you want to stay a family and everything. But you're not sure how," he said. "You make lists, right? Families have holiday dinners to-gether. Families go on day trips. They watch *Wheel of Fortune*, the nightly news."

"I wouldn't know," Renata said. "It's always been just Millie and me."

He did not try to hide his surprise. "But her father—"

"The butcher, the baker, the candlestick maker," she said. She remem-bered how in school some Italian kid, Jerry Iannone, had called her Renata Putana. And Tom Harper had chimed in. What the hell was she doing here? she thought, and stepped back, away from him.

He turned away and pretended to be busy with something.

They were not, Renata thought, kindred spirits at all. She watched him spoon a wiggly blob of cranberries onto a small plate.

"God," she said. "I could have made cranberry sauce. That stuff is awful."

When he looked at her, his face was still covered with surprise. "*Make* cranberry sauce?"

He was still a hunk, she thought. Extra weight or not. She was sure the guy could melt women's hearts.

"Yes. You just buy fresh cranberries and—"

He shook his head, laughing. "Of course," he said. "I never even thought about that." He shook his head again. "Fresh cranberries. Remember in ninth grade? That class trip to Plymouth Rock? Cranberry bogs and the little fake colonial town?"

"Yes," she said slowly. Renata did not have anyone with shared memories. Ninth grade, she thought. Plymouth Rock.

"All I wanted was to sit next to Libby for that long ride back home," he said. His voice was sad, distant. "I only got to within two rows of her."

Renata had sat alone on that trip. Up front, behind the driver while behind her the rest of the class sang—the theme from *The Monkees* and *Gilligan's Island* and *F Troop*. She had known all the words, but when the others faltered, forgetting what the line after "The end of the Civil War was near when quite accidentally . . . ," she had not spoken up. Instead, she had completed the song in her mind, staring straight ahead at the headlights going the opposite way in the dark.

"Now that would be a good day trip for me to take Dana and Troy on," Tom was saying. "A little history. Some cranberry bogs. I mean, they probably think cranberries only come in cans."

Renata put her hand on his arm. "They're too old for that kind of trip, Tom. No teenager wants to spend a day in a village filled with phony Pilgrims."

He seemed surprised. "No? But it's educational. It's . . . history. We'll take Millie too. We'll all go."

He seemed so hopeful, so optimistic, that she said, "Yes. All right. Some Sunday we'll all go."

*Troy lit the candles.* In their soft light, Jenny looked like an angel. Now that she had arrived he didn't even mind that his father had invited this weird woman and her sick kid. Jenny made everything seem calmer, almost normal. She'd brought something called a horn of plenty, a basket filled with colorful little pumpkins and squash and autumn leaves. The squash, she'd told him, were just decorative. Gourds. It seemed silly to grow something you couldn't eat, but he'd accepted what she said and placed the horn of plenty between the candlesticks as a centerpiece.

Jenny squeezed his arm. "Everything looks so lovely," she whispered.

He thought he might burst, he felt that accomplished. And Renata had baked these incredible pies. Wait until Jenny saw them.

During dinner, the phone rang.

"Let it ring," his father said.

But the little kid, Millie said, "What if it's an emergency?"

Then he and Dana and their father exchanged a look. What if it's her? That's what they were all thinking.

"I'll get it," Troy said.

He answered the phone in the kitchen.

"Fuck you, you slimy asshole!"

Troy looked around, nervous, as if everyone could hear all the way in the other room.

"What would you do if I burned your fucking house down? Huh? Answer me, you lying fuck."

He kept his voice low. "Nadine," he said. But he couldn't think of anything else to say.

"Is that little blonde your girlfriend?" Nadine was saying. "Huh? I'll fucking kill her. What is she, twelve? Huh? Answer me, you fuck."

Gently, Troy hung up the phone. He held on to the door frame, to steady himself. He took a few deep breaths. Then he went back into the dining room.

He smiled at everyone. "Wrong number," he said.


*You sure you don't want* to take some of this pie home?" Tom asked Renata.

"Positive," she said.

Renata and Millie had stayed much later than she'd expected. They had watched two football games. Had turkey sandwiches. Played charades. And now she was helping Tom clean up in the kitchen. It was dark outside, and cold. From the living room came the sounds of the Wicked Witch cackling. Everyone else was in there watching *The Wizard of Oz* on video.

"What did we ever do before VCRs?" Tom said.

"Regular old TV," she said. "*Gilligan's Island. F Troop.*" She bit her lip to keep from saying more. The day had gone too well to ruin it. And standing here in the too warm kitchen with Tom, she felt an intimacy that she did not want to lose.

He turned to her, clutching a plate to his chest. A fine crack ran across it. "This was really nice," he said. "I mean, today. Everything." He laughed that self-conscious laugh.

"Yes," she said. "It was."

A thought popped into her mind. I hope he kisses me. Her heart sped up. She felt her cheeks burning. *I hope he kisses me.* She shook her head, girlishly, to get rid of the idea.

"It's really nice," he was saying, "to be, you know . . ."

"Yes?" *I hope he kisses me.*

"Friends," he said. That laugh again. "To be friends," he said.

"Friends," she said. But still the thought stayed. She was wondering how he kissed. What he would do first. A small gentle one? A deep passionate one?

Tom said, "I could really use a friend."

"Me too," she said. "Definitely."

He picked up another plate, concentrated on rubbing it dry. "So many women are, like, sex fiends or something," he said. "You can't imagine. And sex gets in the way of being friends, I think."

She nodded with exaggerated enthusiasm. "Absolutely. The two don't mix."

He was smiling at her, a broad honest smile.

"I've got to go," she said suddenly. She had to get out of there.

"Oh. Okay."

She felt all turned around. She stumbled, trying to get out of the kitchen as quickly as she could.

"Slow down," Tom laughed from somewhere behind her.

The living room was dark. Dana was upstairs with a friend of hers, Caitlin, who had shown up a few hours ago. But Troy and Jenny and Millie were all sitting together on the couch. They had stopped the movie, leaving Dorothy frozen, asleep, in the poppy field.

"I don't have a daddy," Millie was saying.

"That's all right," Troy said. "I don't have a mother."

Millie gasped. "That's much much worse," she said.

At the door, Tom kissed Renata goodbye on the cheek. It was as quick and dry as a brother's would be. She clutched Millie's hand and hurried away, to the safety of their car.

*ibby had fallen head* over heels, hopelessly, in love. Although it wasn't fair to compare, and women's magazines always advised against it, she couldn't stop herself from doing it. Jeremy versus Harp. It was like night and day. In some ways, she decided, Harp was still like a boy. He loved TV and sports. He guzzled beer and talked about cars. He loved action-adventure movies and the *Sports Illustrated* swimsuit issue. Why, he subscribed to that magazine just for that one issue! Even the way he made love was still like a teenager, all rough and eager.

Jeremy was a man. He had a chest thick with hair and made slow careful love. Later, at work or on the freeway, Libby could actually get dizzy remembering it. And he read! Serious books by writers like Kafka and Chekhov. Books most people only read in school because they had to. He had never seen *Bewitched* or *The Munsters* or *I Dream of Jeannie.* He had never seen *Butterflies Are Free.* He liked jazz, Ben Webster and Dexter Gordon. Libby was certain he was the man she had been waiting for her entire life. She spent hours in the library, reading up on everything he talked about.

She was certain now there was a bigger reason for her coming here. It wasn't about becoming an actress at all. It was to meet Jeremy, to have her eyes opened. When she thought of all those women her age, the ones magazines did stories about, she felt as if she was getting in on their secrets. They read the *New Yorker* and listened to jazz and watched movies with subtitles. Libby realized she had gone about everything all wrong. Jeremy was setting her straight. Jeremy was smart and talented, an intellectual. He was also married.

"Separated, actually," he told her.

This after it was too late and she was already in love with him. Then she remembered. "I am too," she said. "I'm married too."

He seemed almost pleased. "Kathleen is a harpist. In the symphony. Beware of musicians," Jeremy said. "Especially harpists."

"Tom is a mechanic," Libby said. "I got married too young. He's back in a small town in Massachusetts, waiting for the Red Sox to start playing again, drinking beer and playing poker with his buddies." She felt a little guilty describing Tom that way. But everything she said was true.

"How awful for you," Jeremy said. "Did he beat you? That sort of thing?"

"Nothing like that," Libby said. "He's just completely dull. Not at all evolved."

"In a way," Jeremy said, "that's even worse."

———

151

*There was a dark side* to Jeremy. He brooded and drank straight vodka. He had insomnia. She sometimes found him hunched over his computer, unshaven and drunk. If he caught her watching him like that, he threw things at her—shoes, the empty vodka bottle, pens. She imagined that this was what it must have been like to be in love with Poe or Chopin, scary and exciting. It was frightening, but Libby thought that was part of being creative. Hadn't she locked herself in her room for days at a time back home?

For a while, Libby had written poetry. She had followed the guidelines from a book called *How to Find the Poet in You*. The book had exercises at the end of each chapter, which she did carefully. In a few months' time she had written a sonnet, a haiku, a limerick, and a free-form poem. She thought they were beautiful. She'd read them out loud to Tom, and he'd loved them. The sonnet had almost made him cry. She sent them out to magazines listed in *The Poet's Market*. No one bought them. But now she wondered if maybe she was like Jeremy, too deep, too artistic for the commercial market.

More and more she was afraid that he would make fun of her. He was going through an especially bad case of writer's block and the smallest thing could set him off into a tirade. Last week he had refused to go out in public with her because he thought she looked cheap. "Go back to your mechanic if you're going to dress like that," he'd told her. She had on her favorite dress too, the electric blue spandex one. Sometimes, after a movie, he called her stupid. He told her she didn't understand real art. The truth was, despite her excitement at first, she still got sleepy when she had to read subtitles. It took her forever to finish one *New Yorker*, and as soon as she did, yet another appeared on her doorstep. They seemed to multiply at a very rapid rate.

On days she didn't see him, Libby snuck off to a multiplex movie cinema and went from theater to theater watching what Jeremy called "junk." Then she ate at a Big Boy. She marked Excellent for every category on the comment card: COURTESY, CLEANLINESS, QUALITY OF FOOD.

Libby worried about losing Jeremy to the harpist. But what worried her even more was how lately, at night, she found herself missing Tom and her kids. She even found herself missing Holly and her house. She had chosen everything in that house carefully, studying swatches of fabric and wallpaper samples for weeks. There had been a time, very long ago, when she had loved that house and everything in it.

When she closed her eyes Libby sometimes got a clear image of winter there, of the way the cold air tasted in her mouth, the snow in the woods and the ice clinging to the trees like crystal. She had read somewhere that palm trees were not even indigenous to California. This fact troubled her. She developed a litany of trees back home, trees that belonged there. Maple, birch, pine, and elm. Maple, birch, pine, and elm. Reciting their names at night helped her fall asleep.

"Again," *Dana said.*

Caitlin did not hesitate. "The day after graduation—"

"The day *of*—"

"Okay," Caitlin said. "The day *of.* We get in my car, just the two of us and one suitcase, and we hit the Mass. Pike—"

"Out of town," Dana said. She sighed and stared up at the winter sky. In Australia, she thought, people gazing upward saw a whole different sky. They saw Gemini, Cancer, Leo.

"And we get us an apartment in the East Village and dress in black and go to foreign films—we have to start calling them films instead of movies— and we need to maybe stop shaving under our arms."

Dana frowned. "Really?"

"Maybe."

For their entire lives Caitlin had been in charge. She always made their decisions and plans—whose birthday party to go to, whose to avoid, which haircuts to get and whether or not they should have long nails, suntans, pierced ears. Having Caitlin there to do these things always made Dana feel safe and sure.

This was their New Year's resolution. To firm up their plans. To figure out their escape. After work on Friday nights now, they climbed the fire escape to the roof of Pizza Pizzazz. Closer to the stars, Caitlin had said the first night they did this. Now it was a ritual, as if doing this over and over would make their plans really happen.

Caitlin finished off the last of the pizza they'd brought up there with them. The special, a four-cheese one called Quattro Formaggio. Gorgonzola, mozzarella, fontina, and Parmesan. "And we'll paint the walls, like, red. Something wild. Bright. And we'll go to Nell's and that place I read about in *People.* What is it? The Robert DeNiro one?"

"The Tribeca Grill," Dana said. She loved the way that sounded. "Tribeca Grill," she said again.

Caitlin stretched out flat, and smiled. "I'm going to get my pictures taken here. Bring my portfolio with me. And you could make a demo tape of your songs before we go. That way, we can take that city by storm, right off." She made her thumb and forefinger into a pistol and shot at the sky. "Bang," she said.

*New Year's resolutions.* Plan escape. Plan new life. Leave 'em laughing when you go. That was what Dana had tucked into the corner of her bedroom mirror, written on a piece of hot pink notebook paper, the ends all curly, the lines straight and blue.

Caitlin said she should get a belt and put notches in it, the way guys did. For Christmas, she had even given Dana one as a joke. What Dana didn't tell her was that she did make small lines on the back of that belt. Already there were a lot. Caitlin always told her she should be a rock star. And rock stars, Dana told herself, were wild. They wrecked hotel rooms and drank strong whiskey. They had experience. They looked tough. She started to wear a black leather jacket, thick black eyeliner, and dark lipstick. She always wore her ripped jeans and the belt with the secret lines. She was growing her hair but for now teased it real high and messy, spraying it so it didn't budge. So when she woke up in the morning in somebody's dorm room, it looked exactly the same. She drank Jack Daniel's, straight, and called it Jack.

Every Saturday night, after work, while Caitlin went off with Kevin and Mike and Mike's new girl, Trudi Martinez, Dana went to another party at Williams. She changed guys every couple of weeks. She made sure Billy saw her. After Justin there was Rick, then Harry, who was actually Justin's cousin, although she didn't find that out until later. They all told her her skin was soft. Butter, silk, velvet. "Are you protected?" they whispered. Always the same. This week her date was John Somebody from New Jersey. She didn't need to drink very much before she started to rub against them. All she needed was for Billy to notice.

She never felt bad until Sunday night when she was home in her own bed. Sometimes, after she washed off her makeup and combed out her hair and put on her old candy-cane-striped pajamas with the feet in the bottom, she would get into bed and sob. She never knew for sure why she was crying, and it never made her feel better. The only thing that helped was to think about that summer day when she and Caitlin would drive out of town.

Dana told Caitlin every detail about the sex. How some guys had long thin penises, and some hooked a little in one direction. How some were pink and some were dark. She told Caitlin how to have an orgasm. How if you got on top and made round motions, pressing against the guy, it never ever failed. You should keep notes, Caitlin told her. Or a diary or something because when you're famous they'll publish it. Your memoirs. Dana had laughed, but really she couldn't think of anything worse than everybody knowing about what went on in those dorm rooms in the dark.

*John had a reddish face,* thin lips, and pale hair. He was a little too thin, and too tall to whisper to.

"So I decided to do my senior thesis on my Irish ancestors and spent all last summer touring there by bike. You can never start your research too soon."

She was amazed by how much they talked. All of them. Like they were going to be great friends. Like they'd keep calling her three weeks from now. She finished her glass of Jack and refilled it from the small flask she carried in her jacket pocket. She thought the flask added character, made her seem tough.

"Have you visited there?" John asked her.

She wanted to tell him the truth, that she'd give anything to go any-where. But she narrowed her eyes at him instead and turned on the act. "Are you fucking serious, man?" she said. She laughed loud so Billy could hear her. "I've never been farther than exit nine." She stood on tiptoe so she could see him better. "But," she said, "my father wants to take the whole family to Plymouth Rock."

John nodded. "Well, sure," he said. "That would be interesting."

She rolled her heavily made-up eyes at him, then turned them upward. "Give me a fucking break," she said.

*The ride to Plymouth Rock* was long and boring and hot. Renata's kid, Millie, couldn't get a chill because she had some kind of disease that was a big mystery. So Tom kept the heat turned way up and Dana sat sweating in the back seat, next to Troy's stuck-up girlfriend. Jenny kept saying inane things like "This is so exciting!" or "Plymouth Rock! I can't wait." She was from some distant state that started with an M. Montana or Minnesota. One of those states that seemed like a big blank square to Dana. Not unlike Jenny's mind, Dana thought, smiling to herself. Blank and square.

Dana had been with John again last night. Thinking about him was not very exciting. So far, he was the dullest of the bunch. So she closed her eyes and thought about Billy instead. She imagined him coming over to her at one of the socials and telling her he was going crazy with jealousy. "I left Melissa," he'd say. "I have to have you."

From the front seat, Renata's and Millie's voices sounded like annoying bees buzzing around the car. It was hard to even daydream with them around. They never stopped talking. They were into this great mother/daughter friendship thing. They made Dana sick.

"Ooooohhhh," Jenny squealed. "Only ten more miles. I can't wait."

*Renata cornered Dana in* the candle shop.

"I told your father this trip would bore you to death," she said.

Behind them, women dressed like Pilgrims, in long gray skirts and white bonnets, were demonstrating the Colonial technique for candlemaking.

Dana narrowed her eyes at Renata. She didn't trust her. "Oh, yeah?" Dana said. She pretended to yawn. "Well, I think it's fascinating." She hesitated, then said, "Fucking fascinating."

Renata did not even blink. "Well," she said, "I think it's a real bore." And then she walked away. She was so big, she had to stand sideways to squeeze past the rows of tourists watching the demonstration.

Dana watched her walk away. Renata, she decided, was one of these fake I'm-your-friend types. Nothing bothered her. Not swearing or smoking cigarettes or anything. As long as you thought she was hip, that was enough for her.

"Guess what this is?" Millie said, appearing suddenly at Dana's side. She held out a candle.

"A candle?" Dana said.

Millie laughed. "Of course it's a candle. But what flavor?"

Dana sniffed it. "Blueberry."

"Right," Millie said. She took Dana's hand as easily as if they walked hand in hand all the time. "Let's find some other flavors," she said.

Her hand was warm and dry, so small that Dana could practically feel all the bones in it. It was like holding a skeleton's hand.

Millie stopped along the way to sniff different candles. Each time she made Dana guess. Cranberry. Vanilla.

"Chocolate?" Dana guessed, tired of the game.

Millie laughed and shook her head. Who, Dana wondered, would let their kid get a haircut like Sinead O'Connor's? Only Miss Cool.

"Spaghetti?" Dana said, sending Millie into a fresh fit of giggles.

She saw her father watching the fake Pilgrims make candles. He actually seemed interested. Now he was even asking a question.

"Give up?" Millie said.

Dana sighed. "Yes," she said. "I give up."

Millie's eyes twinkled. "It's belly button!" she said.

Without even thinking about it, Dana started to laugh too.

"*For the first week,*" Caitlin said, "we'll play tourists. You know, go to the Statue of Liberty and the Empire State Building. Stuff like that. And then we'll pretend we wouldn't get caught dead doing that stuff. Like it was beneath us."

Dana blew her breath out in long streams, to watch it turn into steam in the cold night air. It was supposed to snow, and the sky was already cloudy, blocking out the stars and moon.

"You know what I really want to do?" Caitlin said.

When she talked, Dana watched her breath fog the night air too.

"Hear a symphony. A whole orchestra playing something really beautiful. Violins and everything."

"Do you know," Dana said, "that they cost like eighty dollars? And you don't even know the names of all those instruments."

"Man," Caitlin said, "we have got to really start saving money."

Dana already had almost four hundred dollars in her sock drawer. Since she had started dating these college boys, she never spent any money. She laughed at the word "dating." "Ha!" she said out loud.

"Ha what?" Caitlin said.

"Ha ha."

"You are so weird sometimes."

Dana looked away from her and up at the starless sky. "Want to go to one of these college things with me tomorrow night?" she said, trying to sound offhanded about it.

"What?" Caitlin said between bites of pizza. "Does this John guy have a friend or something?"

"I'm not seeing him anymore," Dana said. Sometimes she was amazed at how she could control her voice, make it sound any way she wanted. "It's this guy Warren. And his brother from some prep school. They are loaded. Warren drives a Porsche."

"No kidding?" Caitlin hesitated.

"It's just for a goof, right?" Dana said. "I mean, we just want to get some experience before we hit the big city."

"Uh-huh," Caitlin said. "What would I tell Kevin, though?"

"Fuck him. Who cares? Tell him he's an asshole. Tell him he's a neanderthal. Tell him he's history."

"It would be nice to spend a Saturday night doing something else. You cannot imagine what it's like having to talk to that slut Trudi Martinez. I mean, she hardly even knows Mike and she's like a rabbit with him."

"Yeah," Dana said.

"I mean," Caitlin said quickly, "she's not after adventure. Like us. That's why she's such a slut."

"Uh-huh," Dana said. Sometimes, on those Sunday nights when she was alone in bed, she used that word too. She thought, I'm a slut. She called herself other names to see how they felt. Sometimes that was what made her cry. She wondered what her mother would say if she knew. She probably wouldn't even care. That's nice, she'd say, and go back to staring at herself in the mirror while Lite-105 played sappy songs in the background.

"You won't be mad if I don't go, will you?" Caitlin was saying.

"No," Dana said. "It's not that much fun anyway."

"In New York we'll be out together every night, right?"

Dana turned her head away from Caitlin, out of the light. She did not want her friend to see that she was crying.

"Okay," Troy said to Nadine. "I'm here. Now what do you want."

He had agreed to meet her in the diner in town. He figured he was safe in public. He figured he could get her off his back once and for all. It was a snowy Saturday morning. One of those days when Troy felt as if he was living in a postcard of New England. He would get this over with Nadine and then surprise Jenny by showing up with a toboggan and taking her to Strawberry Hill.

Nadine looked bad. All nervous like a wild animal. Her eyes were too shiny and Troy knew she was on something big time.

They had both ordered coffee, but Nadine didn't even touch hers, except to dump in six packets of sugar and then to stir it over and over until Troy thought he'd go nuts.

"I need you," she said, her eyes darting across his face. "I mean it. How could you do this to me?"

She was wearing a sleeveless Danskin, despite the freezing weather and the snow. He could see goose bumps on her arms, and her nipples standing out, hard against the black fabric. He made himself look away, but it was too late. He shifted in his seat.

"I didn't do anything," he said. "We broke up. That's all."

"I see you everywhere with that blond girl," Nadine said. Her eyes were getting teary now.

Troy looked around the diner nervously. He didn't want her to start bawling in public. But the waitress was reading the *Boston Globe* and smoking a cigarette and the two guys at the counter were staring at their plates.

"So what?" he said. "Look," he added, his voice low, "why don't you put your coat on?" She'd come in with one of those fake rabbit coats, a white one with black patches everywhere.

"Can we get out of here?" she said. "I'm starting to get really upset."

Her voice sounded too loud and the waitress glanced up from the paper, frowning. "You want more coffee?" she said.

"No," Troy said, standing. "No. We're going."

He put some money on the table, and grabbed Nadine by the arm. He knew he was being rough with her, but he didn't care. He was starting to feel weird. Last week, he'd surprised Jenny with a scrimshaw ring. They'd seen it when they were in Plymouth that day, and while she was watching a demonstration on blacksmiths, he'd run back to the store and bought it for her. When he gave it to her last week, she'd told him she was never going to take it off. Ever, she'd said.

Outside, the wind howled and the snow hit them in the face, all cold and wet. Still, Troy could see that Nadine was really crying now.

"Don't," he said. "Come on. Stop."

She tried to talk, but all that came out were little gulping noises.

Troy took her arm again and pushed her toward his car. He didn't want to be seen standing here on Main Street with her like this.

Inside, he turned the radio on. Jenny always liked Lite-105, and it was still on that station from last night when they'd gone to a party together. Since Plymouth, they'd started to see each other on Friday and Saturday

159

nights. He and Nadine used to play the hard rock station. Now, the Eagles were singing "Desperado." But she didn't seem to notice. She was too busy crying.

Troy pulled out of the parking lot and started driving around, real slow because the streets were so slippery. He could hear the toboggan tumbling around in the trunk. He kept thinking about how he and Nadine used to get drunk and speed around town. Even last winter she'd roll down the window and stick her head out and sing at the top of her lungs with the radio. Later, her face against his thighs would still be cold.

He heard a groan and looked up, surprised. So did Nadine. It had come from him.

She had taken her coat off again. He would not look down past her neck. He made himself think about all those nights parked in front of Jenny's house, making those endless circles over her sweater. She had more sweaters than anyone he knew. They all looked the same too, soft colors with snowflake yokes. When it was real cold, she wore a matching turtleneck underneath. After he gave her the scrimshaw ring, she'd let him move his hand under both sweaters, to her bra. But that was all.

"Stop right here," Nadine said. She was still crying.

They were on a back road somewhere near the quarry. When he turned the car off, the windshield was immediately covered with snow. It blinded him. For a moment, with Nadine whimpering beside him like that, Troy could almost pretend nothing else existed. He could forget the pretty blond girl from Minnesota and the scrimshaw ring. The weight of whatever it was he was trying to prove seemed to lift, to leave him. His mind felt all blurry and when Nadine leaned toward him and pushed her lips hard against his, he thought he could do almost anything out here as the snow fell and hid them from sight.

Nadine tasted like gum and smoke, a combination that was as familiar as the smells of his mother, all Beautiful and coconut hair spray.

"We could go and get some Wild Turkey," Nadine was saying, her mouth close to his ear.

Something sent a shiver up Troy's spine and made him push her away. He kept his arms on her shoulders and looked at her face. She looked a million years old. Jenny, Troy thought, had skin that felt like ice, all smooth and cool.

Nadine tilted her head and narrowed her eyes. He could see the jagged orange line under her jaw where her makeup ended.

"What?" she said.

It sounded gruff and indistinct. Like "Wha?" He thought of the way Jenny and her parents spoke. Sometimes he went home and looked up the words they had used. Words like lackadaisical and procrastinate. Words that kids in the college track at school memorized for SAT tests.

"It's that girl, right?" Nadine said. Her whole body seemed to collapse like a quarterback who'd just been sacked. One minute running fast and proud, full of purpose. The next minute, defeated.

Troy could not look Nadine in the eyes and say that it was not Jenny exactly. That instead it was that jagged line of makeup under her chin, and the late shift at the Dixie Cup factory, and the tattoo he knew rested between her shoulder blades, and the sound of that one word, "Wha?" So he just shook his head, as if he had no answers, and started the car, and slowly made his way down the slippery road.

Renata did not think that men and women could be friends. Sex was always there somehow. Yet Tom Harper was not letting on that there was even the slightest hint of an attraction between them. He appeared at her door on his way to work and shoveled the long driveway that led to the road. He always came with jumper cables when she called him from parking lots with a dead battery in Jack's car. He even showed her how to use the cables, bending close to her, his breath coming out in little white puffs as he carefully explained how to hook them to the battery and when to call to the other car to start up.

Then one night he appeared at her door with a new battery for the car. A funny kind of gift that made her feel special. She stood behind him and watched as he replaced the old one. Renata had wanted to hug him when he was through, to press him close to her. But something in his eyes stopped her from doing anything more than smiling and telling him thanks.

Always, after he left her house at night, she'd sit sipping the beer he'd brought, and wonder how he could keep it so platonic. Renata knew she was not at all beautiful, certainly not in the way Libby was. But men had always been attracted to her. She knew she had a certain sensual appeal. Maybe *he* was just not very sexual. Maybe that was why Libby had left him. But then she'd think of his slow smile, or his hand on her back guiding her through crowds on the Sunday trips they sometimes took, and she'd think that surely he felt that current too. The slight charge that passed between them.

"Are you in love with him?" Millie asked one night as they stood at the door waving goodbye to Tom. Her voice sounded almost hopeful.

"Don't be silly," Renata told her.

But that question buzzed around her head all night. It kept her awake. She always gave him food when he left. Mexican casseroles, stews and cakes. Troy had told her that he was a terrible cook. That he served mashed potatoes with lasagna. That all of it came from boxes or cans.

Tonight she'd given him stuffed shells with an extra jar of her homemade tomato sauce. Renata found herself thinking that he needed taking care of. She kept seeing Millie's face, the way it looked when she'd asked, "Are you in love with him?" Of all the things Renata was trying to give Millie—toys and ice skating lessons and Sunday trips to historic places—what she had not ever been able to give her was a family. It was not something Renata had even considered before.

Sometimes, like now, the quiet here could be maddening. It kept her awake. She missed the sounds of sirens, of voices in the street below her, the church bells across the street and the noisy trucks collecting garbage, dropping off newspapers. Renata turned on the light and tried to read. But she found herself wondering again what it would feel like to kiss Tom Harper. How those big hands would move across her body. The sound he would make when he had an orgasm. She imagined him as a slightly clumsy lover. Like a teenager, passionate and a little rough.

She tried to focus on the book opened in her hands. It was by an English writer she had never heard of before. She tried to make sense of the words, but she kept thinking of those big hands of Tom's.

She sat up in bed and said out loud, "This is ridiculous."

Without thinking about it, she got up and went downstairs to the telephone. The house was not insulated well and felt freezing after her warm bed. Renata shook a little as she dialed. From the cold, she told herself, listening to Tom's telephone ringing across town.

Was it her imagination or did his voice sound hopeful too? His hello held a funny kind of excitement and it wasn't until later, after she'd hung up, that Renata realized he was hoping that it was Libby calling, forgetting the time difference, maybe ready to say she'd made a mistake, that she missed him and was coming home.

"Tom," Renata said. "Hi. It's me." Her teeth were chattering. She added, "Renata Handy."

That made him laugh. "Awake at three in the morning too?" he said.

He had a lovely voice. Not especially deep but there was something in it that was charming, she thought.

"Ben Casey's on channel five," he said. "Juvenile diabetes."

"Listen," she said, taking a breath. "Why don't you come here for dinner tomorrow night?"

"Okay," he said.

It was that easy. She stopped shivering. "Good," she said. "Good."


*Renata felt like a different* person. Like a girl in a book who is making her first dinner for a special man. She made a careful list of what to get. Candles and flowers and perfume and new underwear. She would make beef Stroganoff. He liked red meat. He was always ordering hamburgers and steak when they ate out. She bought new sheets. Masculine ones with bold stripes across them in red and dark blue. She bought albums that made her cry— Patsy Cline singing "Crazy," an old Joni Mitchell, the Beatles's *Love Songs*. She let Millie stay overnight at Rosie Rodriguez's, which she'd been begging to do.

While she vacuumed and dusted Renata imagined how perfect this plan was. They were supposed to go to see a matinee of *Beauty and the Beast* tomorrow anyway. Tom would already be here. And they would get in the car and pick up Millie and drive right to the movies together. They would exchange secret looks. In the dark their hands would touch.

Renata looked around the house. Breakfast! she thought suddenly. She put on her coat and drove all the way to Great Barrington for freshly ground coffee and croissants. This must be what it felt like before the prom, she thought. The car filled with the smell of the coffee. The radio was having a Fleetwood Mac hour of music. Renata sang along with Stevie Nicks. When she caught her own reflection in the mirror it surprised her. She had not looked this happy in a long, long time.


*Tom took in everything* with his eyes. Renata saw in that instant that he was not at all childlike, as she sometimes imagined him. He was very much a man. He knew exactly what she had in mind. His face gave away nothing, but she saw the change in the way he studied her seduction scene.

"I always liked Joni Mitchell," he said finally.

Renata felt suddenly embarrassed. Somehow she had made herself believe that he was an innocent, that she had to take charge if anything was going to happen between them. But now, standing here awkwardly in the middle of the living room, with most of the lights out and a table set for two and Joni Mitchell singing "Chelsea Morning," Renata knew that she had been all wrong.

"Smells good," Tom said. He tossed his jacket on the couch. It was an old jean jacket with a plaid lining. She could almost see him wearing that very same one, leaning against the radiator at the end of the hallway in high school, laughing when she walked by.

"Hey," he said. His hand cupped her face, the way she had been hoping for so long now.

Renata closed her eyes and leaned into his hand. It was rough, calloused. A hand that changed mufflers and jump-started cars.

"It's okay," he said.

She opened her eyes and backed away from him, taking his hand in her own for an instant, then letting it go.

"I don't know how to say this," he said. He looked down at the clean floor.

"Don't," she said. "Don't say it."

On her way to the kitchen, she flicked on each light switch that she passed.

Dana *did not bother to* look at the boy who was sitting on the floor in the hallway beside her. She just puffed hard on her cigarette and concentrated on how she was going to get all the way home in the middle of the night.

"I see you here every Saturday night," the boy said. "You're always with a different guy and you're always watching Billy."

That made her look at him. "What's it to you?" she said. When she exhaled she made sure a good portion of the smoke hit him in the face.

He laughed. "Nothing," he said. "I just like to watch. If you want to be a writer you have to observe." His voice sounded tough. He hesitated over the word observe, as if it was new to him.

Dana looked back at the floor. Her date tonight, whose name she was trying to forget, had been careless and fast. Then he had rolled off her, lit up one of her cigarettes, and said, "Thanks. You don't mind sort of, you know, getting out pretty soon, do you? I can't sleep with people I don't know." A part of her wanted to scream at him, to say "Who the fuck do you think you are?," to tear her cigarette out of his mouth. But she was afraid if she tried to talk she would start to cry. Hard. The way she did at home in bed on Sunday nights. So she had waited a few minutes and then she'd wrapped the blanket around her and gotten out of bed and dressed as fast as she could in the dark corner while he sat there and smoked. "Hey," he'd said as she left, "thanks again."

"You ever read Jack Kerouac?" the boy was saying.

Dana sighed. "I don't really feel like talking right now," she said.

"Where's Marc?"

"Who?"

The boy laughed again. "Marc? Your date?"

"Marc, my date, is asleep," she said. "Okay?"

The boy shrugged. "It's okay with me," he said.

She went back to feeling sorry for herself. When she finished her cigarette, she lit another one right away.

"So did you?" the boy said.

She looked right into his face. "What are you, dense?" she said. "I don't want to talk to you."

He pointed to her cigarette. "That'll kill you, you know."

She rolled her eyes. "Who are you? The fucking surgeon general?"

The boy cracked up. He was a real laugher.

"Oh, brother," she moaned. "What a moron."

"Let me guess," he said. "You're upset about something. Does it have to do with Marc?"

"I wouldn't waste my time being upset about Marc. Okay?"

"Okay with me. So why are you sitting out here then?"

"Why are you?"

"I just came out to take a leak and I saw you so I thought I'd say hi. I've been wanting to meet you for a long time, like I said. But I figured you had the hots for Billy and I hate complicated situations since I plan on leaving Massachusetts ASAP."

Dana could not believe this guy. "Number one," she said, "I do not have the hots for Billy. Number two, I am also leaving Massachusetts so I have no intention of getting into anything complicated either, and number three you grin and laugh far too much to ever be a serious anything."

He stuck out his hand for her to shake. "Roald Vachon."

"Roald?"

"Do you want a ride home or do you plan on sitting here all night?"
Dana sighed again. She shook his hand. "I need a ride," she said.
Roald grinned at her. "Let's go."

*Roald reminded her of a* giraffe, all tall and skinny with a long neck and
yellow hair. He had big teeth. In fact, it looked as if he had too many teeth.
And his nose was too long. Despite all this, he was kind of attractive. Maybe
it was that stupid grin. When he grinned, it took over his whole face. He
became all teeth and mouth. But not in a bad way. His eyes were kind of
nice too. Droopy and dark blue, like a lake at night.

His car was a jalopy. Dana had to sit with her feet on the seat because
there was a big hole in the floor on her side.

Roald talked the whole way to her house. He was from Lowell, Massachusetts. "Like Kerouac," he said, all proud as if he had something to do
with that. He was in college on a scholarship. He worked at a Cumberland
Farms most nights until ten. His father was in prison. "Last time I heard,"
Roald said. His mother smoked too much and had emphysema. "Which is
exactly what you'll have if you don't quit now." He had a sister who was in a
nut house and a brother who was also in prison. "Last time I heard," he said
again.

This all sounded familiar to Dana. Not the details. But the way they were
told to her. All rough and proud. The same way she talked about her family,
her life. When they finally got to her road, she let him drive her all the way
to the house instead of being dropped off and walking the rest of the way as
she usually did.

Before she got out of the car, she touched his hand lightly. "You don't
have to talk that way," she told him. She did not put on her tough voice. She
just spoke like herself. "Not to me anyway."

She saw his Adam's apple jump around like a yo-yo in his throat. Then
he nodded.

"Thanks for the lift," she said.

He leaned across the seat. "You want to hang out sometime? Maybe like
next Saturday?"

"Yeah," she said.

"Cool," Roald said.

He waited until she got safely in the house before he drove away.

---

*"Hi. Dana?"* *The voice on* the other end of the phone sounded unfamiliar.

"Yeah?" Dana said.

"You don't know me but I'm a friend of Marc's. Marc Young?"

"Uh-huh."

"I'm actually calling from Dartmouth but I'll be in Williamstown this weekend visiting some friends and Marc told me you might . . . uh . . . show me around."

Dana was sitting at the kitchen table writing a book report on *The Great Gatsby*. She studied her notebook. "Jay Gatsby," she'd written, "spent his whole life trying to get the things it would take for Daisy Buchanan to fall in love with someone like him."

"Marc said you were . . . really nice."

"He did," Dana said.

"Oh, yes. Absolutely. So I thought maybe Saturday night we could, you know, get together."

Dana closed her notebook. She imagined all the boys' faces in front of her own and the image made her queasy. And then something else popped into her mind. That first kiss she ever had, with Mike. When he'd pulled away, there were smudges of green on his face from her witch makeup.

"You asshole," Dana said. "How dare you? How dare Marc give you this number and how dare you call it?"

"But Marc said—"

"I'm not a dating service here, you know," she said.

"I—"

"Goodbye, asshole," Dana said. She hung up fast. She smiled.

L̲ibby waited until Jeremy's mood improved before she showed him her poems. She came home from work one night and found him in her apartment making chicken satay, threading the meat onto bamboo skewers, mixing the peanut sauce. "Jazz Samba" played on the stereo. That was always a good sign. He even gave her a long kiss hello. "How do you put up with me?" he murmured to her. "I'm such a bear."

After dinner, when they'd finished a bottle of wine and Jeremy opened another, Libby decided to do it. She got the poems from her underwear drawer. Her hands shook slightly.

"I want to read you something," she said.

He kissed her neck with those long slow strokes of his. "I had a break-through today," he said. "Act two cuts right to the heart of the matter now. I pulled it off."

"That's great," Libby said. When he leaned into her, the paper wrinkled between them.

"How does it feel to have such a genius for a lover?"

She laughed, tugging at her poems. She would start right off with the sonnet, she decided.

His thumb circled her nipple. Sometimes Libby wished her brain and her body were better connected, that she could tell herself not to grow wet at his touch, or keep her nipple from hardening and tingling like this until after she'd read him the poems. Bodies always betrayed you, she thought, and carefully dropped the papers, wrinkled and creased now, to the floor.

*When can I read your* screenplay?" Libby asked him.

It was very late. Jeremy was in a much better mood, better than she'd seen him in a long time. That meant he felt sexier, and their lovemaking went on longer. His moods were starting to bother her. Even now, lying beside him and feeling sexually satisfied, Libby found herself remembering Tom almost fondly.

Jeremy yawned and stretched. "When it's done," he said. That was always his answer.

"You know," Libby began, "this acting thing isn't quite working out. I mean, I did get that floor wax commercial . . ." She swallowed hard, re-membering, then continued, "But I think I might get back to my poetry."

Jeremy didn't say anything. Even in the dark she could see him staring straight ahead. For a moment she was afraid he had fallen asleep and she nudged him with her elbow.

"Poetry," he said, his voice flat.

Libby leaned over and turned on the light.

"God," Jeremy said, "I hate when you do that. Just turn on the light that way."

"My husband could sleep with the overhead light on. I'd stay up and read and it never even bothered him."

"Ah!" Jeremy said, "the mechanic. Or was he a saint?"

Libby pulled the sheet around her, covering herself. Jeremy had told her that Kathleen wore white cotton gloves all the time, even to bed. Harpists, he'd told her, have to be very careful about their hands. At the time, she had shuddered, remembering Tom's grease-covered hands. The contrast had seemed important. But now she almost missed them, and could remember quite clearly the way they gripped a football or held a bat, the way they felt the first time he touched her breasts.

"Libby?" Jeremy was saying.

Her name always sounded funny coming from his mouth.

"If it says Libby Libby Libby on the label label label you will like it like it like it on your table table table," Libby sang.

"What?"

"It was a theme song for canned fruit or something. Libby. Everyone in school used to tease me with it."

He touched her hair softly. "My little small-town girl. The things you've endured."

"It was funny," she said. "When they did that. It was like my name was special or something."

"Having fruit cocktail named after you?" Jeremy laughed.

She took a deep breath. "Anyway, I thought maybe I could read you one of these. A sonnet I wrote."

He agreed, reluctantly, to listen.

In an oral presentation, she knew, you should lower your voice, articulate, and read ten times slower than you think you should. Libby did. She read softly and slowly, careful to stress her iambic pentameter. She did not look up until she was finished.

"This is a joke, right?" Jeremy said.

She did not blink, afraid that if she did tears would start to come.

"Who really wrote that? Someone from Von's? Or that teenage daughter of yours?"

Libby rolled the poem into a ball and threw it, basketball style, across the room. "Yes," she said. "Dana wrote it. She actually thought it was good."

Jeremy laughed. "Save the poor darling. Get her out of Massachusetts and away from the mechanic fast."

Quickly, Libby turned off the light.

"For a minute," Jeremy said, "I thought you were serious."

She closed her eyes. Maple, she said to herself. Maple, birch, pine, and elm.

# Spring

*Spring in New England meant* rain and mud. Renata started to think of it as monsoon season. There were leaks in all the rooms. The house was damp and began to smell like a cellar. But she reminded herself how she used to hate having to walk all those blocks to the subway in the rain in the city. This is better, she kept telling herself.

And then Millie started to lose her balance and drop things again.

And Renata blamed the cold night air. The constant rain. How Millie came home from school wet every day. How one night the ceiling in her room had leaked and she'd slept the entire night on wet sheets.

Renata called the school.

"Millie has the flu," she told the teacher. "I guess it's going around?"

"No," the teacher told her. "Everyone's fine."

She went into Millie's room and sat beside her on the bed. "It's the same thing everyone's got, honey."

It was amazing how quickly it came back. In twenty-four hours her skin had grown pale and warm. Her eyes seemed to shrink into her skull. Her new growth of hair, soft and downy, seemed to get sparser. Renata stroked her daughter's head. Wasn't it just a few days ago she was admiring Millie's hair? Commenting on how the color was even more vivid than before? Shinier and healthier?

"Too bad we weren't ducks," Renata said. "Then we'd love this weather, right? And no one would get sick from it."

"Mama," Millie said, "people are people and ducks are ducks."

"Well, I know that. It was just a game. Just a silly game."

When Millie fell back asleep, Renata went to the kitchen and made chicken soup. She cut carrots and celery. She made homemade stock. Soup makes people better, she told herself. Chicken soup cures everything.

The next day, when Millie said her head hurt bad, Renata called the school again.

"Millie won't be in today," she said. A chant had started in her head—the tumor is gone, the tumor is gone, the tumor is gone.

"I hope she feels better, Mrs. Handy," the teacher said. Her voice was sympathetic. "Millie's such a frail thing—"

Renata hung up the phone before the woman finished her sentence. Millie is not frail, Renata thought.

Out loud she said, "Frail? Ha!" Millie could run very fast. She could dance like John Travolta in *Saturday Night Fever*. Exactly. And she didn't even get out of breath. Why, she ran up and down the stairs all the time. She was not frail. She just had the flu. Who wouldn't get the flu with weather like this?

Renata sank into a chair, suddenly exhausted. She leaned her head back and closed her eyes. She could feel the chair's broken springs pressing into her back and neck. She moved against them, returning their pressure until they felt more than uncomfortable, until they actually hurt. Renata let out a gasp, not of pain but of realization. She could not pretend. Her little girl had a tumor in her head.

L_ately *Tom liked being home* alone. He could play his old scratchy records without anyone complaining. He could sing along with them, with Frank Sinatra and Mel Tormé, the songs that made Libby roll her eyes whenever she heard them. The songs that made Dana and Troy groan. He could dance and sing in his underwear and pretend he was with a beautiful woman. A stranger. He'd sing "Strangers in the Night" in her ear. He'd hold her close. Spin her around a few times.

He knew he was a terrible dancer. But alone like this, with his invisible partner, he felt like Fred Astaire. There was something to be said for time to yourself.

"Doobie doo doo doo," he sang, imagining long hair, a small waist. He twirled her. He pulled her back toward him.

When the phone rang, he considered not answering it. Boys were always calling Dana. Different boys all the time. Then there was Troy's old girlfriend who was always calling and hanging up. Why bother answering the phone?

But it just kept ringing and ringing. There was always the hope that it would be Libby. He pretended the feeling wasn't hope. He called it dread. But every single time he picked up the telephone his breath caught and there would be a split second before the person spoke when Tom thought, Please. Be her.

"Hello?" he said. He told himself the feeling was dread. He did not want her back, he told himself. She had walked out on him and never even left him a note.

When he heard Renata's voice he told himself he was happy, not disappointed.

Renata was not making sense. Behind her he heard the static and voices of people being paged.

"Whoa," he said, feeling conspicuous in just his Jockey shorts. "Where are you? What's going on?"

"Millie," she said, her voice flat and distant. "She's in the hospital in Albany. I'm calling from there."

"I'm on my way," he said. "Hold on."


*You think you can make* your child safe," Renata told him. "But school buses run off the road. Crazy men shoot up people eating hamburgers. Just last year, in New York, a tornado hit an elementary school and killed children." She looked at him, her eyes wide. "A tornado," she said. "In New York."

Tom nodded. He really wanted a cup of coffee, but he didn't want to leave Renata. This was too bad to leave her even for a minute. Millie had gone into convulsions. She was in intensive care.

"Every day," Renata was saying, "in New York City, children are killed by stray bullets. Asleep in their beds, or playing on the swings. And a bullet hits them and kills them. Just like that."

Tom nodded again. He wished the doctor would come and talk to them. Outside, he heard a clap of thunder.

"When Millie was first born," Renata said, "this woman who lived down the hall from me had a baby just a little bit older. The woman's name was Lakeisha and her daughter was named Krystal, after this character on *Dynasty*. And Lakeisha and I would take the babies to Tompkins Square Park in their strollers, you know. And we'd sit there and talk about how much they ate and if they slept through the night. Things like that. So one morning I dress Millie and I go and knock on Lakeisha's door and see if she wants to take Krystal to the park and she opens the door and says right point-blank, 'Renata, my Krystal's dead. She's gone.' And I thought I'd misunderstood. I said, 'Pardon me?' like I was in charm school or something. 'My Krystal,' she said. 'My little baby girl. She's dead.' " Renata said, "SIDS."

"Uh-huh."

"Crib death. She nursed her and put her down for her nap and next thing she knew she was dead. I mean, how much safer can a baby be? And it still didn't matter."

A doctor came in finally. He looked exhausted. He wore a dingy blue coat and his eyes were bloodshot.

"We're doing an MRI," he said.

Tom wished the guy would look at them. Make eye contact.

"An MRI?" Tom said.

The doctor glanced at him with his red eyes. "You the father?"

"No."

"Is the father here?"

"I'm all she's got," Renata said.

The doctor glanced up again, then looked back down. "Magnetic resonance imaging scan," he said. "MRI." He started to leave.

"The big doughnut," Renata said. She did not look at Tom or the doctor. And then, as if she was surprised that she'd talked out loud she did look up at them, her eyes red-rimmed and puffy, and said, "That's what Millie called it last time. The big metal doughnut."

*By the time they left* the hospital, it was raining hard. Tom had forgotten to turn off the stereo so when they got to his house, Sinatra was singing "Witchcraft" at the top of his lungs. He didn't turn it off. Instead, he poured Renata a big glass of scotch.

She was staring straight ahead. She did not even have a coat with her, so he had wrapped his around her shoulders. But they were both drenched.

"Drink this," he told her. "And then you'll take a hot shower and try to sleep."

She emptied the glass in three big swallows.

"She has something real bad," Tom said. "Cancer or something?"

Renata didn't answer him.

So he led her gently up the stairs. Dana and Troy were on the senior class trip to Boston and wouldn't be back until Sunday night. He had imagined a weekend of Sinatra and working on an old T-Bird at the garage.

But now he was wishing the kids were home so he could see them, see that they were all right.

He handed Renata a clean towel, turned on the shower for her. But she didn't move.

This is shock, he thought.

And carefully he undressed her. Her blouse was buttoned crooked, as if she'd gotten dressed in a big hurry. No bra. No panties. No jewelry. No socks. Just old jeans and a pair of boots. Your kid goes into convulsions, you know she's got cancer or something, and you get her to the hospital as fast as you can, he thought. Harp kept that idea in his mind so he wouldn't think of the other, more obvious thing—the way Renata looked standing there naked like this. He adjusted the water temperature and helped her into the shower.

"We run out of hot water fast here," he said, although he knew she wasn't registering anything he said. "It's a very temperamental heater."

He shivered in his wet clothes.

"The hell with it," he said, and undressed down to his underwear then got right in the shower with Renata.

Even with the water streaming over her, he could tell she was crying.

"Hey," he said.

Her shoulders and chest started to heave, big jerky motions that broke his heart.

"She could die," Renata said.

"No," he said. "No."

But of course she could. He had known all along that something was wrong with Millie. And now that's what the doctor had been trying to say. It's why he couldn't look them in the eye.

Tom wrapped Renata in a towel, and quickly dried himself off. He got the bottle of scotch and brought it into bed with them.

"Little kids shouldn't die," he said.

He put his jeans on, and a sweatshirt, and got under the covers with her. She didn't bother with a glass. She drank right from the bottle.

"Did I tell you about this school in New York?" Renata said. Her words were slurred slightly. "Upstate? Hit by a tornado. All these little children were killed."

"I know," he said.

She rested her head on his chest, and that's exactly how they fell asleep.

At some point in the night she whispered to him, "Don't leave me alone. Please."

And he whispered back, "I won't."

"I just think *black walls* are creepy," Dana said.

"Not just black," Caitlin said. "Black with like Day-Glo painted stuff and a black light. It'll be cool."

They both looked at the clock beside Caitlin's bed, and then at each other.

"Three more minutes," Dana said. She squeezed Caitlin's hand.

Caitlin nodded. "We could paint cartoon characters and stuff."

"Sure," Dana said. "Now I see what you mean."

They kept holding hands, waiting. In the bathroom, right down the hall, on the counter near the sink, sat a tube of Caitlin's urine mixed with some chemical from an early pregnancy test kit. If she was pregnant, their lives, their plans were over. No New York, no great careers, no nothing.

"Ninety seconds," Dana said, and she squeezed Caitlin's hand again.

"I could get an abortion," Caitlin said.

"Five minutes ago you said you couldn't."

"I couldn't."

Dana tried to picture Caitlin married to Kevin, having a baby with him, living in some dumpy house in Holly with pantyhose drying over the shower rod and empty beer cans everywhere. She shuddered.

"You don't even know how to cook or anything," she said.

Caitlin rolled her eyes. "You can buy premade stuff. Anybody can figure out macaroni and cheese or tuna casserole. Cooking is beside the point."

"I know." In New York, they were going to have Chinese food delivered, the way people in movies always did. Handsome men would take them to fancy restaurants. At sunrise they would eat bacon and eggs in diners, still dressed in their evening clothes. "Anybody can read directions," Dana said.

"I think it's time," Caitlin said. "You go and look."

Dana walked as slow as she could to the bathroom. She crossed her fingers. She thought about how Caitlin's period was two weeks late. Caitlin had read from a book called *What to Expect When You're Expecting*. "Nausea. Vomiting. Food cravings." Last night, after work, she'd made Dana examine her breasts for telltale signs—darkened nipples, swollen veins. But they looked as small and flat as ever.

Our lives are over, Dana had thought.

But when Caitlin said almost those exact words, Dana had laughed. "Don't be so dramatic," she'd told her.

She could not imagine a baby inside Caitlin. If it was her, she'd get rid of it without blinking an eye. She did not want a preppy kid with nice teeth smiling back at her the rest of her life, reminding her every minute of all those nights with all those boys. She shuddered thinking about it.

"Why aren't you saying anything?" Caitlin called to her.

"I didn't look yet," Dana said. Then she walked into the bathroom and took a breath.

"It's fine!" she yelled. "You're fine!"

To herself she said, soft and fast, Thank you thank you thank you thank you.

Caitlin came running down the hall, screaming as loud as she could.

Dana held the tube out to her. "No brown ring. No baby."

Caitlin didn't even bother to look. Instead she sang "New York, New York" real loud.

Dana threw her arm around her friend's shoulders and together, like two girls auditioning for the Rockettes, they kicked their legs high, out of sync and off beat.

*t was spring. For the* first time in months, Tom felt, finally, alive. His body and mind tingled constantly and that fog he'd been walking around in finally lifted. If someone had told him that someday he would have Renata Handy move into his house, that she would be his lover, he would have laughed. It would have seemed like the funniest thing in the world. Yet here it was, happening to him and not funny at all. I'll just stay one more night, Renata kept saying, until now her clothes were hanging where Libby's used to be, her car was parked in the driveway, and her alarm clock sat glowing at him from the night table.

Tom did not love Renata. This was an entirely new feeling for him, almost primal. He was startled to see her in his bedroom sometimes, dressing for work or to visit Millie in the hospital. Sometimes he felt guilty as he watched her. His heart would race and his mouth would go dry. She needs a place to stay, he'd tell himself. She needs to be around people until Millie is better. But he knew those were just excuses. The truth was, he liked having her here. He liked the sense of feeling that fog lift away.

Sometimes, as he lay beside Renata, both of them sweaty and worn from their lovemaking, Tom felt as if that foggy feeling had descended on him long before Libby ever left. It sounds to me, Renata told him, like you settled for a lot less than you should have.

And "settled" described his life to this point perfectly. His routine at work, with Libby, everything had a downward feeling when he looked back at those days. Even his weight had settled around his middle. But Renata changed everything. He had never felt so sensual with someone. When he was away from her, at the garage, he could not concentrate on mufflers or transmissions. He could only think of the way her skin felt, of her long fingers on his back, her strong legs around him. She was a noisy lover, and this still startled and excited him. I feel like I'm a teenager, he told her. Like I'm in high school.

In one week, Millie would be home from the hospital. This thing she had, this neuroblastoma, was hard to treat. No one could agree on what was best. But since the radiation hadn't worked, the doctors had decided to operate and do still more radiation. The surgery had been tricky, but Millie had pulled through. Her head looked like a road map and she'd lost most of the use of her right arm and leg. "If we got it all this time," the doctor had said, "that's a small price to pay."

"Of course you got it all," Renata had told him.

Now she spent her days getting a room ready for her. She painted the walls a bright yellow. She had a hospital bed delivered. She moved in toys and books from the other house, driving back and forth every day. Tom would come home during lunch and find Renata rearranging things again. Or cooking them all dinner. Now, when he opened the door and walked into his house, it smelled like fresh paint, like spices, like the flowers Renata placed in jars and bottles everywhere. It smelled, he thought, like a home.

*"I don't get it,"* Renata said, frowning. Sometimes when she frowned she looked like a completely different person. Someone with worries Tom could never even begin to understand.

Tom cleared his throat and looked down at the map spread before them on the kitchen table. It was one of his favorites, a map of the eastern seaboard made before Route 95 had been built. The route from Maine to Florida was carefully traced in dark green ink, small Xs marking points of interest or places to stay the night. In a masculine penmanship, written in the sea near Savannah there was this notation: "Ma's—grits, ham, biscuits, gravy, 99 cents."

"Well," Tom said finally, feeling Renata waiting for him to respond, "I collect them. Maps," he added, even though that was obvious.

Renata's long index finger traced the road to Florida. "So," she said, "you took this trip?"

Tom sighed. He tried not to remember the way Libby used to love to pore over maps with him. How her cheeks would flush with the idea of where they led. Think of the things she *didn't* do, he reminded himself. Think of how good this house smells right now.

"I know it's crazy," he said. Slowly, carefully, making sure all the creases matched up exactly, Tom began to fold the map. "Maybe I missed my calling," he said. He forced a smile, feeling its phoniness all over his face. "Maybe I should have been a mapmaker."

Renata placed her hand over his, the old map dangling half folded between them. "Cartographer," she said. "That's what it's called."

"Jesus, Renata," he said, pulling his hand free, "I know that."

He turned away from her. The map was a neat rectangle in his hand now. Folded like that, no one would guess the secrets it held, the neat lines that led to Savannah and beyond, the small roads, the bridges, the Xs and 99 cent breakfast at Ma's. Libby used to memorize routes, the names of cities and towns along the way.

Tom figured that when she left Holly, she had not needed to consult a map. She had her route planned long ago, with alternates and scenic diversions. She knew, from all his old maps and triple A Triptiks customers had brought him, what was under construction, where there were fast-food restaurants and areas of interest, and where, at night, weary from the day's driving, she could check in somewhere with a pool and color TV and sleep until the next morning when it was time to move on again.

Behind him, Renata began to hum a song he could not identify, its melody foreign and unfamiliar.

R̦oald had practically become Dana's best friend. They talked on the phone constantly. They went to the movies every Friday and Saturday night.

To foreign films with subtitles. To the big multiplex in Pittsfield. They argued about them afterward. He gave her lists of movies to watch at home on the VCR. You, Roald had told her, are a neophyte.

They read books too, exchanging them back and forth. He gave her lists of those too, and Dana spent time after school in the library, reading. She even started reading the encyclopedia, beginning at A. She also wrote down odd facts that she thought would be good in conversations in New York. Did you know that the cow has seven stomachs? she would say to Roald. Did you know that James Madison was the shortest U.S. president? That Carl Sandburg called Chicago the hog butcher for the world? What are you doing? he asked her. Trying out for *Jeopardy!* or something?

Now, on the telephone late Wednesday night, Dana told Roald, "My father is having an affair with Renata Handy. She is now our resident Amazon and weirdo."

"How do you know it's an affair?" he asked her.

"They are upstairs doing it right now. They do it constantly. That's how I know."

"Ah," Roald said. "It."

"Yes, it," Dana said. Every night she heard the bedsprings creaking. Every morning her father walked into the kitchen grinning. Renata grinned a lot too.

"When did this start?" Roald said.

"It's totally gross."

"I thought you claimed sex was amazing."

"If you saw Renata Handy you'd understand. She's like six feet tall and fat." Then she added softly, "My mother is beautiful. I don't see how he could do this."

"Horniness," Roald told her. "It makes for strange bedfellows."

"I guess," she said. Above her, the bedsprings quickened. June, she reminded herself, was only ten weeks away.

*Tom picked up the telephone* and called the operator.

"I need the area code for California," he said. He whispered when he spoke. Upstairs, Renata was sound asleep.

The operator's voice was kind. "Which city?" she said. "They have a lot of area codes."

"Right. Of course." He swallowed hard. "Los Angeles."

"Two-one-three," she said. "Have a good night now."

His fingers trembled slightly as he dialed the phone.

This operator was not as patient.

"There is no Libby Harper in L.A., sir."

"But there has to be." What was it that women who lived alone did? he thought suddenly. "L. Harper," he said. "Try just the initial L."

"There is no L. Harper either, sir," she said.

"There has to be," he said again. But the operator had hung up.

Tom did not put the receiver down. He heard the dial tone, and then a loud beeping. It was like she'd disappeared, he thought. He could try other cities. San Francisco. New York. Where else did actresses go? Burt Reynolds had some kind of theater in Florida somewhere, didn't he? With computers couldn't they somehow centralize all these operators so he wouldn't have to keep calling for area codes of every city and then redialing each time?

Then Tom realized something.

He dialed information in Los Angeles again.

"What city?" the operator said. It was a man this time.

"Los Angeles," Tom said. Despite the beer, his mouth suddenly felt very dry. "Libby Holliday."

"Hold for the number," the man told him.

A computerized voice came on and told him where he could reach his wife. He laughed. Wife. She was not even using her married name anymore. Libby Holliday, he whispered. And the smiling housewife waxing the floor disappeared. Instead he saw the young blond girl who sat in front of him in English class, who begged him to drive his car faster, faster, whose charm bracelet left small imprints on his naked arms—a ballet shoe, a sweet sixteen, a small silver car.

He did not dial the number. He repeated it to himself all the way back upstairs to bed. Renata was awake. She tossed the covers off and opened her arms, as if she were waiting for him.

I t was funny how *Libby* thought a person shouldn't just walk away from a relationship without an explanation. She knew, of course, that she had walked away from her entire family without telling them why. But she felt they understood, that in all the years of her unhappiness they had almost come to expect her to leave someday.

She did not know why Jeremy had stopped calling her. And she thought she deserved an explanation. He did not return her calls. She wrote him a letter, made sure it was cheerful and upbeat, and signed it "Warmest regards" so as not to seem pushy. He still didn't respond.

Her friend Janice said, "Spring, and a man's fancy turns to love."

"Is that supposed to make me feel better?" Libby said.

Janice only shrugged.

It didn't seem like spring to Libby. She was used to the changes that came in New England—the sudden burst of warm air, the rainy nights, the bits of bright green appearing in unexpected places. Here, there was just more of the same. People were always bragging about the weather, but Libby found it dull and uninspired.

All those years she'd imagined coming West, she had pictured vivid sunsets over the Pacific, limousines taking her everywhere, a sense of excitement that never went away. She had found none of that. In Holly, she had a place. People knew her. Sue rolled her eyes at Libby's big schemes. Dana and Troy shied away from her altogether and Tom loved her, no matter what. Foreign films and thick books with small print didn't take the place of any of those things.

Sometimes she saw herself on television, mopping that floor, the spray of stars shooting from it. She had it on video, but catching it by accident between *Jeopardy!* and *Wheel of Fortune* was even better. There she was, spilling into people's homes across the country. But even that moment was short-lived. Eventually she had to go back to Von's or write a letter to movie theater owners protesting the price hike. Eventually she had to face herself.

When Ashley got a regular role on a new sitcom and Heather got a replacement part on a soap, Libby quit acting class. Right away two new young girls with gobs of hair and tight black clothes replaced them. Libby had had enough. Now, without acting class and Jeremy, her nights stretched before her endlessly.

She started to listen to late-night talk radio. She especially liked this woman, Doctor Bobbi. Her voice was like maple syrup, soothing and sweet. At the end of each phone call, Doctor Bobbi always said, "Hang in there, babe. Someone out here loves ya." No matter how bad the situation, she said that. It made Libby think of Tom. Through all these years, that had always been his message to her. She had hardly appreciated it.

One night, after calling Jeremy every hour and hanging up when his machine picked up, Libby called Doctor Bobbi. She was put on hold. On the radio, while she waited, a woman was talking about how her mother had left her and her sister when they were very small, and now they wanted to go and find her.

"I heard Sally Jessy will do that for you," the woman said. "Hire a detective. Everything." She had a slight speech impediment, a lisp, that made her sound even more pathetic.

"The point is," Doctor Bobbi was saying, "do you really want to confront this woman who left you twenty-five years ago? Who did the most heinous thing a mother can? Desertion? Abandonment?"

The caller was crying now. Libby started to cry too. She had done that to her children. And Doctor Bobbi was saying it was the worst possible thing. She tried to imagine this woman's mother. Perhaps she had felt that she would die if she didn't leave too. No one seemed to care about that. Here was the daughter now, grown up, seemingly all right except for this little lisp.

A voice clicked onto the phone. "Your call is up next."

Libby hung up. Her hands were trembling. She tried to picture Troy, with all those awful tattoos and his red-rimmed eyes. There had been a time when they were close. He used to make her laugh when no one else could. The image she got, though, was of him as a newborn, all red-faced and wrinkled. Dana had come into the world kicking and screaming, but Troy had been calm. He had looked her right in the eye.

For an instant, she thought about calling home. Just to see how everyone was doing. And just as she thought that, the phone rang, startling her. She half expected it to be Troy on the other end, as if they had communicated by mental telepathy.

Libby was surprised to hear Sue's voice instead. She glanced at the clock. It was after midnight in Massachusetts. Something must be terribly wrong. The face of the teenage Troy came to her then, loomed right in front of her. Didn't mothers have omens like this? As she had sat remembering him as a baby, something bad was happening to him. She knew he drank too much, took who knew what kind of drugs. He was always getting into trouble, a bad boy, the kind she avoided when she was a teenager.

But Sue was talking about something else and it took Libby a few minutes to understand.

"Wait," she said, calming down. "Are you talking about that big old weirdo Renata Handy? The one from school?"

"Yes!" Sue said, frustrated. "Renata Handy has moved into your house. She's living with Harp."

Libby couldn't catch her breath. "But he loves me," she managed to say.

"They're having an affair," Sue said. "He shows up all over town with her and her daughter."

"Renata Handy and her daughter are living in my house?" Libby said.

"And there's something wrong with the kid. Leukemia or something." Sue took a drag on a cigarette, exhaled long and slow. "Renata is still as big as a house too. With those gypsy clothes. She told Dee-Dee that her husband died in the gulf war but I doubt it. I mean, really."

"How could he do this to me?" Libby said, more to herself than to Sue.

"Libby, don't get mad or anything, but you did leave him. The guy's been a mess. You should see how he looked, unkempt, all unshaven and drawn. Like a zombie. Like a guy with a broken heart."

"Thanks for telling me," Libby said. She didn't know why, but suddenly she was angry at Sue. "As if I didn't know he was upset." She wondered if Sue would betray her too, start hanging around with Renata, double date with them.

"I'm sorry," Sue was saying. "I thought you should know. If you ever thought about coming back, you know, maybe this would be a good time."

"I'm not coming back," Libby said. "I have a life here, you know."

"Yeah, well. Good night, then."

Libby hung up the phone. Once, back in school, Renata had drawn her a picture, like a Peter Max one, all psychedelic swirls, of a boy and girl growing out of a flower. "It's you and Tom," she'd said, in that stoned way she used to talk. Libby had not known what to do with it—two naked people popping out of a lily, their hair all orange and purple. She had laughed, shown it to everyone so they would laugh too. Then she'd thrown it away.

Doctor Bobbi was saying, "Good night, Los Angeles. Hang in there and remember, someone out here loves ya."

*All Libby could think about* was Harp making love to Renata Handy. It disgusted her. Once she even got up the courage to call home, but when a little girl answered the phone she hung up. Janice didn't understand what all the fuss was about. "Renata Handy is ugly," Libby told her. "And weird." But Janice still didn't get it.

She tried to make Libby feel better anyway. She set her up on a few blind dates and came over to watch *L.A. Law*. But nothing helped. Just when she'd start to relax, the sight of the two of them together would slap

Libby in the face again. She called Sue two or three times a week. "Are they still together?" she demanded. "Yes," Sue told her. "Yes."

Janice got tickets to the ballet. "It'll make you feel better," she said. "It's *Giselle,* where all abandoned women get their revenge."

"I was not abandoned," Libby told her. But she went along anyway.

The ballet only made her more depressed—all those lovely young ballerinas, leaping high into the air. She used to hope that Dana would become a ballerina. But Dana always did the exact opposite of what Libby wanted. The way she dressed and cut her hair, it was almost as if she wanted Libby to dislike her.

At intermission Libby said she wanted to go home.

"But you'll miss their revenge," Janice said.

Janice, with her hair dyed a strange flat black and her dark red lipstick, looked like a creepy stranger to Libby. Glancing around the crowded lobby, everyone suddenly seemed like a creepy stranger, and Libby yearned for something familiar—her back yard, the road leading to her house, the sound of Tom's voice.

Her eyes settled then on a familiar face, Fu Manchu mustache, shaggy brown hair. Jeremy. His arm held firmly to the waist of a woman with ripples of long red hair. She wore black evening gloves and Libby knew it was his wife, Kathleen.

"I've got to get out of here," Libby said. She thought if she didn't leave this minute, she would get sick, throw up right here during the intermission of *Giselle.*

Janice was saying something Libby could not understand, as if she was speaking a foreign language. Libby pushed past the crowd of people, and out the door, where she stood gobbling the dirty air for a very long time.

*Jeremy was not hard to find.* All she had to do was call the production company he sometimes worked for to find out that he was building a fake cantina in the desert for a Mexican restaurant commercial. Libby drove the two hours to the site, then sat in the car and watched as the crew finished building the cantina—fake adobe walls all cracked and stained brown, tiled floors and terra cotta tables. Actresses in off-the-shoulder peasant blouses and brightly colored ruffled skirts pretended to serve margaritas to other actors pretending to eat dinner and have fun. All an illusion.

Libby saw Jeremy standing off to the side, drinking a soda and watching. He looked like everyone else, a workman in a T-shirt and jeans, not at all like a brilliant screenwriter, which Libby doubted he even was. She got out of the car and made her way toward him, the sun hot on her neck and shoulders.

"Hello," she said.

He didn't seem surprised to see her there, in the middle of the desert at a fake cantina.

"So this is what you do," Libby said, motioning toward the set.

A muscle in his jaw twitched at that.

"You could have told me you'd gone back to Kathleen," she said. "A gentleman would have told me."

He finally looked at her full in the face. "I didn't really have anything to say. After a while you just bored me."

He'd said that to hurt her, she knew. And it worked.

Jeremy pointed to the fake cantina. "All make-believe. Tricks. Out here, there are tricks for everything. To make turkey look moist and brown and the cherries in pie shine." He turned back to her. "You don't belong out here, Miss Libby Holliday. You belong at home baking cakes and watching *I Dream of Jeannie* with your mechanic husband."

"*I Dream of Jeannie* hasn't been on in years," she said. "And I think you know that. Everyone knows that."

"Maybe." He touched her cheek for an instant. "Go back home to Connecticut."

"It's Massachusetts," she said.

"Okay."

"At least there things are exactly how they seem. People know where they stand."

"Okay," he said again.

Libby made her way back across the hot sand. She wished she hadn't worn high-heeled sandals, they made the going tough. But she wouldn't stop to take them off until she was back in her car. Then she sat and watched until they were finished shooting and the crew tore the whole thing down, until the desert grew cold and there was nothing left standing.

"Trust me," Jenny said. "I'll quiz you every night and you'll practice in this book and it'll be a breeze."

She smiled that glorious smile of hers. Huge orthodontist bills, Jenny had told him once.

"Which first?" she was asking him now. "Math or English?"

"You know," Troy said slowly, "some experts think SATs are dumb."

She laughed. "What experts?"

He tried to remember. Finally he shrugged. "I don't know. I saw it on *60 Minutes.*"

"You nut," Jenny said. She squeezed his hand, gave him a soft quick kiss on the cheek. "They mean for poor children. And it's IQ tests, not SATs."

"I thought—"

"Besides," she said, "for the schools you'll be applying to you won't even need to score very high."

He wanted to tell her that he didn't want to go to any school. He wanted to graduate and work with his father and maybe in a few years build a house. What he liked to read were carpentry magazines. To look at pictures of floor plans and half-built homes, to read about the choices of wood you could use, to study the way rooms open onto each other. Troy already had ideas for the house he would build. There would be skylights and a big stone wall that separated the living room and the bedroom, so there could be a fireplace in both rooms. And he wanted a big kitchen with one of those islands in the middle.

"Even if you go to the community college for a year," Jenny said, "you can always transfer. Maybe you could even go to a school near me."

"In Michigan? Somewhere like that?"

"Sure," she said. "Why not?"

Troy studied her perfect face. The smooth white skin. The blue eyes and little turned-up nose.

"You're so beautiful," he said. His voice was almost a whisper. He kissed her, but she pulled away, smiling.

"First we study for the SATs," she said. "Being the world's best kisser will not get you into college."

Troy nodded. He wondered if she really thought he was the world's best kisser. He wondered if she liked skylights in a house, and big fireplaces with pillows in front of them.

"I remember now," he said. "It was like, how can a test ask for a word that means the same thing—"

"A synonym," Jenny said.

"—the same thing as sofa when the answer is davenport. No one's heard of a davenport. I mean, who says davenport? Right?"

She didn't answer him. She was too busy writing something in the practice book. Finally she looked up at him.

"Ready?" Jenny said.

"The four food groups," Renata said as she put dinner on the table.

"Whoopee," Dana said.

"If you eat from the four food groups every day," Renata continued, "you'll stay strong and healthy."

The sign they'd hung for Millie was still in the doorway. WELCOME HOME. And, Dana thought, Renata and Millie had really made themselves right at home. Everyone was acting like they were one big happy family when really, they all knew the real truth. They were a bunch of strangers pretending.

Renata even tried to act as if she was her mother all of a sudden. She came into Dana's room to say good night. She asked her about school and how Caitlin was doing and if there were any boys she liked. But Dana refused to play along. She just kept reading and planning her move to New York City.

"I might take the SATs," Troy said.

Renata smiled. "That's great."

Dana groaned. She wanted to tell this woman she did a bad June Cleaver act. Instead she got up. "Great dinner, Mom," she said in her best sarcastic voice.

Her father looked at her all sad, as if she was breaking his heart. "Dana," he said.

"No," Renata said. "It's all right."

It was Millie who giggled. "She's not your mother," she said.

Dana looked right at Renata. "No kidding," she said.

*"They think they're the* Brady Bunch," Dana told Roald.

They were at a restaurant near the college, eating hamburgers and drinking beer.

"All I know is in two months I will never have to deal with any of them again," she said.

"How long do I have to wait for the mayonnaise?" he said. "Everything's getting cold." Roald had a disgusting habit of putting mayonnaise on his french fries. Lots of mayonnaise.

"Why don't you just use ketchup like everybody else?"

"Because," Roald said, dragging each word out, "I am not like everybody else. And neither are you. But, you start thinking like that and you'll end up right here in Massachusetts for the rest of your life. Remember that."

The waitress slid a jar of mayonnaise across their table and kept on walking.

"Thanks," Roald called after her. "That's what I like. Service with a smile."

Dana opened the jar, and spooned heaps of mayonnaise all over her french fries.

"That's right," Roald said. "Just like in Brussels."

*"Mais bien sûr,"* Dana said. She stared out the window, onto the dark street. Sitting here, at night like this, she could almost imagine she was already there. She squinted her eyes, trying to see the distant city lights.

*All Millie did was sleep.* Renata told Troy not to worry, that it was from the trauma of that long surgery. Sometimes he babysat for her so Renata and his father could go to a movie or something. He knew that Dana hated the living arrangement they had, but he loved it. It was the first time since his mother had left that it felt good to stay home. Sometimes he even reminded himself that he never stayed home before his mother left. That maybe this was the first time ever that it felt good.

Dana closed herself up in her room all the time, reading weird books or talking on the phone to this new friend of hers, Roald. If Troy tried to even talk to her, she stared at him all hard and cold. She'd hung a map of New York City on her wall, and circled different sections in red. But when he asked her what the circles were for, she ignored him and just kept reading *Slaughterhouse Five.* She did manage to tell him how far behind he was. "On what?" he'd said. "Vonnegut. Kafka. Everything." "Uh-huh," Troy had said, and left her room.

He was happy to spend nights, as he was doing right now, with Millie sleeping upstairs and Renata and his father at the movies. He told Jenny he'd be studying those SAT review books she'd given him. But really he was revising the plans for his house. Every now and then he went upstairs and stood in the doorway and watched Millie breathe. He liked the rise and fall of her chest. It made him believe it would never stop, that she would grow up and be fine someday in the future.

That's what he was doing when the doorbell rang. Watching Millie breathe and imagining her as a teenager, with long chestnut hair and beautiful white teeth.

He heard someone come in the back door and call hello. Troy watched for two more breaths before he went downstairs. Caitlin was standing in the living room, studying his drawings. She was all dressed in black, a long sweater with tights and flat shoes that made her look like a kid.

"Dana's not here," Troy said. He took the drawings from her right away.

"As usual," Caitlin said. She sat on the couch, tucking her legs up underneath her. "Roald again?"

She pronounced his name real loud and fake and Troy laughed. He went and sat beside her. "Yeah. Roald again," he said.

"I think he's gay," Caitlin said.

"They're both weird," Troy told her. "No offense."

"Are you kidding? I never even talk to her anymore. And when I do, I don't even understand what she's talking about half the time."

Troy nodded.

"And," Caitlin said, "to top it all off, Kevin broke up with me. He got all strange because of this New York thing." She took out a tube of bubble gum–flavored Chapstick and spread it on her lips. It smelled sweet. "Can I hang out here awhile? Maybe watch TV or something?"

"Sure," Troy said. "I'll make popcorn."

She smiled at him, her lips all shiny and sweet. "Great. Thanks."

They watched MTV for a while, then *Back to the Future 2* before she asked him what the drawings were. He wasn't going to tell her at first, but he liked having her here with him. It reminded him of when they were kids and the three of them would always be together. Even when they were real young, and Caitlin was a skinny freckle-faced kid, Troy used to think she was beautiful. He used to give her rings from the bubble gum machine and she'd wear them even after they turned her fingers green.

"Why are you looking at me all weird?" Caitlin said.

Troy felt his cheeks grow hot. "I wasn't," he mumbled.

"Well, stop it," she said.

She was always bossy. She would pretend to be a sergeant and make him and Dana march and jump over fences. She always picked the television shows they watched and the games they played. Somehow he'd stopped noticing her. Maybe it was when she and Dana started playing with paper dolls or those stupid Cabbage Patch kids they used to carry around all the time. But Troy also remembered how even after he stopped hanging around with them, he still thought there was something about Caitlin. Something a little sad underneath those freckles and all that smart talk.

It was still there, too. That sadness. He could see it right now as she sat here applying and reapplying that bubble gum Chapstick with her bony little hands. Not a morbid sadness, but the kind that you have to really look close to notice. She was funny too. And that's probably what most people saw, a funny sassy girl who acted as if she knew it all.

"You're doing it again," Caitlin told him. "You're looking at me like you never saw me before. Can't you do something else?"

So Troy got the drawings and brought them over to the couch, spreading them across both their laps.

"It's a house I want to build someday," he said softly. "I keep re-arranging it, making changes and stuff."

"What are these?" Caitlin asked him.

"Skylights."

"Mmmmm," she said. She traced the shape of them with her fingertips.

"And this is a big fireplace that takes up a whole wall," he said, shuffling the drawings so she could see better. His face was more sure now.

"So it's like in two rooms?"

"Exactly!" he said. "And wait until you see this great kitchen. See, it has one of those islands in the middle."

"Those are so great. Becky Barnett's house has one of those."

"I guess stuff like this seems dumb to you. I mean, with your big plans to go to New York and stuff."

"Yeah," she said. "Dana and I are going to paint our walls black." She held on to the drawings. "They say that some apartments in New York have the bathtubs in the kitchen. Can you imagine?"

"No," he said. He watched her studying the drawings. He tried to imagine what it would feel like to kiss her. Quickly he picked up the remote for the television and jumped through the channels.

MTV came on again, the new Madonna video.

Caitlin jumped up and started lip-syncing with Madonna. She knew all the moves. The more Troy laughed the more she camped it up. When the video ended, Caitlin was lying on the floor with her arms outstretched in a perfect Madonna pose.

Troy looked at her. When they were really little, maybe five or six, he used to have a crush on her. She used to wear these really long braids with tiny colored ribbons on the ends. He reached up and touched her hair. It was all rippled now, like waves. "Remember your braids?" he said.

Caitlin got to her feet. "Of course I do. I mean, they were on my head, weren't they?" She swatted at him. "You nut," she said.

He was thinking again what it would feel like to kiss her. He could smell that bubble gum stuff.

"Remember when I used to have a crush on you?" he said.

Caitlin nodded.

Standing there like this, it seemed to Troy as if the air was crackling, as if the room had been shot with an electrical jolt. Once, on television, he'd seen a guy get electrocuted at an accident scene. The man had been trying to get to the people trapped in a car and he'd stepped on live wires that had been knocked to the ground. The jolt had lifted the man's body off the ground, sent smoke from his ears and mouth. Even though Troy knew the man was dying, he'd felt a thrill. The power of that jolt of electricity was what he sometimes got when he took great speed, or the first time he got a tattoo and the needle pricked him hard. It was, he'd always thought, what love was supposed to feel like. And here it was now, right in front of him, the air sizzling and crackling as Caitlin stepped toward him, a quizzical look on her face, her eyes narrowed, her head tilted slightly.

Then the door opened and Dana came in, wet with rain, and the moment was over. Troy reached a hand out as if to find that electrical current, to touch it. But there was nothing there. Just the cool wet air that Dana brought in with her.

"April is the cruelest month," Dana said.

"What does that mean?" Troy asked her.

Dana rolled her eyes. "T. S. Eliot," she said.

Caitlin and Troy looked at each other and shrugged. For an instant Dana even thought something passed between them. But then it was gone.

"Where were you?" Caitlin said. "With Roald?" She pronounced his name in that same way and Troy laughed.

"We went to see *Grand Illusion*," Dana said. She rubbed her hair with a kitchen towel to dry it. "Only the best movie ever made."

Troy looked at Caitlin. "I like *Terminator 2* better," he said.

"Oh, yeah," Dana said. "A real masterpiece. I'm going to go change. Are you going to stick around?"

Caitlin shook her head.

"Okay. See you tomorrow at school."

"Right," Caitlin said.

"Yeah," Troy said. "See you tomorrow at school." Even after she left, for some reason he couldn't stop grinning.

*Troy started to follow* Caitlin at school, to bump into her and pretend it was an accident, to wait outside her classroom door until she emerged, looking puzzled to see him there. Sometimes when he was with Jenny he would grab her to him and kiss her hard, waiting for that jolt. It never came. She felt as good as ever, but he wanted that feeling he'd had when he stood in front of Caitlin that night in his living room. At night he dreamed of that man he'd seen on TV. The way his body flew off the ground, the way his eyes looked so surprised and his mouth flew open as if he was saying, "Oh!"

On Fridays in art class, Mrs. Graham always taught them art history. Everyone thought it was the most boring thing in the world. She showed them slides and talked about Impressionism and the Renaissance. Usually half the class went to sleep, hidden in the dark classroom. Mrs. Graham would shout "People! Wake up!" and bang on the screen with her pointer.

Troy tried to pay attention, even though all those paintings of madonnas and kings were boring. Jenny liked art. Her parents had framed prints from museums all over the house and she could talk about different exhibits she'd seen. She loved one painting called *American Gothic*. It had a weird-looking couple holding a pitchfork and made him think of an old cornflakes commercial. But still he tried to pay attention. A while ago he really had liked one of the slides. It was of wet-looking water lilies in pastel colors. "You like Monet?" he'd asked Jenny that night. "His water lilies?" Her eyes had brightened and she gave him one of her great smiles and said "Yes!" with such enthusiasm he'd been sure she would let him move his hand under her panties that night. He'd been right.

So he tried hard to stay awake, to pay attention to Mrs. Graham's boring slides. Today they seemed especially boring, her nasal voice droning on and on about something he couldn't quite focus in on. The next day were the SATs, and Jenny was all excited that he was taking them. Thinking about that made his stomach feel tight, like he was getting ready to be punched. That had been Houdini's trick, he knew. To tighten his stomach muscles so he could take a punch. The trick had failed him. It was a punch that had ultimately killed him.

Troy blinked hard and tried to focus on the slides. Suddenly, right there in front of him was the most incredible slide. A woman holding flowers and a man kissing her, floating right up into the air. Troy leaned forward in his seat, studying it. Was it the power of that kiss that had lifted the man—jolted him—off his feet like that? he wondered.

"Who painted that?" Troy blurted.

The jocks in the row behind him laughed.

"Wake up, Harper," someone shouted.

"Chagall," Mrs. Graham said. "Thank you for asking, Troy." And then she clicked her remote control and the picture was gone, replaced by one of a man playing the violin on a roof.

When class ended, Troy pushed his way down the corridors to Caitlin's locker. There was only one more period left and he knew she had study hall, which meant she could leave for the day. He had History, which meant he couldn't but he didn't care.

She was already walking toward the door, her neon-colored high-tops squeaking against the waxed floors. Troy caught up with her, grabbing her arm to stop her.

"What is wrong with you?" she said. "Why do you keep following me around? Where's that girlfriend of yours anyway?"

The sunlight was pouring through the window, almost blinding him so that her face was practically a blank, outlined by sun.

"Let's go," he said.

"Where?"

"I don't know," Troy told her. He tugged on her arm, urging her outside.

"What is wrong with you?" she said again. She leaned against the school, her face in focus now.

"The other night," Troy said. "At my house. I felt this . . . this thing between us."

Her cheeks turned pink. "So?"

"I haven't even really paid attention to you for so long and—"

"So? I haven't paid attention to you either, you know. I mean, I do have a life too. A job. Plans."

"I know," he said. "I just have to kiss you. That's all."

Caitlin glanced around. "Now?" she said. "Here?"

He did it. He took her by the shoulders and pressed his lips to hers and it was exactly right. He was that man in the Chagall painting. He was flying, soaring even.

When the kissing stopped, Caitlin pushed away from him.

"Listen to me, okay?" she said. "I felt it too, that night at your house. All I've been imagining was this. Kissing you. But you have a girlfriend and I'm going to New York City and that's that." She walked away from him, fast. She turned once. "Besides," she told him from a safe distance, "I would never never fall for a guy from this hick town. Do you understand?" She didn't wait for him to answer. She just kept walking.

Troy watched her go. He could not stop smiling.


*"I brought you something,"* Troy told Jenny.

They were in Dunkin' Donuts. It was seven a.m. and in one hour Troy would be in the high school cafeteria taking the SAT test.

She smiled at him. "A present?"

"Sort of," he said.

Slowly, he unrolled the blueprints, smoothing them with his hands.

"Drawings?" she said.

She raised one eyebrow at him. She had told him that she'd practiced that in front of the mirror for years. It seemed like a silly thing to do, he thought.

"Of?" Jenny said.

"A house." He looked at her light blue eyes, her soft skin. "I did these," he said.

She brightened. "You could become an architect. That would be something."

Troy shook his head. "No. It's a house for me. I want to build it. I have the exact spot too. It's on a hill with this incredible view. I want to show you."

When Jenny ate doughnuts, she nibbled in circles until she reached the filling. Then she opened the center and licked out all the jelly or cream. That's what she was doing now, licking the jelly from the middle of the doughnut.

"Fine," she said. "Sometime we'll go and look."

Troy swallowed hard. He tried to think about all the math she'd taught him. There was a whole section in the SATs called problem solving. He could never make sense of it. If four men are on a train and the train is going two hundred miles an hour . . . He cleared his throat.

"I sort of wanted to show you now."

She laughed. "You nut. The SATs are in less than an hour."

"I know," Troy said softly.

Jenny looked down at the blueprints. "Oh," she said.

"I would wait for you to finish college," he told her. He did not sound very convincing.

She twisted the scrimshaw ring he'd given her, around and around. "Oh," she said again.

At night, *when she could* not sleep, Renata created a different life for herself. Millie was better and she and Tom were married. Dana and Troy were theirs and Libby Holliday didn't exist. In this other life, everybody was happy.

Lately, though, ever since Millie had come home, Renata's fantasy life seeped into the daytime too. She made meals from an old Betty Crocker cookbook—chicken Divan and Waldorf salads and canapés shaped like stars with olive faces. She spent the afternoon waxing furniture, polishing floors, Windexing windows. She watched *General Hospital* with Millie and spent hours wondering how the characters' lives would turn out.

Only Dana, with her heavily lined eyes and teased hair could bring Renata back to reality. One look from Dana, and the fantasy ended. One look, and Renata remembered everything—why she had left Holly in the first place, and why she had come back. It was funny how when she first saw Dana she had been surprised at how unlike Libby the girl was. But now, Renata could see Libby Holliday in Dana's eyes, in the way she held her head and the way she frowned.

Renata thought a person should face her enemy head on. So one warm May afternoon, while her chicken pot pie baked in the oven, Renata walked into Dana's room to talk to her.

Dana was in her usual pose, sprawled out on her bed reading. This time it was *Leaves of Grass*.

"I have a feeling," Renata said, "that you don't like me."

"Brilliant observation," Dana said.

She had a way of talking as if everything she said was an aside. It drove Renata nuts.

"I'm not trying to take your mother's place," Renata said, suddenly feeling like one of those soap opera characters.

"Don't worry," Dana said, "you couldn't even if you tried. She's beautiful and thin and—"

"And she walked out on this whole family," Renata said, imitating Dana's aside technique.

Dana threw her book down on the floor hard. "Look," she said, her voice a near scream, "you can't just take over our lives. You can screw my father and you can move in here but you can't adopt us. You can't make us your family."

On *General Hospital,* Renata's character would have slapped Dana right across the face. Renata thought about that, about how it would look and sound and feel. But all she did was sigh, and sit down on the very edge of Dana's bed. It was a twin bed, with an incongruously feminine pink chenille bedspread.

"I don't want your family," Renata told her. "Millie does."

"That is really low," Dana said. "Blaming your conniving on a sick kid. On *your* sick kid. I suppose it was Millie who wanted to screw my father too."

Renata shook her head slowly. "You're just like I was. A real tough kid, right? I bet I could tell you things about yourself that you think nobody knows."

Dana was on her feet now, standing, fists clenched, in front of Renata. Renata focused on the way her knees poked through the holes she'd torn into her jeans, on the small red heart embroidered on one pocket.

"Don't you understand?" Dana was saying. "I can't be like you. You aren't my mother."

Below the heart were Dana's initials in white spidery letters. DLH.

"I left this town for New York when I was seventeen," Renata said. "I was going to set the world on fire."

Dana's fingers were moving back and forth, as if she was kneading bread.

"By then," Renata said, "I really had slept with almost all the guys people thought. I figured it was a way to be happy. I was that sad a kid."

Slowly, Dana bent and picked up the book. She smoothed the pages and laid it gently back on the bed.

"I could maybe help you," Renata said. Her voice sounded hopeful. "I just want to be your friend while we're both here. While we're all here."

"I don't need another friend," Dana said.

Renata studied the girl's face. She'd seen lots of teenagers like Dana walking around the mall when she was working at the bookstore. They all looked so tough at first glance, and so young if you really looked at them closely. Like Dana now, all clear smooth skin and scared eyes.

"What do you need, then?" Renata said quietly.

Dana forced a laugh. "Me? Nothing." She swept her arms across the sad little room. "Can't you tell? I've got everything."

Renata wondered if she should talk about all the boys who called here for Dana. Not as many lately, but Renata understood what was happening. It had happened to her, after all. Confusing sex with love, or with feeling loved at least. In fact, Renata wasn't sure she'd learned the difference even now.

"Maybe," Dana was saying, "the real question here is what *you* want. Maybe this isn't about me at all."

Renata smiled at her. It was funny how sitting here with Dana was almost like going back in time and looking in a mirror. How she wanted to take this girl in her arms and give her comfort, protect her not only from the world, but from herself.

"You don't have to be related to someone to be like them," Renata said. She had to press her arms close to her side to keep from going over to Dana and wrapping them around her. "That's what friends are, right?"

"Did my father tell you to talk to me?"

Renata shook her head.

"I'll never like you," Dana said, but she did not sound at all convincing. "Or be like you."

Renata inched toward her. "Tell me," she said, her voice low, her heart breaking for this girl with too much makeup and funny hair. "What do you want?"

Dana narrowed her eyes. "To send my barbaric yawp over the roofs of the world."

A challenge, Renata thought. She picked up the book. "Walt Whitman," she said.

And finally Dana smiled, a little. She sighed and sat on the bed beside Renata, still keeping a safe distance.

"New York is as hard as here," Renata said. "Don't think you're going to move there and everything will be different."

"But I'm moving with Caitlin. We have such great plans. I mean, we practically have our apartment all decorated and everything." Then she added, "I want to see it. That's all. I want to have a pastrami sandwich delivered to my door at three a.m."

Renata reached over and put her arm around Dana's shoulders. "I know," she whispered.

---

*Libby answered on the* second ring. Her voice slapped him in the face. It sounded exactly the way it always did. People who spoke to Libby on the telephone sometimes thought she was a young girl. Is your mother home? they'd ask her.

"Who is this?" she was saying.

Tom pressed the phone to him, as if he could feel her through it.

"Libby," he said. "Libby, it's me."

She didn't say anything. This, he thought, was worse than if she'd hung up.

He laughed nervously. "I feel like it's the first time I ever called you. Do you remember that? I practiced for a week. I highlighted parts of *Romeo and Juliet* to talk to you about. Well," he added, laughing again, "parts of the Cliff Notes for *Romeo and Juliet*. I never could read Shakespeare. But you know that already." He was babbling. Stop it, he told himself. Ask her questions. "Are you . . . all right?"

"Yes," she said.

Good, he thought. Questions are good. "I saw you on television. In that floor wax commercial?" Those aren't questions. Damn it, he thought, get a grip. He closed his eyes, tried to think.

"You did?" she was saying. "You watched?"

"We all did. You looked so great."

"Really?" she said.

"God, Libby, come home. I miss you so bad."

"Don't," she said. All the softness was out of her voice then.

"Would you think about coming home at least?"

"It would be a little crowded, wouldn't it?"

She knew. He closed his eyes again.

"How could you?" she said. "Of all people to bring into my house?"

"You left us. What did you expect? Libby—"

"And don't think I don't know that voice," she said.

"What voice?"

"That sleepy after-sex voice you have right now."

"How could you know it?" he said, starting to shout. "Since you never wanted to make love I'm surprised you remember anything about it."

"Goodbye, Tom."

Then he was shouting, loud. "That's right. Hang up. Run away. Don't try to fix anything."

"You're the mechanic. I'll leave the fixing to you."

When he heard her hang up, he started to bang the phone against the wall. He banged so hard that all of the insides fell out. Wires and pieces of metal. Still he kept banging until there was nothing left to bang and he had to kick the wall instead.

"Fuck," he said finally, and slumped against the wall. That was when he saw them, all of them, shadowy figures in pajamas standing in the doorway, watching.

"I . . ." he started, but it seemed so hopeless to continue.

"We heard," Renata said. She turned toward the kids. "It's okay now," she told them.

When they left, shuffling back to bed, she did not move toward him.

"Tell me something," she said. "Could you ever love anyone like that again?"

He shook his head.

"Answer me," she said.

He tried to make out her face in the darkness, but couldn't.

"No," he said finally. "No."

*ibby quit Von's and she* was running out of money. For the first time in a long time, maybe in her whole life, she did not have a plan. Some people from work had told her she should think about moving up to Seattle. "Lots of opportunity up there," they'd said. On television there was a show about a little town in Alaska where everyone seemed attractive and happy, well read and cultured. But Alaska and Seattle did not seem like the answer.

When Harp called her she thought her heart might burst right out of her chest. She even forgot for a minute that he was living with Renata Handy in the house he'd built for them and their family. Instead, she thought about the first time he ever called her. She was fourteen years old, in her room studying American history, the Mayflower Compact. Her mother knocked on her bedroom door and said, "There's a Tom Harper on the phone for you." That night Libby had played it so cool, taking her time to walk down the hall, as if it meant nothing. But it had meant everything.

Tonight when he told her he'd been thinking of that first phone call too, Libby had suddenly remembered everything—the first time he'd kissed her and how she used to think she could kiss him forever, how her lips used to feel bruised from all those kisses.

But then the sound of his voice, gravelly as an old gangster's, reminded her of what was going on, of how he'd probably snuck out of bed with Renata Handy just to make this call. Once, Libby had read about how anthropologists have this theory that an embryo imitates evolution during the nine months before it's born. How it starts like a tadpole and then a fish, all the way to a human. That was how she felt that night. In about nine minutes she and Harp recreated the whole twenty years of their relationship—from that first excitement to all the anger and bitterness, right up to her leaving him.

When she hung up, Libby went and looked out the window. It was a funny thing, that window, there was nothing out there to see, just a little path and more apartments. But she looked out it anyway, into the night. In the apartment directly across from hers, framed in the window, she watched as a young couple kissed. They kissed for a very long time, and when they finally pulled apart, Libby saw that they were two men.

She watched as one led the other away, into another room, leaving the window lit but empty. She could make out a framed print on the wall, the kind you buy at a museum. But she did not recognize the artist. Standing there like that, Libby knew she did not want to stay here anymore. She did not want to go to Seattle or Alaska. She wanted to go home. But Harp had betrayed her and she had betrayed him. That did not seem to be something two people could ever forget.

Summer

Troy could tell Caitlin anything. That first night, when she finally agreed to go for a ride with him after weeks of avoiding him, sometimes even running away from him, they sat up all night drinking wine and talking. He did not even touch her. They just sat side by side in the spot where someday soon he would build a house, and they talked.

With Nadine it had been all sex and wild adventures. With Jenny he had tried to be something he was not. But on that first night with Caitlin he was the man who soared when he kissed the woman in that painting. He was the man who got the electrical jolt and flew into the air saying "Oh!"

She told him everything too. She said, "No one would believe it but I'm terrified of everything." She said, "I don't get what the big deal about sex is. It doesn't feel like much at all." She said, "I wish I had known my father. That I had looked into his eyes even once."

When the sun came up they had not decided anything out loud. But they both knew that everything was different.

*Dana and Caitlin sat on* the roof of Pizza Pizzazz, waiting for a meteor shower. Tonight was supposed to be the best night for viewing them. Roald had wanted Dana to go with him to Mount Graylock, but she felt that maybe she'd been ignoring Caitlin too much these days. Now that they were together, waiting for the sky to explode, Dana found herself wishing she had gone with Roald. He would point out constellations, tell her how many light-years away the planets were, explain what was causing the meteor showers to happen.

Caitlin, however, was not even talking. She didn't even seem interested in watching them. "But it's a scientific phenomenon," Dana had said. "And it's beautiful." And she kept checking her watch as if she had something more important to do.

Lately, Dana had been losing her patience with Caitlin. Caitlin was starting to act like all the goofy girls from school they used to laugh at. The ones who never read, who talked about makeup and clothes and boys, who could not even name the vice-president of the United States. Maybe she was jealous of Dana's friendship with Roald. But he made Dana feel like somebody. He made her think.

But Caitlin only shrugged or played with the ends of her hair in response.

"Don't tell me you're mooning over Kevin?" Dana said.

That made Caitlin laugh at least. "Oh, no," she said. "Not even a little." "What then?"

Caitlin laughed in that silly way she'd developed lately. She shook her head.

Dana sighed real loud so that Caitlin would know how exasperated she was. But still Caitlin didn't say anything more.

"Roald said—"

"I am so sick of Roald," Caitlin said. She wasn't even looking up at the sky.

"Well, I'm sick of you," Dana told her.

Caitlin took her hand and squeezed it. "I know. That's okay."

"That's okay?"

"I met this guy," Caitlin said. She seemed to choose her words too carefully. She looked up at the sky then, but not as if she was waiting to see meteors rain down on them. It was more like not wanting to look at Dana. "I can't stop thinking about him. Sometimes, after we've been together, you know, made love, I feel like he's burned an imprint on me. Like I can still feel him." She hugged herself and smiled. "I was going to tell you but it's complicated."

"Is he married or something?" Dana said. She was thinking about those words—"made love." They sounded too serious. That wasn't how they usually described sex. Her throat felt dry and she too stared hard at the sky.

Caitlin laughed that weird new laugh again. "No," she said. "It's not like that."

"Good sex is making you weird," Dana said. "When he comes to visit you in New York I'll wait in the diner on our corner. I'll dress all in black and drink bad coffee and read John Donne's love poems while you reach new sexual heights. Then the three of us will walk through rain-soaked streets together and watch the sun come up."

"You are such a romantic," Caitlin said.

Off in the distance, the sky lit up.

Dana pointed east. "One more month," she said.

Caitlin didn't answer.

"Roald is hitchhiking cross-country," Dana said. "It could take him years. He wants to stop in little towns in Montana and Colorado and work at weird jobs. Isn't that exciting?" Dana said.

She was starting to feel that things were really going to happen now. The oil can on her bureau was almost full of money. Her cap and gown were hanging on her bedroom door. She had a box of books to bring with her and a poster of Neal Cassady and Jack Kerouac that Roald had given her.

"Our life," Dana said, "is around the corner, waiting to happen."

She grabbed Caitlin's hand and squeezed it in her own. Despite the warm weather, Caitlin's hand was ice cold.

"Cold hands, warm heart," Dana said. She squinted her eyes, as if their futures would reveal themselves to her right there on the roof of Pizza Pizzazz.

The postcard from Nadine said simply, "Wish you were here. Love, Nadine." Not very original. The postcard wasn't either, just a sunset on a beach in Florida. Still, Troy could feel her watching him from all those miles away. He even double-checked in the Rand McNally Road Atlas, tracing Route 95 with his finger from Massachusetts to Miami, to reassure himself that she was far away from him. He wondered if he'd ever feel safe again when someone like Nadine was roaming around, knowing him even from this distance.

He looked over his shoulder too much, watched cars that drove behind him for a familiar face. He kept the postcard folded into a tight square in his wallet, like the St. Christopher medals the Catholic kids carried around for safe journeys. Nadine told him that once she'd taken a crowbar to some guy's car windows. She'd smashed every one because he'd treated her bad. Troy tried not to think of that story. He tried not to think of any of Nadine's stories. They all made him shiver.

The only time he felt safe now was when he met Caitlin, late at night. It was true that they had sex, but what he thought about more was the talking they did. He always brought the plans for the house and she brought magazines—*House and Garden, Country Living, Elle Design.* They argued about things like what color a kitchen should be and the benefits of wall-to-wall carpeting versus hardwood floors. But Caitlin always ended up by saying, "It's going to be a beautiful house."

And when she said it, Troy knew it was true. It would be. He could see the years unfold neatly, the way one room opened onto the next on his blueprints. He'd work for his father and save money and slowly build the house. It would take years to get it right, but he could live in it pretty quickly. He'd only need a couple of rooms. When he was with Caitlin, naked and stretched out on a blanket in the woods, he could close his eyes and see all of it as clear as the moon and Big Dipper overhead.

"I never thought I'd like a black bathroom," Caitlin was saying, "but it's very chic. And then you could change the accents to any color. You know, red or white or hot pink."

He traced her ribs, silently counting them, the same way he sometimes traced the road to Miami on the map.

"Bathrooms," he told her, "should be green or turquoise. Water colors."

"No," Caitlin said.

"Blue maybe." Her hipbones were sharp. "And it should have a Jacuzzi and a bathtub big enough for two people."

"A round one," Caitlin said.

"Right."

She sighed. "Well, really, a house needs more than one bathroom. One could be black."

Troy closed his eyes and saw it, the years ahead of him, the house. He smiled and held Caitlin tighter to him. He wanted to tell her not to go to New York, to stay right here with him. But he didn't. He just pressed her to him, feeling the goose bumps that ran up her legs, and her sharp hip digging into his thigh.

"It will be the most beautiful house ever," she whispered.

Renata came home from work with brochures of faraway places. Club Meds on South Pacific islands, villas for rent in Spain and Portugal, ruins in Greece and Turkey.

"A family vacation," she said. "You and me and Millie. I'll use every penny I have so we can go."

She had not talked to him, not really, since she'd heard him on the phone with Libby. At night and on his lunch breaks and in the early morning they'd made love harder and more frenziedly than ever. She whispered things to him then. Do anything, she whispered. Do everything. But in daylight, out of the bedroom, they hardly spoke at all.

Until today when she spread the travel brochures before him like an exotic smorgasbord.

"Every kid should see the world," Renata said. "We'll pretend we're a real family," Renata said. Her voice was rushed, as if she didn't have time to explain. "We'll buy tacky flowered shirts. Identical ones. And Instamatics. And Bermuda shorts. Millie can start a souvenir collection. You know those plastic domes? When you shake them fake snow falls? She can collect those."

She dropped onto the chair beside him and covered her face with her big square hands.

"Oh God," she said. "What if they didn't get it all?"

When she started to cry, he still could not think of anything to say to make it any better.

$S$*ue looked surprised when* she saw Troy at the door.

"Something wrong?" she said.

In the bright morning light, he could see she had lots of freckles, like Caitlin.

"No," he said. "I just came to take Caitlin for a ride."

He followed Sue into the house. It was small and run-down, but somehow the place managed to be cheery. There were yellow curtains on the windows and plants everywhere. Caitlin had told him that her mother had fixed it up when she first got married and never changed a thing.

Caitlin was in the living room and when Troy walked in she looked up and smiled and blushed.

"Hi," she said.

Sue frowned. "What's going on?"

Caitlin wore baggy jeans and a sleeveless black bodysuit. She looked beautiful, Troy thought.

"I want to take you for a ride," Troy said.

Sue touched Troy's hand lightly. "When you were born," she said, "I thought, Wouldn't it be great if these two ended up together. Your mother, on the other hand, had different ideas."

Troy laughed. "She always had different ideas."

When Sue looked at him then, she knew. "Your mother," she said, "is not always right."

*Troy and Caitlin went to* the land every day. They marked off rooms. They told each other "I love you" constantly. "Say it again," Troy whispered to her. And when she did, he'd whisper, "Again."

"To think," she told him, "all this time you were right there in front of me."

"I was smarter when I was five," he said. "I knew then you were the one for me."

But then at night, alone in his room, Troy worried about the summer growing nearer and Caitlin leaving him behind. For as long as he could remember, Caitlin and Dana had been making plans to go away together. And lately those plans seemed even more definite. Dana had started to buy the *Village Voice* and circle apartment and job possibilities. She sat with their father at the kitchen table and discussed the best, the shortest route to New York from Holly. It was a short drive, really, but still their father pointed out to her things of interest along the way, scenic routes, a possible place to spend the night. Dana listened but her foot tapped as he spoke, as if she were already on her way.

Troy knew that Dana did not care about battle sites, museums, or factory outlet stores. She only cared about leaving. And beside her would be Caitlin, the *Voice* open on her lap so she could read the classified ads out loud as they drove. The thought of it made Troy crazy. Caitlin would find someone there who knew things he did not—how to order the right wine, what books were on the bestseller list, how to find their way on the subway. He couldn't stand the thought of it. He had to find a way to make her stay.

*"What's the rush?" Troy asked* Caitlin. He had several tactics to try. "You could work all summer and save even more money."

They were at the land, stretched out on a blanket. Caitlin's face was pointed at the sun, smeared with sun tan lotion.

"I suppose," she said. "But we're sort of ready. You know."

Troy moved on to his next idea. "I noticed that the new . . . uh . . . Scott Turow book is on the bestseller list again."

Caitlin opened her eyes. "What?"

"It's even number one."

"Who cares?" she said. And she closed her eyes again.

"You know how my dad has all those maps? He collects them? I happened to notice this New York City subway map. And I think you should probably consider living near an express stop. It seems to me that would save you a lot of time in the long run. Maybe Forty-second or Thirty-fourth—"

Caitlin sat up. "Troy, I don't want to frown. It will give me weird tan lines. So could you just tell me what you're talking about?"

In the sun like this he could see the flecks of color in her eyes, topaz and jade.

"Besides which," she said, "those are terrible neighborhoods. Times Square and something else equally scary."

"Don't go," he said, surprising himself. That had not been on his list at all.

"Don't go?"

"Stay here with me. We'll build a house right here and be together."

"You want me to stay?" she said.

Troy groaned. "I really messed up bad, didn't I?"

Caitlin started to laugh. "Messed up? Are you kidding? You said the exact right thing."

*R* *enata saw Tom differently* now. She could not decide if she had wanted him—loved him even—to make Millie's wish come true or if it had been real. She liked to think it was real for at least a little while, maybe even just one night. But now she saw Tom Harper for what he was—a once handsome boy going paunchy, who still loved his wife.

Sometimes, when Millie slept, Renata thought about other things too. He had not read a book since high school. He ate potatoes with lasagna. His fingernails were always dirty from fixing cars. It was good to think of these things. The others, she knew, would do her no good. So she pretended not to know that he was also kind, liked Sinatra, made her feel special for a time.

She was glad he was there now when she had to meet with the doctors after Millie's follow-up MRI. That she could lean on his strong arm. Even if she was already beginning the process of leaving him, standing there in the hospital hallway she was happy he was beside her.

The doctor shook his head. "You can never tell with this disease. With kids. We want to keep her a few days—"

"What?" Renata said, digging her fingers into Tom's arm.

"Molly," the doctor said, "shows a small shadow at the base of her brain."

"Millie," Renata said. "You mean my daughter, right? You mean Millie?"

He glanced at his papers.

"Of course," he said. "Millie."

Renata felt her heart start to rise, to soar.

"It could be scarring or it could be a return of the mass," the doctor was saying.

But Renata had stopped listening. She let go of Tom's arm and rushed back into the room where Millie sat waiting for her.

"Let's go, Millie," Renata said.

The nurse looked up at her, startled.

"I want to take her now," Renata said.

The nurse patted her hand. "That's all right," she said. "Illness makes people do and say the strangest things."

"Yes," Renata said. She felt she wasn't really there, that she was flying above this room, this town, the entire state of Massachusetts, looking down at it all. "Yes," she said again.

*Doctors, Renata decided, used* words like survival rate and radiation and CAT scan and MRI. They put on stern doctor faces and talked statistics. They handed out copies of medical journal articles and pills for pain. But they did not talk about hope or victory or little girls. They did not know Millie.

She could no longer count how many times she had sat in an office like this one—posters of some body system on the wall, large neat desk with paperweights and Cross pens and silver-framed family pictures, white-coated doctors talking to her, saying the same things.

This time, Renata could not concentrate on what it was they were telling her. Instead, she thought about Millie, the way she looked when Renata had left her at the hospital yesterday. "More tests!" Renata had said, her voice as bright as a stewardess's. "Will you bring my penmanship notebook?" Millie had said. "So I can practice."

"Millie is such a funny kid," Renata said.

She saw the way the doctors looked at each other. One more mother over the edge, that look said. Humor her.

"I told her she didn't have to go to school anymore," Renata said, surprised at the calm in her voice. The poster across from her showed the flow of blood, from veins to arteries to heart and back out. "Do you know what she said?"

It was the female doctor who spoke. "Mrs. Handy," she said, proving they weren't really listening to Renata who kept telling them she was *not* Mrs. Anybody. "Statistics show—"

Renata held up her hand. "Wait," she said. "Let me finish. Millie insisted I send her to school. She wanted to learn to write in cursive. Can you imagine? You're all educated, right? You all know that penmanship is not really important. Not in the bigger scheme of things. But Millie practices hers all the time. She has notebooks full of perfect looped letters. Qs and capital Ls. The kid has beautiful penmanship."

"Mrs. Handy," the woman doctor said again.

"That's another thing," Renata said, standing, edging toward the door, wondering what exactly that smell was that filled every doctor's office. Did they bottle it? Sell it in air fresheners? "I'm not Mrs. Handy. I've never been married. Ever. And I've told you that."

"I'm sorry," a different doctor murmured.

"*Miss* Handy," the toughest doctor said. He even had a serious waxed mustache that he twirled when he spoke. "We cannot offer Millie a high survival rate—"

Renata was shaking her head and opening the door. She had heard this enough. What about faith? she was thinking. There was even a doctor—a famous doctor—who believed in the power of faith in healing. He'd written books about it. Didn't these people know that? There were new examples every day.

She was in the hallway now, pushing past nurses in their marshmallow white shoes and gaggles of more doctors conferring. She was thinking about Lourdes, where people bathed in its healing waters and were cured. She and Millie could go there. They could learn French. Eat escargots. Wear berets. In fact, she would buy Berlitz tapes and when Millie felt better they would both listen to them. *Ecouter et parler.* Renata smiled. That was the name of her French book in school. To listen and to speak.

Outside she paused to catch her breath. A florist's delivery truck pulled up and the driver began to remove flower arrangements. He took them from the truck and placed them on a portable cart that he had carefully unfolded. Daisies and gladioli and roses. Dozens of them. They all had the same message. Held on a sign by a smiling bunny or written in glitter across white fake satin or painted on a wooden stake. GET WELL.

But none of those doctors believed that Millie would get well. Only Renata believed it. Somehow, though, that seemed enough. There were endless possibilities, she thought as the delivery man loaded coleus plants and a small cactus garden onto his cart. A plastic man in a sombrero peeked from behind a succulent. GET WELL was written on the sign he held. GET WELL was written in pink on an entire bouquet of silver heart-shaped balloons.

Didn't these doctors ever read the *National Enquirer* in the grocery line? People were always getting healed in that. Two-headed babies and eight-hundred-pound men and even children eaten by alligators or attacked by pit bulls, everyone in there survived. Why, Renata had even read about a woman presumed to be dead who came to life just as the undertaker prepared to embalm her. These things were miracles. These things happened.

*When Tom came to the hospital* from the graduation ceremonies, dressed in a blue suit that was shiny at the elbows and pulled across his middle, Millie was asleep and Renata was leafing through an old *Redbook*. She held up the magazine.

"I'm learning Dolly Parton's secrets," she said.

She watched as he went to Millie's side and lightly touched her cheek. Like a father, Renata thought.

"How was all that pomp and circumstance?" Renata said. She kept flipping the pages of the magazine, nervously.

Tom shrugged. "Weird," he said. "Watching your kids graduate from high school. I kept thinking, Wait a minute. I just did this yesterday myself." He hesitated, then said, "You'll come back to the house with me, won't you?"

Headings flashed by. How to Crochet a Vest. Ten-Minute Dinners. The Heimlich Maneuver. Natural Childbirth After a C-Section.

"I wouldn't miss toasting the graduates," she said.

"No, I don't mean just this afternoon. I mean I would like you and Millie to stay at the house." Tom did not turn toward Renata. He added, "With me."

"I don't know," Renata said. The magazine felt slippery in her hands. "It's been good, I think."

"The sex," she said.

"No," he said, his back still to her. "Everything. The trips on Sundays and the nights watching TV and eating popcorn." He was a big man, tall and broad. When he finally faced her, it seemed strange that he was crying. He said, "The way you made the house smell like cinnamon."

But Renata just shook her head and kept flipping the pages of her magazine. "Millie and I," she said, "we've got to move on."

"Where?" Tom asked her. "Move where?"

Renata looked up at him, her eyes bright. "Somewhere," she said. She let the magazine slip from her hands to the floor. "Everywhere."

Tom moved toward her, as if to take her in his arms. But she stood abruptly. "There's so much to do," she said. "Better get going."

He stepped back and nodded. "Right," he said, and watched as she moved past him and out the door.

*Caitlin scanned the crowd in* front of the high school. Parents all dressed up, being polite to everyone. Some kids were crying, some shouting with joy.

Dana tugged at her arm. "Come on," she said.

Troy waved to them. "You leaving?" he called.

"What does he care?" Dana muttered. "He's getting to be a real pain in the ass, isn't he? Always coming around lately."

He had unbuttoned his gown and it blew in the breeze as he approached them.

"I want to go to the hospital before the party," he said.

Caitlin nodded.

"So go," Dana told him. She pulled Caitlin away from him.

"I'll see you at the house," he was saying.

"Who cares?" Dana said under her breath.

*"Roald is taking me for* a very fancy farewell dinner as soon as we can get away from my father. He bought a ton of champagne so we could all cele-

brate together," Dana told Caitlin as they drove away. "It sure beats going to one of Cindy Tom's dumb parties and getting drunk and everybody puking everywhere." She glanced over at Caitlin. "Right?"

Caitlin was sitting very straight in the seat, her hands folded in her lap, her eyes staring straight ahead.

"Just think," Caitlin said, her voice flat, "when our parents graduated from high school, they went and got married, practically right away."

"Our mothers got knocked up," Dana said. "They were idiots."

"They were happy," Caitlin snapped at her.

"Right. That's why my mother left. From sheer happiness over life in Holly, Massachusetts."

"They were," Caitlin said, softer now.

Dana glanced over at her friend. "Hey," she said. "I'm scared too. But together we can do anything."


*Dana led the climb to the roof* of Pizza Pizzazz. She had a bottle of champagne and a box wrapped in brightly striped paper tucked under her arm. She reached the roof long before Caitlin.

Below them, girls in those disgusting Pizza Pizzazz uniforms were taking orders for disgusting pizza combinations. Dana held the bottle high. "Goodbye blackened shrimp, goat cheese, and jalapeño pizza," she said. "Hello New York City."

When Caitlin finally joined her, Dana popped the cork and took a big gulp.

"Warm and cheap," she said, "but it does the trick." She held the bottle toward Caitlin.

Caitlin shook her head.

"You're not going to toast blackened shrimp, goat cheese, and jalapeño pizza?"

Caitlin smiled. A weak smile, a smile that was hardly there.

"You're not going to toast New York City?"

"Dana," Caitlin said.

Something seemed to be falling down inside Dana. In her chest, tumbling around. This is not happening, she told herself.

"Here," she said, hearing the nervousness in her own voice. "Your graduation gift."

"I got you something too," Caitlin said.

They opened their gifts in silence.

"A compass," Dana said.

"So you'll always know where you're going," Caitlin told her.

Dana smiled. "You have a real knack for symbolism."

Caitlin held up a crystal apple. It shone in the bright summer light. "It's so beautiful," she said.

"It's inscribed on the bottom. There's a little silver plaque," Dana said. "But don't read it until we get there."

"There?"

That feeling inside Dana seemed to accelerate. "To New York," she said.

"Dana," Caitlin said again.

Dana grabbed Caitlin's arm, hard. "Don't tell me we're not going," she said.

Caitlin looked at Dana. "I'm sorry," she said.

"But all of our plans."

"You can still have them."

"Alone?" Dana said. She wished she could stop that feeling she had. It was like jumping off a high building, she thought. Not knowing if you'd survive the fall. "I can't go alone," she said.

"Yes, you can," Caitlin said. "You're the brave one. All along you've always been the brave one. Me, I need to stay right here. I want to stay."

"No, you don't," Dana said. "You want to leave town, to have adventures. You want to *be* somebody."

"No," Caitlin said, her voice so soft it was like a whisper. "That's what *you* want. I met a guy. We're going to build a house and get married. I don't want to go away."

The feeling was back, only worse. Like skydiving, dropping thousands and thousands of feet from the sky. "But you want to leave. You're the one who always said so."

"Dana," Caitlin said, taking her hand and holding it tight. "The guy. The one. It's Troy."

It was like Dana couldn't get air. She gulped for it, swallowing hard. But her lungs could not get any. Everything was happening too fast, falling apart when it was supposed to come together.

Without even thinking about what she was doing, Dana took the crystal apple and threw it as far as she could. When it hit the ground, it shattered.

"How's that for symbolism?" Dana shouted. "You traitor. You jerk."

She threw the compass then too. They did not hear it hit the ground. Dana turned and ran down the fire escape, away from Caitlin, who sat on the roof, not moving.

————

*Roald came to their house* for champagne, all dressed up for the fancy dinner. They stood away from the others, watching.

"Finger sandwiches," Roald said. He rolled his eyes.

"I want to go with you," she told him. "Cross-country. I want to work at a bar in Montana."

"You know I've got to go alone," he said. He munched on a carrot stick. "Rabbit food," he said.

"But I'm not a bother," Dana said. She sounded as desperate as she felt. "I'm adventurous."

"That's for sure," Roald said. He poked her in the ribs. "Ask any guy at Williams."

"Very funny."

Troy and Caitlin came in with her father then, and Dana watched them as if they were in a movie. She could not hear what they were saying but she could guess. Her father kept slapping Troy on the back and hugging Caitlin and everybody looked all starry-eyed and smiling.

"The happy couple," Dana said.

"What a waste." Roald finished his champagne. "Let's blow."

As they slipped out the back door Dana heard her father banging a spoon against his glass for everyone's attention. She walked faster so she would not have to hear.


*Renata was sitting outside,* in the grass, when Dana got back from dinner. Dana went and sat beside her.

"I'm taking Millie to Mexico," Renata said.

The air was filled with the sounds of crickets and the smell of summer rain on its way.

"I was thinking," Dana said slowly, "that I might stay here after all. I could go to the community college. Study English or something."

Renata took Dana by the shoulders. "No," she said. "You have to go."

"Caitlin isn't coming," Dana said, starting to cry.

"I know all about it."

"I'm afraid."

Renata wrapped Dana in a big hug. "We're all afraid, baby. All the time. But you've got to go and do what you've got to do."

"I can't leave my dad all alone."

"Your dad can take care of himself," Renata said. "Everyone has to take care of themselves."

"I just don't know."

Renata released her, cupped Dana's chin in her wide hand. "You do know. You pack up your stuff and go."

Dana tried to imagine it, the highway that led south, the buildings shining in the sunlight. If she left early enough, she would be there by noon. Her life could start tomorrow. She squinted her eyes. Caitlin claimed it was only starlight that she saw, but Dana knew better.

*Her mother had told Dana* that Sue and Mitch had big plans for their little house. An addition in the back, more children, maybe even horses. She used to point out the beginnings of the extension, a low foundation in back that sat empty now, all weedy and overgrown.

Dana sat in her car in front of the house. She could smell the cherry blossoms from the tree Sue and Mitch had planted. In the early morning like this, with the beginnings of sunlight breaking through the mist, Dana could almost imagine what could have been here.

She leaned on her horn, the sound shrill and loud. Three long beeps, one short one. That's how she and Caitlin always called for each other. In the back seat, she had everything packed in Hefty garbage bags. All of her stuff fit into two. That's how much she was leaving behind.

Caitlin ran out, still in her lemon yellow baby doll pajamas, barefoot, her hair loose.

She leaned into the open window on the driver's side, brushing Dana's cheek as she peered in.

"Traveling light," Caitlin said.

Dana nodded and got out of the car.

Caitlin straightened, hugged herself in the cool morning air.

"It's not too late," Dana told her. "You could still come."

But Caitlin only smiled and touched her friend's arm. Her fingers were cool, the nails polished a pale pale pink. On her ring finger was a gold band with the tiniest diamond in the center.

Almost shyly Caitlin said, "Troy gave it to me. Pretty, isn't it?"

"Yes," Dana said. "It is pretty." She held on to her friend's hand hard, as if everything depended on that connection.

Caitlin squeezed hard too. "Blow them away in New York. For both of us, okay?"

"Okay." She started for the car, but Caitlin called her back.

"Here," she said, holding out the compass. "I went and retrieved it for you."

Dana took it from her.

"Use it to find your way home sometimes too," Caitlin called to her.

When she got back in the car, cherry blossoms covered the seats and floor. Their fragrant smell was everywhere and Dana sat for a minute, breathing it in. Then she put the car in first gear and beeped the horn, three long, one short. She saw Caitlin in the rearview window, still standing there, waving goodbye.

Dana scooped some blossoms from the empty seat beside her, then held her hand out the window, and watched as the breeze picked them up and carried them away.

First, *Renata found the silver* dollar from Mrs. Ramone. Then she carefully taped it over Millie's chest. She thought there should be words to say to make this ritual work. But Mrs. Ramone had not given her any. In Renata's mind, one word kept repeating. Please.

"Millie," Renata said, "how would you like to move to France?"

Millie frowned. "The country of France?"

"Right. The country."

She shook her head. "No."

Renata smiled. "That's okay," she said. "We have lots of options."

She had spent all afternoon in the library. There were lots of places to go and get healed. Not just Lourdes. There was Chimayo in New Mexico. And small towns in Italy, in Florida, and Portugal and Mexico and Canada. She spread out a map of the world, each country a bright hopeful color, each ocean vivid blue.

"Where do you want to go?" Renata asked her daughter. "Where?"

In the end they had decided on Mexico. Millie liked the food there, and it was far away, but not too far. They would learn Spanish, Renata told her. They would buy bright-colored clothing, beads and ruffled skirts. They would walk barefoot. And Millie would get well.

Renata took Millie back to their rented house. They would waste no time in leaving, she decided. They would just go. "Pack up all your cares and woes . . ." Renata sang as they drove.

"Remember?" Millie said. "Remember when I used to ask you if you wanted to meet Prince Charming?"

"Yes," Renata said.

"I still want you to. I want you to live happily ever after."

"We will," Renata told her. "In Mexico. Maybe we'll meet a bandito who will carry us into the sunset."

Millie rested her head against the car window and closed her eyes. She looked chalky, too pale.

"In Mexico," Renata said, pulling into the driveway, "you will get a nice tan. To hell with dangerous ultraviolet rays. We'll live dangerously, won't we?"

Millie didn't answer.

"Won't we, Millie?" Renata said.

"Sure, Mama."

They got out of the car and walked slowly into the house. All of the herbs had died in their box, shriveled and dry. The sight of them made Renata almost double over in grief.

"Our plants," she said. She reached for a branch of rosemary, and it crumbled in her hand. Then she remembered all the planting she had done in the winter, the tulips and crocuses. Renata rushed to the kitchen window, to look out at the back yard. The fruit trees were bare, the borders that she had so carefully planted with bulbs were empty. She had fooled herself into thinking for a while that she could keep things alive here.

From behind her Millie said, "I don't want to go to Mexico."

Renata did not turn to look at her daughter. She only nodded. Even Millie knew there were no miracles this time. At least not for them.

"Let's just go back home," Millie said. "To New York."

"Is that where you want to be?" Renata asked her. She still didn't turn around. She did not want Millie to see her crying.

"Yes."

Again Renata nodded. They would go back to New York then. In this, Millie should be the one to decide.

*E*verything felt upside down to Tom. He thought he wanted Renata to stay, yet when she refused he felt oddly relieved. He thought being alone again would feel sad, almost creepy after all this time with Millie and Renata and his own kids, but instead it felt almost sweet. He stood in his front yard, with the sun beating down on his back and realized that although he would never be as happy as he once was, in a new unexpected way he was almost happy again.

Sometime this past year he had realized that Holly, Massachusetts, was not the center of everything after all. That Renata needed to find a miracle, that Dana needed to chase stars, that he needed to stay right here. A fuzzy image of Libby floated into his mind. Libby, he thought, had needed to leave him.

And thinking that, another idea crept into Tom's mind. Maybe it was time for him to leave too. Not Holly, of course, but this house. He turned to look at it, and in that moment it seemed suddenly different. It was no longer the house where he would find happiness—it did not seem to hold some secret about Libby or himself, it was just another slightly run-down dark green house in western Massachusetts. In fact, in the warm summer breeze, as the trees bent and their leaves glistened golden in the sunlight, the house seemed to almost sigh.

Something had settled in him. Maybe he would sell the house after all, move to one of those new condominiums that had been built where old man Knight's farm used to be. Someone had told him they were nice—wall-to-wall in every room, a dishwasher and microwave, and each unit was cable ready.

He did not want to go back inside the house, so he got in his car and drove over toward those new condos. Westshire, they were called, as if they were in England or something, the name on the sign at the entrance written in fancy scroll. Everything there was neat and orderly, speed bumps and numbered parking spaces. Libby would like it here, he thought. And he knew then that he would still take her back if she wanted to come. But that it would never be the same. He would never be the same. Never again could he love someone—even Libby—that way.

Tom stood there, feeling the new and still unfamiliar hardness in his chest, at the very place where he used to believe love settled, the place that used to warm him for so many years. From the distance came the sound of children splashing in a swimming pool, the smell of hamburgers cooking on a grill. He thought again about life here. He could imagine the feel of the new carpeting under his feet, the smell of fresh paint as he closed his eyes to sleep there, the way a night would feel in a place like this.

L—*ibby was thinking about going* home. Sometimes she imagined a party awaiting her there, the kind that soldiers in old movies got when they returned from a war. Sometimes she imagined slipping in at night, quiet and unnoticed, in the same way she had left a year ago.

The funny thing was, no matter how she imagined it one thing was always the same—her children were still babies in her fantasy homecoming. They were babies and therefore could not be angry at her for leaving them. Instead, when they saw her, they broke into smiles, ran toward her in the awkward way that small children move, let her scoop them both into her arms, whispered "I love you" in a rush of milky breath.

And when she thought that, Libby got immediately sad, because of course it was so completely untrue, impossible. She knew there would be no hugs, no whispered endearments. Just Dana's steely gaze, Troy's look of distrust and betrayal. It seemed unfair to Libby that a person only got one life, one chance. If only she could have frozen time, kept her children small while she came out here to California to try her luck. Then perhaps she could have had the homecoming she imagined.

Tom called her sometimes late at night, each time his voice sounding sweeter and sweeter to Libby. The telephone had a way of making some things easier to say. On the phone, you didn't have to look a person in the eye and watch the pain there. You didn't have to let them see your own pain.

Libby did not want to hear details of her family's life without her. Even when Tom called her on graduation night, his voice thick and sleepy from too much champagne.

"You missed everything," he told her.

She knew he meant the ceremony, their children in caps and gowns, clutching their diplomas, the party afterwards with Sue and Caitlin and Great Western champagne. But she knew too that she had missed much more than that—Cub Scout meetings, weekend camping trips that Tom took the children on while she stayed home, Dana's prom.

"I feel old, Harp," Libby said.

He didn't answer her.

"I've got kids all grown up and I can hardly remember them as babies," she continued. She squeezed her eyes shut, pressed her fingers to her temples as if that could help her remember.

"Oh," Tom told her, "they were beautiful babies, Libby."

A picture flashed in her mind. In it, Libby was sitting on the grass at home, wearing navy blue and white polka dot Capri pants and a white halter top. It was summer and the air was full of summer smells—hot earth, sweet grass, flowers in bloom. And there, in front of her, in a tiny wading pool shaped like a water monster from an old cartoon, *Beanie and Cecil,* sat Troy and Dana. Both of them were young, with fine soft hair and chubby arms and legs. Dana wore a bonnet covered with white daisies, Troy had tossed off a Red Sox cap. They were laughing together, splashing in that pool, and behind them Libby saw Tom, filming the whole scene on a home movie camera, moving closer to them, all slow and steady.

She remembered how she turned toward him, toward that camera and flashed a big smile. A real one too, because at that very moment, she was happy. Remembering it now, Libby thought of it as the last day she had felt happy with what she had.

She told him that on the phone, but he started to laugh.

"That's some memory," he said. "But we never had a home movie camera."

Libby frowned. She twisted the curly telephone cord around her finger, then let it spring free, all the time holding on to the image of that day. "But I remember it all so clearly," she said. "That little pool. And Dana's hat with those daisies. And you capturing it all. In fact, go up to the attic and find that camera. Maybe we never even had the film developed. Maybe it's still sitting up there in a box somewhere."

Tom laughed again. "I'm not going to look for something that doesn't even exist."

Libby felt like the room was starting to spin. She grabbed the edges of the end table and held on tight. "But I remember it," she said again.

"That's the nice thing about memories," Tom told her. "No one can change them for you. Right or wrong."

"Well," Libby said, "I remember that you love me. There's one you can't dispute."

Tom didn't answer right away. In that awful silence, she saw all the miles that had come between them unfold before her. She felt her heart begin to beat hard.

She heard him sigh. "Yeah," he said finally, "I love you."

Something about the way he said it made her shiver. With all the homecomings she had imagined, there had never been one without Tom there, waiting for her, arms outstretched. "I've been thinking about coming home," Libby said, her voice soft.

Upstairs, on her bed in Holly, was a quilt her grandmother had made a long time ago. The pattern was called Tumbling Blocks, because no matter how you turned it, everything seemed to be falling down. That was exactly how she'd felt when she left Massachusetts. When she got in her car, and drove down that road, that feeling had started to finally disappear. She'd felt hope again. She'd felt the tingle of promise, of possibility. Now she imagined wrapping them—Tom, Dana, Troy—in that quilt and holding them close. She imagined them understanding at last.

Tom cleared his throat. "You know," he said, "I've been thinking too. I thought I'd sell the house and buy one of those new condominiums they built over on Knight's Farm."

Libby hesitated. "I would like that," she said, still clutching the edge of the table. "I would like to live somewhere new."

"Uh . . . you get to pick whatever color scheme you want," he said. "Peach or something called aloe—"

"Aloe?" Libby said, wishing she could throw her arms around him. "Aloe would be green."

"Green?" he said. "Really? How about that?"

Even though she felt sad, she laughed at the sound of his voice, at the idea that he was still someone who could be surprised by small things. "Don't decide until I get there," she said.

All he said then was that he wanted to get some sleep. "Too much champagne," he said.

But Libby didn't want to go, not yet. She said, "I just remembered something else. I remember how you came after me when I left for New York that time before we got married. How you swept me off my feet and the next thing I knew I wasn't in New York at all, I was standing in front of a justice of the peace, shaking like crazy and marrying you." As she said it, she realized she was shaking now too. "I don't think I knew what happened until about the third inning of that game we went to at Fenway afterwards."

"That was some day," Tom said, and she knew by the way he sounded that he was remembering too, that it was something they still had together, something that could not be erased.

Ann Hood is the author of *Somewhere Off the Coast of Maine, Waiting to Vanish, Three-Legged Horse,* and *Something Blue.* She lives in New York City, where she is at work on a new novel.